Key to the Past

by

Iona Morrison

A Blue Cove Mystery, Book 8

Key to the Past

Cover Art by *Debbie Taylor*

The Wild Rose Press, Inc.
PO Box 708
Adams Basin, NY 14410-0708
Visit us at www.thewildrosepress.com

Publishing History
First Mainstream Fantasy Edition, 2019
Print ISBN 978-1-5092-2955-0
Digital ISBN 978-1-5092-2956-7

A Blue Cove Mystery, Book 8
Published in the United States of America

Compelled by a strange force pulling at her, Jessie slipped out of bed. The closer she got to the dresser, the harder it was for her to look away. "Kimberly," she called to her. The weeping girl stopped crying. Jessie reached for an antique key, which rested prominently on the dresser. *She hadn't seen it there earlier.* Clutching the key in her hand, a strange electric sensation coursed through her body. *What was happening to her?* She dropped the key to the ground, but it was too late. The room was moving, and so was she. The light, like a huge hand, lifted her off her feet, slowly spinning her round and round. The tempo began to build faster and faster. The light tugged her, pressing her into its current, and then it all went dark.

Dedication

Dedicated to Dennis Hurst and David Morrison,
who are alive in another dimension:
I miss you both in my here and now.

Other books by Iona Morrison

Chapter 1

Jessie Reynolds loved the vibe the moment she pulled up in front of the Brass Lantern Inn. Rich with history, the inn was perfect as far as her eyes could see. Intense blue irises, bright red tulips, and a few remaining yellow daffodils gave color to the flower beds waiting for the blooms of summer to arrive. The large front porch invited her to come in and stay for a while.

Walking up the steps to the welcoming front doors, she paused to take it in. "Awesome. It's even better than the internet ad," she said, taking a deep breath of the cool evening breeze. The gentle wind felt refreshing after her long day of meetings and seminars. What she wanted most right now was a warm bath and a good night's rest. Opening the door, she pulled her suitcase across the threshold with her laptop case slung over her shoulder.

"Here. Let me help you." A tall young man with a nice smile approached her. His large hands reached for the strap sliding down her arm. "I'll be the one taking this to your room." He put the computer case next to her suitcase at the base of the stairs. "Don't worry. I'll watch over them for you."

"Thank you. Do you play basketball by any chance?" she asked, looking up at him. His hands could easily palm the ball, and he was more than tall enough.

He towered over her. If he wasn't playing, the local high school should be kicking themselves. She expected him at any moment to pat the top of her head like Liam used to do when she was a kid.

"I do. How'd you know?" He grinned at her. "My height, right?"

"You're tall enough, but it was your hands that gave you away. I'm sure you can handle the ball with ease."

"I'm good." His eyes lit up. "I never let anyone drive to the basket for a score if I can stop them, but it's hard not to foul when I play tough. My team hates it if I get into foul trouble." He chuckled. "So do I. It's not fun being benched. Coach tells me I have one of the sweetest three-point shots in our division." He jumped, pumping a fake shot, and made a swishing sound. "If you're here tomorrow night, you should come to see me play." He straightened his shoulders, puffing out his chest a bit. "I'm number twenty-three, Brian Miller."

"I might just surprise you, Brian. I love high school basketball, and I'm sure you'd be fun to watch." Jessie reached for her purse on top of the suitcase, smiling at his youthful exuberance.

She walked past the teen to check-in at the front desk, more than happy to be here for the next couple of nights instead of the hotel by the convention center. The city was noisy, and she hadn't slept well. When she booked her trip a few months ago, the inn had no available rooms until tonight. With a train to the city only a few blocks away, she jumped at the chance to take the open reservation.

Located outside of Boston proper, the inn seemed ideal for a romantic weekend getaway after the convention ended. With all the great restaurants she wanted to try, and, of course, all the historical sights she had to drag Matt to see, the Brass Lantern seemed, well, almost perfect.

But the longer she waited for the desk clerk to return the more the atmosphere in the Brass Lantern gave her mixed signals. Oh, the inn was beautiful with its polished brass, rich wood, and furnishings. It even exuded an old-world charm complete with the faint musty smell often found in the older structures she loved. But the air in the room seemed to crackle with inexplicable energy, making her wonder what she had walked into. Either that or her imagination had shifted into full gear.

Rubbing her arms where the goosebumps were now forming, she tapped her foot, quietly admonishing herself. "Don't you dare get involved." Her jaw clenched. She tried to ignore the sound of moaning that seemed to emanate from every corner of the room. Sticking her finger into her ear to block the sound, she subtly ran her hand through her hair when she realized how stupid she must look to the couple sitting in the lobby watching her.

"I'm sorry I wasn't here to greet you, miss, but I'm here now." The woman smiled at her. "You're in the first room at the top of the stairs. Brian will make sure your luggage is delivered."

"Thank you." Jessie signed the receipt the lady handed her.

"If you need anything, don't hesitate to call. My shift is over, and I'm officially on vacation, but Evelyn will be here in a few minutes." The woman handed Jessie a key and information about the inn and surrounding areas. "Pleasant dreams, and enjoy your stay, Miss Reynolds."

Jessie climbed the stairs, hoping to put the moans of the lobby out of her mind. It didn't matter. Either way, she was staying. The Brass Lantern was her home for the next several days. That's all there was to it. After a good night's rest, and sleep, which was what she obviously needed, her plan for tomorrow besides the seminars included watching a high school basketball game. She owed it to Brian Miller. He was a nice kid.

The staff was friendly, and her room was quaint and filled with a collection of beautiful antiques. Whenever she could, she always chose a B&B over a hotel any day. And this one had a high rating, a renowned chef, and evening meals like the Blue Iris Inn, owned and operated by her best friend, Katie.

Laying her head back against the pillows, Jessie planned on savoring this small break from Blue Cove. There was no way she would let her tiredness or whatever she had heard downstairs mess up her mini vacation away from the cove. She missed her boyfriend, Matt, but not the craziness of the past few months. Between cases and plans for Katie's wedding, she was ready for some time to herself. The conference had taken up a few days already with only a couple more to go. Plus, she had scheduled a spa day for Friday—one of the true luxuries she allotted herself. What girl didn't need a facial, pedicure, and manicure to relax? She smiled, shut off the light, and snuggled beneath the soft covers of the bed. The sweet sound of silence lulled her to sleep in no time.

A loud crash awakened her. Glancing at the

numbers on the clock, she vaulted upright, and her heart raced, pounding in her chest. Her hand fumbled in the darkness, knocking her phone to the floor with a thud as she reached for the lamp on the bedside table. Dark soon gave way to the blinding light rushing into the room. Closing her eyes, she blinked several times, trying to acclimate herself to the lamp's brightness. "Only one-thirty, ugh."

The blind spots slowly faded, and the room came into focus. At first glance, all seemed to be in order. Calico chairs and the chintz fabric loveseat were upright and in the same place she had last seen them. The heavy antique furniture hadn't moved either. Paintings were still hung securely in place on the wall. *What was that awful noise?*

Searching the room for the culprit that had caused the loud commotion, her sight landed on the large gilded mirror, which had been on the wall but now lay shattered on the floor in many pieces. "Well, that's not a good sign," she muttered. Lifting the phone from its cradle, she called the front desk.

"How can I help you, Miss Reynolds?" the woman asked as she answered.

"The huge mirror in my room fell off the wall," she explained to the woman. "I have no idea how, but there is glass everywhere."

"Oh, my, dear me, another one. That makes three, but it's been a while since the last one came down." She cleared her throat. No amount of throat-clearing could cover the nervous edge to the woman's voice.

"Excuse me. Are you saying this has happened before?" Jessie's interest was piqued. It didn't bode well for a relaxing time, which seemed to be fading fast.

"Sort of," the woman answered softly. "I can only imagine what is going on. We can't seem to agree about why it keeps happening. Sit tight, and I'll send Carl to your room to clean up the mess. Don't cut your feet. Heaven knows we don't need you to be injured after being scared out of your wits."

Jessie got out of bed, avoiding the area of broken glass. She grabbed her robe and slid her feet into a pair of soft, cushy slippers. As she sat on one of the calico chairs, her mind began to dredge up more than one good reason a mirror would suddenly come crashing to the floor in the room she was renting. A ghost, perhaps. Her foot moved nervously beneath the chair. Where was Carl?

A knock at the door sent her to check through the peephole before she opened it. The man standing in the hallway was a total surprise. He wasn't what she had envisioned as the inn's caretaker. Well over six feet tall, with rippling muscles in his upper arms that were hard not to notice, he instantly filled the room once she opened the door. Rapidly, the large space felt quite small and warm. His cart seemed almost miniature as he pushed it through the doorway with one hand while balancing a broom casually over his shoulder. With his reddish-blond hair curling out from under his cap and intense emerald green eyes which looked directly into hers, he must have set many young hearts aflutter. His roguish grin most likely sealed the deal.

"Sorry to bother you, ma'am. I'm Carl." His eyes traveled slowly over her in an insolent manner. "This big old thing crashing to the floor must have startled you."

"You could say that." She moved back to put some distance between them. "The lady at the desk told me this was the third one. Why are they falling off the wall? Aren't they properly secured?"

"Now that's a good question and one for which I have no immediate answer. If you have your shoes on, come over here and I'll show you what I mean."

Hesitant to get too close to the man, she walked to where he stood and looked at where his finger pointed. "Oh my. The hangers are still in the wall." She hadn't expected to see them intact. Surprising and totally mystifying was the face looking back at her from the broken mirror. Could Carl see the girl in the shattered pieces?

"Yes, they're anchored to the studs—solid, and not going anywhere. Look at this." He showed her on the frame that the wire support was still attached firmly in place and not broken. "It's like someone is lifting the mirrors, frame and all, right off the wall and throwing them to the ground, which isn't possible considering the weight of these things." He scratched his head. He handed her a chunk of the frame to hold. "You can imagine the weight of the frame in one piece with the beveled glass in it. The darn thing weighs, at the least, fifty-five or more pounds."

"I see what you mean. It wouldn't be easy to toss one, and if it fell the weight alone would break the wire and rip not only the hangers out but damage the wall as well." The girl was still watching her.

"Right, and as you can see, there's no damage. Evelyn, the lady who works the desk most nights, swears we have a ghost. This is an old inn and has seen its share of bad stuff over the years. The original owners built it in the early eighteen hundreds. There's a lot of history here. Some good and some not. But I'm not ready to agree with her about a ghost, though. Besides not believing in such wild tales, I've never seen any signs of a ghost." He chuckled.

"You have an accent. Where are you from?" Jessie sat on the foot of the bed while he swept up a few chunks and slivers of glass from the area where she had been standing.

"I was born in Ireland." His head down, he concentrated on sweeping the floor. "Don't want to miss anything if I can help it."

"You mean to tell me you don't think a ghost is possible. Your Irish mythology, with its banshees, leprechauns, and fairies, are magic's fertile ground for supernatural possibilities." She smiled as he frowned.

"Some things you never get away from." He lifted his cap and placed it back on his head. She could sense the war inside him. The subject was uncomfortable for him, and she changed it. "How long have you worked here?"

"I'm the owner," he told her with pride in his voice. "I bought the place recently, and that's why I'm doing the cleanup. There's some remodeling in the works, and I want to turn a profit before I hire anyone else."

"I get it." She nodded as she tugged the belt on her robe tighter. "I'm a new business owner myself." She watched him sweep more of the glass into a pile. "If not a ghost, then what's your theory?"

"There's a logical reason for it. Maybe it's as simple as the foundation shifting." He scooped up a part of the gilded frame. "This antique frame will be hard to replace, though. They don't make them like this anymore."

Jessie listened indifferently to his musings. Boy, could she tell him a thing or two. "I'm sure you're right. There's a good reason for it. I guess you'll know soon enough. Every mystery is solvable, eventually," she told him halfheartedly. She moved to sit on the edge of the chair to get out of his way and let him finish his cleaning. Would time give an answer? It sounded good, but it took ten years for authorities to solve Matt's high school sweetheart, Elizabeth McKenzie's murder. *Slow down.* She shook her head. *We're not talking murder here, only a broken mirror.* But the girl's haunted eyes said murder to her.

"That should take care of it." He emptied that last dustpan full of glass into the trash can. He placed another large section of the gilded frame on top of the broken glass. Carl hesitated at the door and glanced at her. "If you need anything else, let me know." He tipped his cap at her. "I wouldn't walk around barefooted. It's possible I missed some glass. Evelyn said she would give you another room tomorrow after the other guests leave. The mirror is no longer hanging in that room—can't fall that way." Carl walked out the door. "I'm sorry your sleep was disturbed. I hope you can get some rest." He stopped in the open door. "Of course, your stay here will be on the house."

"You don't have to do that." She tipped her head back so she could see his face.

"Yes, I do. I can't have my guests disturbed by loud noises in the middle of the night. Especially pretty ones like you." He grinned. "It's not good for business or my guests' peace of mind. Sleep well." He grabbed the door to pull it shut.

"Thank you. I'm sure I'll be fine." She followed him to the door and slid the deadbolt in place. He turned out to be nice, even if a bit bold.

The Brass Lantern was a pretty inn, but it wasn't home. The Boston area was not Blue Cove, and Matt wasn't here to help either. The ring sliding around on her finger twinkled in the light, flashing its brilliant reminder of their new engagement. She was free to wear her beautiful ring while she was out of the cove area. Holding her hand toward the light, she marveled once again at its beauty and sighed wistfully.

They hadn't made the news public yet. Right now, the reason seemed almost silly for not telling their friends and family, though at the time it had made perfect sense. Okay, if she were honest, it was mostly her idea. Matt simply went along, somewhat reluctantly, with her. He told her she was still dragging her feet. Was she? After the last few days of being apart, she might need to rethink the stupid plan. Not wanting to undercut Katie's engagement party with her own announcement, she had kept theirs a secret. But she wanted her friends to know. Positioning her hand, she looked at the ring again. Grams would be over the top with happiness. Her friends were expecting the news at some point, the town placed bets on when it would happen, and Katie would be thrilled. What had she been thinking? She slapped her palm to her forehead.

The empty supports on the wall caught her attention again. *Okay, now what?* There was no blaming Blue Cove for this mystery. Rooms don't moan, and mirrors don't suddenly fall from the wall. A girl's face doesn't often stare at you from broken glass. Was this a trick of some kind, to scare people, or was there something more going on here? She already knew the answer to her question. If she could shut her mind off, she would rest, but tomorrow she would snoop around and research the history of this inn. Something wasn't kosher, and she wanted to know what. Switching off the light, she laid her head back against the pillows stacked behind her. There was bound to be a body somewhere.

Sleep was the last thing on her mind. The room felt like it was whirling around her. She turned on the light. Impossible, yet it was exactly how she would describe the sensation if she were talking to Matt. What she didn't want right now was a mystery or another ghost. Blue Cove was trying enough. This town would have to work through this mystery without her.

"Get a grip, Jessica Lynn. It's time to sleep," she reprimanded herself. "The room isn't spinning, nothing is out of place, and there is no ghost in sight. An illusion maybe. Let's chalk this one up to an overactive imagination." She shook her head and reached for the light again. Her hand stopped midway. There would be no sleep for her, at least for a while. The energy in the room was too high, and she couldn't settle down even if she wanted to. Nothing moved, and yet everything seemed to be, which made no sense at all.

Hopping out of bed, she grabbed her laptop. Plumping the pillows to support her back, she turned on her computer. She searched for information on the Brass Lantern Inn.

Old with plenty of history, right up her alley, but nothing seemed amiss in what she read. *Wait a minute.*

Her eyes landed on the small footnote in the local paper in an article dated May 1, 1967. *May first—that's tomorrow.* Excitement pulsed through her. "Umm," she mused, "anything is possible." The article stated that the police still hadn't found any trace of Kimberly Ryan, a young woman who worked at the inn and lived in the area. Her boyfriend, Patrick Hamilton, was supposed to pick her up from work at five but was late that day. Authorities thought she had started walking, but she never made it home. Was Kimberly's ghost trying to reach her? In her heart, Jessie knew it was her, and Kimberly had been murdered. With a stroke of a few keys, she could be off to the races learning all she could about Kimberly. Jessie pulled her hand back from the keyboard and closed her laptop, pushing it aside.

This wasn't the time for her to look for another mystery to solve. She let her thoughts drift to the convention, a much safer subject to think about. No ghosts, no missing people or murders, only what was trending in the publishing world. Jessie felt quite proud of herself. Two conference speakers had told her she had done her homework and invested in a perfect location for a successful business. Her five-year plan was on track. Her father would be happy to have that piece of information. He always liked a good bottom line. She had seen several new titles on display from publishers that she wanted to order for her store. Add to that the several helpful tips for her business she had learned from other shop owners, and it had been a successful couple of days.

The distraction wasn't working. She felt conflicted. She wanted to find out more about Kimberly, but she had promised Matt that there would be no cases, no bad guys, only a few days to get acquainted as a newly engaged couple. She refused to spoil their celebration with another crazy premonition. Shutting off the light, she fought through the strange sensation in the room and eventually drifted off to sleep.

Chapter 2

It didn't last long. Jessie awakened a little while later to the sound of two people in the throes of a loud argument. She picked up the phone to call the desk again, thinking it was coming from the next room, but paused as soon as the woman began to cry. Someone continued shouting obscenities, badgering and threatening her. Jessie's anger rose with every curse word. She peered out into the hall. Surely, someone else had to be concerned by all the yelling. There was no one. How could that be? She slipped out of the room, tying her robe closed as she walked. Her hand was poised to knock at the next room but stopped when she was met with silence. Great. The fight was in her mind. Closing the door to her room, she got back into bed.

She pulled the pillow over her head to stifle the noise as the yelling began once again. It didn't help. Light spilled out from under the closet door, illuminating the room, inviting her to check inside. *You will not look.* There was nothing normal about what was happening. Forcing herself to remain in bed, she turned over on her stomach and refused to move. The voices grew louder and the light brighter until she couldn't take it anymore. Slipping out of bed, she walked out of the room in her robe into the silence of the hall. If there was no other room, she would sleep in her car if she had to. *Enough is enough.*

****

Had he ventured out on a bogus assignment? Damn. He could be home sitting in his favorite chair instead of on some fool errand. Never had his trusty companion led him astray before, but the longer he sat here, he wasn't sure about anything. Brass Lantern Inn, tonight his guide had told him—be there and wait. Maybe he should give up and call it a night. Folding his newspaper, he started to stand, but the vision coming down the stairs caused him to fall back in his chair. Lifting his paper to cover his face, he watched her without the danger of being seen. The force around her was strong. A lovely sight with tousled hair. The guide was right—she could be trouble and necessitated watching. She was unaware of him—good. It freed him to listen to their conversation, which disturbed him even more.

****

"Is everything all right, Miss Reynolds?" the desk clerk asked as Jessie moved slowly down the stairs. "It's late, dear, and you should be asleep."

"If only," she said longingly. "Have any of your other guests complained about the room I'm staying in?" Jessie plopped down on one of the open chairs in the lobby, rubbing her tired eyes.

"No." Evelyn dog-eared the corner of the page and closed the book she was reading. "There are no complaints about that room specifically." She peered over her glasses at Jessie, a frown emphasizing the deep-set wrinkles on her face. Her light brown hair pulled tight off her face in a bun didn't do anything to soften her stern features. If it wasn't for the spark of light in her pretty brown eyes, Jessie would have packed and left the inn right that moment.

"What do you mean? You've heard something, haven't you?" Jessie jumped up at seeing Evelyn nod. "Have you had other guests say they heard voices or saw strange lights? How about large mirrors falling off walls, waking them in the middle of the night? You did tell me this was the third one."

"Yes, I did, but I'll not admit it openly. Guests won't like hearing there're strange happenings going on here. Besides, it's been quiet for about a year. You're the first who talked about voices and a strange light, though."

"Well that's just great. Another first for me," she mumbled under her breath.

"Every year, for the past few years, a mirror crashes to the floor in the middle of the night as the month of May approaches. We have no idea why. I think we have a ghost, but Carl thinks I'm silly. I'll leave it to you to decide."

"What do you know about Kimberly Ryan?" Jessie asked her.

"You've heard about her? Who told you?" Evelyn clicked her pen on and off. She eyed the guest sitting behind his paper warily.

"No one told me anything. I read something in the local newspaper about her."

Lowering her voice, she bent her head toward Jessie. "It's a bit of mystery to the folks around here. People have added to the story over the years. No one knows what is true, or what's an urban myth. The previous owner believed that Kimberly's ghost roamed the inn. Mollie Flynn was a bit on the strange side, with all her talk about the little people and magic. Her sightings were one of the reasons she sold the inn, besides getting too old to run it anymore. She retired to Florida and wanted to set her grandson Carl up for the future. He's a straight shooter and doesn't hold to his grandma's ways. She was positive we had a ghost. He won't even talk about it as a possibility. I agree with him only because I'm not sure the ghost story makes sense."

"Why, if you don't mind me asking?" Jessie found herself hanging on everything Evelyn said.

"Kimberly wasn't murdered here. She simply disappeared. Doesn't a ghost usually haunt the place of their death?"

"I have no idea." Jessie shook her head. "Unless, of course, she wants someone to help solve her disappearance, so she can rest in peace."

"I never thought of that angle before. The authorities believe she disappeared walking home. Kids often hitched a ride back then, or so I've been told, and maybe she got in the car willingly with the killer. Although Linda Cranston, who worked here with her at the time, told me once no one ever saw her leave work that day. Who knows? But every year whenever we get near May first, strange things start to happen and continue throughout the whole month."

"Does Linda still live in the area?" Jessie asked.

"Yes, she lives in a small home near the outskirts of town. She's older and doesn't get out much anymore. I was young at the time and only got interested in Kimberly after I came to work here. I'm about to retire. I wish they could solve the case, but it happened such a long time ago."

"What do you think happened, Evelyn?" Jessie

asked her pointedly.

"Well, just between you and me—" She glanced quickly around the lobby. "—I believe she was murdered here, all right. I've seen too many things not to believe there's a ghost on the premise. I've watched that ghost show on TV, and we have one. Tell anybody else I said that, and I'll deny it." She pushed her glasses up on her nose. "Carl wouldn't be happy with me for talking to you about all this."

"He told me that you thought it was a ghost," Jessie told her.

"Wow, he told you that? He gets upset if I even mention the word ghost." She shook her head. "I'm surprised."

"He told me earlier when you sent him to my room." Jessie rested her elbows on top of the counter with her face propped between her hands. She closed her eyes for a moment. The only thing missing was a body. "I saw something strange as he was sweeping up the glass."

"You look tired, Ms. Reynolds. Shouldn't you be getting to bed?" Her manner turned brisk. She eyed the man who peeked over the paper. "Things should be quiet before long." Evelyn reached in the drawer and handed her a pair of earplugs. "These should help do the trick. If you want, we can talk more tomorrow. Goodnight, Miss Reynolds."

"Goodnight." Climbing the stairs back to her room, she was too tired to figure it out why Evelyn's nature suddenly turned frosty or why the atmosphere at the Brass Lantern was charged with a strange kind of energy. Was it possible Evelyn had seen the girl in the glass? Tomorrow would be soon enough to ask her. She might need to find a different place to stay, but she didn't want to.

There was no doubt about it. Kimberly was murdered somewhere in this inn. Jessie knew it. She jotted the name of Linda Cranston down on her notebook, writing several other observations under Linda's name, and placing the pen over the top of the notebook when she was done. She wanted to remember her thoughts in the morning. Her curiosity stirred, she wanted to satisfy it.

The earplugs and her eye mask would do the trick. She reached for the light to shut it off. Sleep wasn't going to come easily, and her mind wasn't going to be quiet. Some nights went that way. The people in the closet weren't sleeping either.

****

Watching her walk up the stairs, his senses heightened. The aura around her challenged him. What had she seen? Rubbing his hands together, the excitement of the possibilities intrigued him. This one could cause trouble, but the thought of the confrontation thrilled him. Life had been a bit mundane as of late. This could test his skills on many levels. Yes, he was going to enjoy the contest. He licked his lips in anticipation as he left the inn, but not before booking a room for a couple of nights.

Chapter 3

Wide awake, she glanced at the clock and stretched. "Too early," she muttered, rubbing her eyes. In truth, she had slept little. Whatever had gone on in the closet didn't stop until the morning light streaked into the room through the tiny opening in the curtain. "Finally." She sighed, pulling the earplugs out of her ears. "The wonderful sound of silence."

She reached for her ringing phone, eager to tell Matt everything about her crazy night. "Good morning."

"Hi, sweetheart," Matt's deep voice said. "I've missed you. I can't wait to see you tomorrow."

Oh, how she loved the timbre of his deep voice. "I've missed you too." She flipped through her hastily written notes.

"How's the conference?" he asked.

"Great. I'm looking forward to the main speaker today." Jessie began to tell him about what she'd learned. Even to her ears, she sounded distracted.

"What's going on, Jess? Your heart isn't in this conversation."

"Nothing…Well, okay, maybe something." She began to tell him about the mirror and the strange occurrences in her room.

"It's probably the shifting foundation like that Carl fella told you." Matt didn't sound convinced. "No work, remember."

"I know, and I'm trying hard not to get involved. A foundation shift could account for the broken mirror, not the girl watching me from the broken glass. But as soon as I got back to my room last night, I did a little research. On May 1, 1967, a young woman named Kimberly Ryan went missing from this inn. She worked here and was waiting for her boyfriend Patrick to pick her up. He was late, and the story is, once he finally arrived, she was gone. No one ever heard from her again," she said, her voice filled with excitement.

"What has that got to do with you, or us for that matter?" he asked.

"I have no idea. You know how it is with me once these folks try to contact me. I've tried my best to ignore it all. Still, I have to admit I'm intrigued."

"Tell me what you're thinking. Maybe if we go over it, our weekend won't be ruined. Or should I find a new place for us to stay?"

"I've already thought about finding a different place. I'll give it one more night. Besides, I scheduled a spa time for me tomorrow. I want to look perfect when you get here."

"You always look perfect to me."

"That's sweet of you." Her lips curved into a smile. He always managed to say the right thing.

"I'll trust your decision about the inn. I know how you love those places."

"Right, and this inn is not only beautiful, but the food is amazing too. You know me, and how much I enjoy good food." She chuckled.

"If you think the room is okay then it's bound to be great."

"Have you read anything about the sixties or heard stories from your parents or grandparents?" she asked, her mind racing on to things she was learning.

"Of course. They were turbulent years," Matt said.

"I know. Besides the assassination of several key figures in politics, there was the Vietnam War, which most of the youth were protesting. Every generation experiences change, but the generation growing up in the sixties and early seventies saw lots of them. It was a decade of protests, a real cultural revolution." She paused to take a breath and then raced on. "Woodstock, for heaven's sake, and some of the strangest clothing designs I've ever seen. What were they thinking? I do like the music though. I need to ask Sadie to tell me some stories about the sixties. I couldn't believe the articles I read on Woodstock. It just happened." She continued as fast as the ideas popped into her head.

"You're digressing. Focus, sweetheart. What does any of that have to do with us?"

"I have no idea. I only know that Kimberly Ryan's disappearance has me hooked. It's hard to ignore crashing mirrors and strange voices coming from the closet. And I've tried, believe me. It's even harder to ignore the girl in the mirror. So far, I haven't had to open the closet door. I have to this morning to get dressed. I should be fine because it's quiet now."

"What do you mean you should be fine. If you're concerned, ask someone to open it for you. Don't go looking for trouble."

"I'm not looking for trouble, and I'm not afraid to open the door by myself. All I'm saying is once I do there may be no turning back. Who knows what'll I find?" Jessie chuckled. "Hopefully, the dress I'm wearing today if it didn't get destroyed during their loud argument."

"Who was arguing?" Matt asked.

"I have no idea. Weren't you listening to me? There was a fight going on in my closet."

"I heard you, but I wasn't sure if you were serious."

"You're kidding, right? I'm the same girl who had a ghost throwing books in my store. Of course, I am serious. There was something strange going on in that closet last night."

"We'll try to figure it out after I arrive. Does that sound good to you?"

"Sounds perfect. I love you, Matt. I have to get dressed, or I'll be late for the morning session." After their goodbyes, the room seemed empty without the sound of his voice. She slipped her phone into her robe pocket.

Sitting on the edge of the bed, she slid her feet into her slippers before standing and wending her way to the bathroom. After using all the delay tactics she could think of, she walked to the closet and reached for the knob. The strange sensation creeping up her arm caused her to pull her hand back again. Whatever had happened in the closet last night, the energy was still there. A jolt of electricity raced through her as her fingers curled around the doorknob again. Jessie yanked the door open. Stepping inside, she reached for her dress, and the door slammed shut with a bang behind her. No amount of turning or cajoling would budge the door. It was stuck. Thank goodness, she'd put the phone in her pocket. A wise last-minute decision. Jessie called the front desk once again. Carl had to take the door off the hinges to set her free. He promised to move her things to a new room before she returned in the evening.

****

Jessie returned to the inn later in the evening after dinner and one exciting high school basketball game. Brian Miller wasn't bragging—he had a sweet three-point shot, and he was hot tonight. His final three-pointer came seconds before the buzzer sounded, leading his team to an awesome victory, and she had been there to see it. What a shot. The ball swished through the basket, all net. The crowd went wild, running out of the bleachers onto the court. Jessie smiled, taking it all in. She had screamed and cheered right along with everyone else. Miller waved when he saw her and tried to make his way over to her. The crowd pressed, and she left before he succeeded. The perfect way to end a day of seminars and all things business with some high school enthusiasm. One of the best games she had seen in years.

Carl had kept his word, and she had a new room. Evelyn had moved her things for her. Thankfully, the only mirror in this room was the one connected to the dresser. Firmly attached, it wasn't going anywhere unless the ghost could throw the dresser with it. Jessie tugged on it to make sure. This mirror was ornate in an opulent and yet eerie way. Two skeleton heads on wooden staffs adorned the carved sides, with a wooden pentagram in a circle floating in the center arch of the mirror. It would have been almost beautiful with its arches and beveled glass on the top, except for the unusual carvings, which caught her attention. Not her style and a bit on the creepy side.

She slipped into a pair of jeans and a soft T-shirt. She curled up on the bed with her computer as Kimberly Ryan called to her, and Jessie had to find out more about the girl. Her fingers flew over the keys, researching everything she could find on Patrick Hamilton and Kimberly Ryan's lives. As she read the local paper's archives, she saw photos of them. Patrick was a nice-looking young man. He was handsome in a West Coast surfer kind of way. His hair cut reminded her of the early sixties bands she had seen—almost like someone had used a bowl to cut it. The article said he was never considered a suspect in her disappearance. His fair looks were in stark contrast to the beautiful young woman in the next photo. Jessie studied the girl's picture on the screen. Kimberly had a delicate beauty— porcelain skin with expressive velvety brown eyes that went perfectly with dark hair tossed artfully over her shoulders and down her back. Kimberly Ryan was simply stunning.

From all the accounts Jessie read, Kimberly was a soft-spoken, generous young woman. She was working at the Brass Lantern, paying her own way through college, and maintaining a high grade-point average. She even found time to tutor a few kids at the local elementary school who were struggling in math. *What happened to you?* There was no way Jessie could walk away from her.

The articles Jessie read wouldn't leave her mind. She laid her head back on the pillows plumped behind her. Going over every detail, she tried to bring Kimberly's life into focus. How could a young woman simply disappear, never to be seen or heard from again? If she was murdered, they should have found a body by now, or maybe not.

Kimberly Ryan wanted Jessie to know what had happened to her. Jessie's last lucid thoughts before she fell asleep were of a lovely young girl facing her death alone and those haunted eyes staring at her from the broken glass. A testament to her shattered life. Rolling onto her side, Jessie closed her eyes and went to sleep with Kimberly in her thoughts.

The sound of a woman's soft weeping awakened her. Disoriented, Jessie was mesmerized by a bright light that flowed from the mirror into the room. Were those wings she saw behind the girl? Kimberly Ryan wept and gazed at her from inside the mirror. Compelled by a strange force pulling at her, Jessie slipped out of bed. The closer she got to the dresser, the harder it was for her to look away. "Kimberly," she called to her. The weeping girl stopped crying. Jessie reached for an antique key, which rested prominently on the dresser. *She hadn't seen it there earlier.* Clutching the key in her hand, a strange electric sensation coursed through her body. *What was happening to her?* She dropped the key to the ground, but it was too late. The room was moving, and so was she. The light, like a huge hand, lifted her off her feet, slowly spinning her round and round. The tempo began to build faster and faster. The light tugged her, pressing her into its current, and then it all went dark.

****

He knew the exact moment she had slipped through the portal. His gut churned. It wasn't the greasy diner food messing with his innards. Damn woman. Now he had to go and find her. She could mess everything up. He had a profitable arrangement. One that had paid him well for decades. Still, each time he went through the gate, it affected him. He had no idea how many times he could travel back and forth. Would it eventually kill him? He knew of no one besides himself who had ever gone through the portal and came back alive. It was possible she was already dead. He could hope, but doubt remained. The force around her was strong, and he couldn't leave anything to chance. He began the process. As soon as he crossed over, he began his search.

Chapter 4

"Have a great weekend and try to chill if you can." Dylan walked into Matt's office. "We'll take care of everything on this end. Things should be quiet with Jessie out of town." Dylan chuckled. "At least this week has been." Dylan leaned his shoulder against the wall. "How's Boston holding up with her in town?"

"It's fair to say trouble may have found her again." Matt shook his head and proceeded to tell Dylan about the mirror crashing to the floor and the girl staring out of the broken glass. "Add to the mix strange voices all night long with a bright light coming from the closet, and I think you can see where I'm going with this. Jessie did a little research and found out one of the employees who had worked at the inn went missing in the 1960s. They never found the girl or her body. She seems to believe the girl's ghost found her."

"What do you think?"

"I'm trying not to think about it, but it's safe to say I see my romantic weekend slipping away fast." Matt stood, grabbed his briefcase, and shoved in a file. Old habits die hard. "In fairness to Jessie, she never once looked in the closet and even left the room in the middle of the night to get away from the voices, but I know my girl, and she's intrigued. If she is, then I'll soon be involved too. The thing is I've been calling her all morning and haven't got her yet. I've left several messages, which has me concerned."

"No worries. She's probably busy at the convention."

"Nope, that was over yesterday. She told me about something she'd scheduled for today. I wasn't listening. All I kept hearing was another case had found her."

"She's shopping. That's what they all do. I hope you both can stay out of whatever is going on and enjoy a quiet weekend. You've earned it." Dylan turned to leave. "Don't forget our engagement party in two weeks. It's at Liam's and Connor's place. Live music and all. Should be a fun time. Liam promised to throw us a great party, and I know he won't let us down."

"With Katie or you constantly reminding us every week, there's no way we'll forget it. We'll be there and ready to celebrate." Matt walked down the hall with Dylan. He stopped to talk to a few of his officers in the lunchroom.

"Back on Tuesday, Joe. You know how to find me." Joe nodded at him and waved him on. Matt walked out of the station. He was ready for his days off. He removed his jacket, throwing it across the seat as he got to the car. It had only been a few days of not seeing her, but to him, it had felt like a lifetime.

What he didn't want right now besides another intense case was anything to ruin the special plans he had prepared for Jessie. It was meant to be their personal celebration of their engagement before they made it public. The smile spread across his face. She had made his day after she had told him yesterday how fun it was to wear her ring every day this week. He was taking it back to the jeweler's on Tuesday to have it fitted. He turned on the engine, cranked up the music, and latched his seatbelt. He should be in Boston in a few hours.

"Hey, bro, what's up?" Matt answered his phone.

"Not much. How are things on your end?" Evan's voice came across the line.

"Right now, quiet. I'm on my way to Boston to spend the weekend with Jessie.

"Who's taking care of her store while she's gone?" Evan asked.

"Peyton is still in town. Between her and Audrey, Jessie has it covered."

"I'm thinking about heading to the Cove next week." Evan told Matt what he was contemplating. "I'm considering possibly opening a photography business and gallery there. I'm doing the research on it now."

"Sounds like an interesting plan."

"I'll keep my gallery in the city too. At least that's my plan for now. How long will Peyton be there?"

"I have no idea. I'll have to ask Jess."

"Don't ask. I was curious that's all," Evan said. "Will you be around next week?"

"I should be back on Tuesday." Matt crossed his fingers. "Consider working for me as our photographer while you're contemplating. Marcy is leaving soon, and we'll need someone to photograph crime scenes."

They talked about it for several minutes before Evan hung up. Matt grinned. He would have to tell Jessie that maybe there was more to this whole Peyton-Evan story than met the eyes.

Mile after mile he watched the scenery go by. According to the last sign, he had about twenty miles to drive. *Why wasn't Jessie calling him back?* It wasn't like her. Surely, she had gotten his message by now. A few minutes later he answered his ringing phone. Finally, relief filled him.

"Matt, how far are you from Boston?" Dylan asked.

"Getting close now. Have you heard from Jessie?" Matt exited the freeway when the GPS said to.

"Not exactly, but Carl Flynn from the Brass Lantern Inn called. He found your name with the letters ICE beside it on her phone. The number was the station's phone."

"In Case of Emergency. I told her to do that." Matt had a sinking feeling. "What did he want?"

"I don't know how to tell you," Dylan said.

"What? Don't leave me hanging." A few expletives flew out of his mouth.

"Jessie is okay. At least, I think she is," Dylan replied. "I can drive up there if you want."

"What do you mean you think she is?" Matt shouted into the phone.

"This is where it gets strange." Matt heard Dylan take a breath. "The officer who took the phone from Carl wouldn't tell me much, and I couldn't make sense of anything he did say. I took down the number he gave me. Contact him when you get into town. I texted you the number and the name of the fella."

"Gotcha. I'll call them as soon as I can. I'm almost to the inn. It's a little north of the city. I'll get back to you as soon as I find out what's going on. No need to worry anybody yet."

"I'll wait to hear from you, but if you want me to drive up there say the word," Dylan repeated the offer.

"We'll wait and see." Matt hung up. He would

welcome another case if it meant Jessie would be all right. *Jess, I have no idea what's going on, but I'm on my way, sweetheart.* Matt drove as fast as he could to get there.

****

Jessie awakened with Matt's voice in her head, which made no sense. Her fingers skimmed up and down her side making sure she was in one piece. Something had happened to her, but at the moment she couldn't remember what. She was afraid to open her eyes, but they fluttered open with her need to see. Where was she? Nothing about the room seemed familiar. How did she get here? *Think, girl.*

"Thank God, you're alive. I wasn't sure you were still with us. I found you lying in the field this morning. Like sweet manna from heaven with a beautiful face. That must have been some trip you were on." The bearded stranger raked his hand through his long hair, separating the strands as he did. He stood in a group of women, all staring at her.

"What trip?" They were all dressed in the oddest clothes. She had seen the style before, but where? Her brain was fuzzy.

"You know—acid, LSD, baby. You get my drift." The man leaned close to her as he spoke. The girls behind him peered over his shoulder, bending with him.

"I've never used acid in my life." Her heart began to race. Who was this odd-looking stranger? He needed to back away. His face was inches from hers, and his breath wasn't nice. The smell was different. In fact, the air seemed infused with whatever it was.

"You were hallucinating big time. I figured you must have gotten some bad stuff." He looked at the girls, shaking his head. "We've all had one or two bad trips." They nodded in unison with silly smiles on their faces.

Weird, and getting stranger. The whole scene was wrong. Who were these people? She struggled to sit up. "I need to get home."

"Cool it, beautiful. Easy does it." He pushed her head back on the pillow. "Where would home be?"

"I-I don't know." Jessie rubbed her temple. Why couldn't she remember?

"We can't help you get home if you don't know where it is, now can we?" He gave the others a strange look. He whispered in one of the girl's ear, and she smiled.

"You can stay here with us until you're feeling better," the girl said. She sat on the edge of the bed. The flowers woven through her light brown hair matched the flowers on her skirt.

Where is here she wanted to ask, but Jessie held her tongue. She didn't want to appear weak or afraid. She was both. One thing was clear to her—this was somehow tied to Kimberly's disappearance and the vision she had of her. This strange group watching her might be involved. Instinctively aware something was not right, she knew one thing—she wanted to get out of here soon. Her life depended on it.

"Do you know your name?" the girl beside her asked. "My name is Clover, and the girl bringing you water is Essence. The man talking to you earlier is our leader, Skylar."

"Where am I?" Jessie glanced around the eclectic room—a mishmash of hanging beads, fringe, burning incense, and bean bag chairs. A dream, or a time warp, and these folks were stuck in it.

"This is Rainbow Ridge Commune." She placed a cold cloth on Jessie's forehead. "We welcome anyone on their journey of enlightenment. What brought you to us?"

Jessie had no idea how she ended up there. "What day is it?" Jessie tried to stifle the panic rising inside her. Her fist clenched at her side, and her toes curled in response.

"Why it's Monday, May eighth. Don't you remember?" She gave Jessie an odd look. "Surely you remember the day. Did you get hit on the head?"

She struggled to make sense of what Clover said. "No, my head is fine." She closed her eyes. *Think, Jessie, think.* She asked the next question that popped into her mind. "What year?"

"It's 1967. You've got to be teasing me, or can't you remember for real?" Clover appeared confused. "Are you sure you're all right? Maybe Skylar needs to take you into town to the doc's office."

Fighting back the sick feeling inside her, Jessie answered Clover. "Don't worry, I'm fine. My day has been peculiar is all. I left home early this morning searching for someone and haven't had any luck yet." Equally sure it wasn't on May eighth, but a Friday, and not in the year 1967, she tried hard to remain calm in the face of rising panic. Never mind the fact she hadn't been born yet.

It had to be connected to the key. Her mind raced on, trying to figure out how she had got to the Rainbow Ridge Commune in 1967. And how, oh how, was she ever going to get back home? The strange light and the girl in the mirror had something to do with it. Matt would never believe her, and she had no explanation. More depressing than that was would she ever get back to him or how would he find her? She shut her eyes, trying to keep the tears stinging her eyes from rolling down her cheeks.

Chapter 5

Matt had talked to the authorities on his arrival into town. They wanted him to see what they had found at the inn after the emergency call came in. Matt had no idea how to explain it all to Dylan as he talked to him. Standing in her room at the inn, he found it hard to believe what Carl Flynn, the proprietor, told him. What had Jessie said to him last night? He tried to recall her exact words and wished he had listened to her more carefully. She wasn't here, but he could sense her presence everywhere in the room. Her belongings were still in plain sight waiting for her to return.

"Has anyone touched anything?" His fingers skimmed over the silky dress hanging in the closet. Her robe, draped across the foot of the bed, waited for her to put it on and wrap herself in its warmth. Her slippers still lay in the same place where she must have kicked them off. The bed covers were thrown back. She must have jumped out of bed. *Tell me the story, sweetheart, so I know how to help you.*

"Only Officer Macintyre," Carl told him. "He came in and looked around for a few minutes and then left. I had only moved Ms. Reynolds out of another room yesterday after she got stuck in the closet."

"She was trapped in the closet?" He couldn't remember her telling him that piece of information. He wasn't that distracted talking to her last night. She had talked non-stop about a high school basketball game and some kid named Brian.

"Yes, the door slammed shut and wouldn't budge. She went in to grab her dress and the door jammed. At least she had her phone. We're still trying to figure out how it happened." Carl raked his hand through his hair. "If you don't mind me saying, this has been a couple of bizarre days. I always laughed at Evelyn, my night clerk. Her talk about us having a ghost was on the peculiar side to me. But now, I'm not sure of anything."

"Have you ever seen this before?" Matt picked up the key laying on the ground in front of the strange looking bureau. The warm sensation vibrated up his arm, invoking the memory of touching the fetishes in Palm Springs. The sensation remained long after he placed the key on the top of the dresser. It explained a lot to him. Relief washed over him. If anyone asked him why, he wouldn't be able to give them an intelligent answer. Jessie would return to him. He was sure of it, or at least he wanted to be. He had to believe she'd be back.

Carl shook his head. "I've never seen it before. It's not one of ours. Should I get rid of it?"

"No. As of now, this room and its contents are evidence. Something transpired here last night, and we have to try to figure out what, until Jessie is able to tell us herself." As odd as it seemed, he knew the key was the link to what had happened in this room.

"Good luck getting her to talk. No offense, man, but I doubt she'll be talking anytime soon the way she looked when they carried her out of here."

"You might be surprised." Matt smiled to himself and took another quick look around the room. Hell, nothing surprised him anymore. Jessie had kicked his logical approach of case solving to the curb more than once over the past year. It might be harder to figure out what happened to her without her nearby to talk to him. Still, if he knew his girl, she would find a way to let him know what was going on.

Matt wanted to talk to Reba Thompson and found it hard to believe he was even entertaining the idea as he searched for her number. She would know what to do. He saw Jessie's notebook and pen and grabbed them off the nightstand. He put them in his briefcase. He packed up her computer and would take it with him for safe keeping.

Carl gave Matt the key to the room. "The chief of police, Sam Macintyre, said you were free to come and go from here as needed. He wants all the help he can get. He's never seen anything like this before, and neither have I. If word gets out about this, my inn will be worthless. I wish I had never bought the damn thing now."

"I can't believe I'm saying this, Carl, but I don't think you'll need to worry about it. I could tell you some strange things, and this is another one to add to the list."

"I sure hope your fiancée will be all right. I doubt she'll ever want to stay here again. I wouldn't blame her if she sued me for everything I'm worth."

"She might surprise you. She's a sweet person." Matt placed her phone and charger into the case with her laptop. He needed to keep it charged for her.

"If you're finished with me, I have work to do." Carl walked toward the open door, bending his head as he crossed the threshold.

"Go ahead. I have a few phone calls to make. I'll sit here and take care of them before I leave."

"Be my guest. I don't want to be in here any longer than I have to be," Flynn called over his shoulder from the hall.

Matt sat in one of the chairs. This had been an odd morning, and he hoped Reba would have a few answers for him.

****

"Matt Parker, I've been expecting your call. I know something has happened to our dear girl. I've been thinking about her all morning."

"You're right." He explained what he had found out so far. "I know Jessie would call you first if she could."

"Of course, she would. I'll tell you what I'd tell her. She'll be fine but will experience some unusual things before this case is finished. She's in two dimensions."

"What the hell does that mean? Pardon my language." Matt's free hand clenched into a fist.

"No problem. I know you're upset. Somehow our girl crossed through a portal or gate into another time dimension. Don't ask me how. We'll both know soon enough."

"What should I do? I mean, I have no idea how to handle this."

"Sure, you do, young man. You will solve the case the way you always do—reason, research, using your logic, and of course, listening to her. She'll be talking to you. She's been communicating with me all day."

"What if I can't hear her?" Matt uttered the words aloud, facing one of his fears.

"You'll hear her fine. Listen to your heart, son." Reba paused. "Matt, I have one warning, though. There is a darkness that causes me to shudder whenever I think of the inn. Something bad has happened there, and it's more than the missing girl. She is the way to something bigger, and it's been going on for many years."

"Reba, I wish I understood how you know all this stuff." Matt ran his hand through his hair.

"The same way Jessie does. It comes to us if we're required and leaves us when we are no longer needed." Reba chuckled. "I have a feeling you'll be seeing and hearing things new to you before this case is over."

"Jessie mentioned to me seeing a girl watching her from the broken glass. I wonder what that means."

"I'm sure we'll know soon enough. Each spirit has its own way of communicating. Good luck, and call me anytime. As soon as Jessie is back among us have her call me. You only have to remember another dimension, for now. Understanding will have to come later."

"I'll have her call." He frowned. Reba had expressed it perfectly. Understanding would come with the safe return of Jessie. He placed the next call. His hands still shook. In two dimensions, damn, and he had thought nothing could shock him anymore. "Hey, Jeremy, this is Matt."

"What's up?" Jeremy responded. "Let me guess. You're in the heat of another strange case."

"You could say that." Matt explained what he knew so far. "I need you to research the Brass Lantern Inn." Matt gave him the name of the suburb outside of Boston where it was located. "It's an old inn, lots of history, and maybe with something still unsavory going on there."

"Are you freaking kidding me?" Jeremy whistled long and slow.

"My exact question. I guess we'll know when she tells us."

"Damn, I don't understand. How can she be in two dimensions? An altered state? Trans-dimensional portals are only a theory. Fantasy stuff, not real." Jeremy paused. "Impossible."

"What the hell are you talking about?" Matt jumped out of his chair and paced.

"A form of technology that supposedly opens dimension barriers allowing individuals to travel between them with ease. I find this fascinating. Maybe it isn't only a theory." Jeremy whistled again. "Nobody will ever believe this."

"I'll have to get back to you on the subject of whether it's theory or reality. If—and when—I can figure out what you're talking about. Right now, the idea of two dimensions has me stumped."

"Look it up online. It's fascinating reading if nothing else." Jeremy sounded excited.

"Sounds good, but I might have to pass and take your word for it. I'll keep you up to date on what I find." After he hung up, Matt took another look around the room. He tried to visualize what might have happened there. The dresser had the strangest mirror he had ever seen. If only these walls could talk. Before he left, he grabbed the key off the dresser and pushed it into his briefcase. Jessie wanted him to take the key— he knew that much.

Chapter 6

Jessie remained quiet, pretending to sleep, able to observe her surroundings without being noticed. In no time she had figured out that Skylar seemed to control the girls. Clover and Essence were emotionless. Following close on his heels, they did everything he demanded.

Skylar was a legend in his own mind. She knew his type—puffed up with his own importance. His long stringy hair looked as if he hadn't washed it in weeks. The jeans he wore had patches on top of patches. Add to them a flowered cowboy shirt, an embroidered vest, and his style made absolutely no sense at all.

Whatever he wanted, the girls did for him. As she lay there, he had asked plenty of them. Jessie wanted to stand and scream at the girls to wake up before it was too late. They wouldn't listen; they were enthralled with him. They followed Skylar in an almost trance-like state. How did Kimberly fit into this if at all? After all, wasn't Kimberly the reason for being here?

There were many troubling things about Skylar, but his stormy gray eyes topped the list—angry, empty, and cold as steel. Jessie had only seen eyes like his on the face of a cold, calculating killer. She shuddered. Hopefully, she would know the reason for being in this situation soon.

What she found intriguing, even though he was not

a handsome man, he was surrounded by beautiful young girls. How were they taken in by this con artist? She had rolled her eyes more than once at what he told them. Skylar was a master manipulator.

The girls seemed to be his empowered minions, their personalities stripped slowly away. Before she left the commune, which had to be soon, it was important for her to understand why they followed this crazy man. She took care to observe him and not be noticed while she did. He sat in a chair, with several young girls sitting at his feet hanging on his every word. Preaching to them of personal freedom, he managed to make his followers dependent on him and under his control. Every one of them was fixated on each of his words. Was this some kind of weird cult? Every generation had them, and the sixties obviously were no exception.

After listening to him drone on for what seemed an eternity, she was relieved when the man stood to leave. "Clover, take care of our guest. Make her comfortable. You know what I mean. I want her to stay with us." He left the room, closing the door with a bang behind him

Finally! What had he meant to make her comfortable? Coming from him she didn't like the sound of it. She opened her eyes and stretched her arms over her head. Clover skipped across the room.

"You're awake. I was wondering how long you would sleep." Clover sat on the bed beside her. "You missed all the wisdom our leader shared with us. How are you feeling?"

"Much better. I need to go home." Jessie lifted her head off the pillow.

"You're free to leave whenever you want to, but Skylar would like you to stay with us." Clover smiled at her. "I want you to stay with us for a while too. Skylar will take care of you. He knows so many wonderful things."

That's exactly what she was afraid of, but she didn't say it out loud. "Why do you stay?" Jessie swung her legs onto the floor and sat up. "Don't you miss home and your family?"

Clover shook her head. "Skylar is my home. He is love. He knows the way for us to live a better life."

"It seems to me he is using you and piece by piece destroying who you are."

"You don't understand." Tears clouded Clover's eyes.

"You're right. I don't. Please, explain it to me. I want to understand."

"I was living on the streets. Skylar found me and brought me here. Girls like me don't have many options. I'd have nothing without him. He gave me a roof over my head and food to eat. My parents kicked me out of the house at fifteen. This is my family now. Essence is a sister, and so are all the other girls. You could be too if you stayed."

"I have family who would miss me. If I don't return, they'll have the police out looking for me." Jessie hoped she could find her way back to them.

"Skylar could hide you from them. He does it all the time.

"But I want to go home," Jessie said. "Why don't I see any other guys around beside Skylar?"

"Oh, there aren't any. Skylar is protecting us from men who want to hurt us."

Some protection. She knew it was true that women in the sixties had few rights. A woman couldn't even get a credit card until 1972 without her husband signing for it. It made Jessie thankful to all the women who fought for their rights. She couldn't imagine living in any other time. Still, she wanted to know why Clover stayed. "But don't you desire to marry and have a family someday?" She looked Clover directly in the eyes.

"Of course, I do." Clover smiled, folding her hands in her lap in a demure manner. "We are being groomed to be Skylar's brides."

"All of you?" Jessie knew her eyes had to be as big as saucers. She was shocked.

"Yes. He already has several wives. The kids on the compound are from his marriages."

Jessie shook her head. "That's against the law."

"Skylar obeys a different law. He tells us we aren't subject to the laws of this land." Clover glanced at the door when Essence walked out.

Little did he know. "Why would you want to share your husband with another woman?" Jessie ran her fingers through her hair.

"It has to be this way. Skylar must have many wives to fulfill his mission on this earth, and we have been chosen to help. It's an honor." Clover pressed her skirt with her hand, straightening the fullness over her legs.

"I just bet he does," Jessie mumbled under her breath. "Many wives indeed. What a crock." If she stayed much longer, she would lose her mind. This was the past, and she couldn't change it. Concentrate on the future, she reminded herself. "Clover, has a girl named Kimberly Ryan stopped here on her travels? I've been looking for her. She's my friend." Jessie hoped she sounded convincing. "I heard she might have come this way." Jessie pulled out a picture of Kimberly from her pocket. She had no idea how it had got there or why she knew to check.

Clover looked at the photo of Kimberly, a dark shadow crossing her face. "Put that away! Don't let Skylar see it. He'll go nuts. He carries one in his wallet. She was destined to be his number one wife, but she refused to marry him. They had a big fight, and he left her by the side of the road. He drove back to apologize, but he couldn't find her. He is looking for her replacement. Who knows—it could be you if you stay."

"I have to leave soon. I'm sure my fiancé is looking for me." The hair standing up on the back of her neck told her she had to get out of there now, before Skylar got back. "I hope someday you'll find out you don't need this place or Skylar."

"He'll look for you. Skylar doesn't let go of what he wants, and he told me he wants you. I'll help you, but you must hurry. He'll be back for lunch shortly." Clover glanced at the clock. "He'll be angry with me that you're gone."

"I hope he won't get too mad at you, but I must go." Jessie stood and followed Clover.

Clover led the way through several smaller rooms to a large kitchen/dining area. "I'll tell Skylar you slipped away when I went to get you a glass of water. Quick. He won't watch for you to leave from here." Clover showed her a door hidden in the pantry. "Skylar uses this door to leave the compound when the cops are coming in the front door looking for him."

"Thank you." Jessie left, hoping Clover could be free from Skylar too. She moved quickly out the door and across the field. There was no doubt in her mind he would try to stop her if he saw her. With no thought of where she was going, she started to run.

"Matt, if you can hear me, find me. I have no idea where I am."

****

Matt stepped into the open elevator and pushed the button, riding it up to the fourth floor where the doors opened in front of the nurse's station. Damn, he hated hospitals. Most of life's dramas and heartaches played out behind many of these doors. At least the color scheme in this hospital was better than most.

He stopped at the door to room four twenty-seven. Hesitant, he braced himself, pushed the door open, and walked in. Matt searched for any clue on her face that Jessie was present as soon as he walked in the room. "Where are you, sweetheart?" He gazed at her prone rigid form. "I brought the key. I'll keep it safe until I know what you want me to do with it. Reba said you're in two time dimensions, whatever that means. That's more your line of expertise, not mine. Will you ever come back to me?" He raked his hand through his hair. "I wish I knew what you saw and how this happened. How can I help if I don't know where to begin?" He brushed his lips across hers. He felt her steady breath, but no response to his kiss.

She didn't stir or move a muscle. Her face was as beautiful as ever, but there was no sign she even recognized his voice.

"How is she doing?" the nurse asked as she walked into the room pushing her cart.

"The same." He watched as she checked Jessie's vitals.

"Everything is normal. I think she'll be awake and telling you quite a story before you know it."

"I sure hope so."

"Of course, you do." She patted his hand. "There's the call button if you need anything. If she wakes up, you call us right away."

"You can count on it." Matt pulled out his computer and typed Kimberly Ryan's name along with the name of the town into the search window. Several articles popped up for him to read. He checked police records for girls who went missing in the same year and month. The more he read about the sixties the more he was convinced it would be hard to figure out what had happened to Ms. Ryan. There was a whole street culture, but no social media to keep tabs on people as they moved around.

Jessie was quiet, and he needed her to talk. Reba said there was something still going on, and somehow it was all tied together. The local authorities were grateful for his help and had given him carte blanche to be a part of their investigation. Kimberly wasn't on their radar; they only wanted to know what had happened to Jessie at the inn. It was up to him to work the Ryan end of the case until Jessie was back from wherever she had gone to. The first person he needed to talk to was Kimberly's boyfriend, Patrick, if he was still alive. He had to be in his late sixties or seventies. A quick check showed that Patrick was still in the area. After a call, Matt scheduled to meet him at noon tomorrow for lunch. Now all he had to do was figure out how Kimberly fit into what Reba said was still happening today. It would have been nice if Reba had told him what that something was.

****

48

Making it through the portal alive, he knew when he got to Rainbow Ridge that she had been there ahead of him. The woman was gone now. Undetected, he didn't even need to ask. Skylar's anger resounded off the walls. Clover cowered with the other girls. Any item within the proximity of his foot not heavy enough to remain stationary flew across the room. Several furniture pieces felt the fury of his punch during his tirade, including the side of Clover's face. Her eye, already swollen shut from the damage Skylar had inflicted, turned purple in the time the stranger stood there observing. When Skylar heard why he was there again, he would come unhinged. He found the thought humorous. How he loved this secret game he was playing. Maybe he should wait. Damn, there was no need for him to contend with Skylar's anger. Let the search begin. He would find her and only tell Skylar if it was necessary. The man and his guide left quietly before someone in the group saw him.

Chapter 7

Jessie had no sooner left Rainbow Ridge than she found herself outside of a café on the outskirts of a small town. She had no idea where or how she had gotten there. There was no rhyme or reason to what was happening. She was only a passenger on this journey, and quite frankly she was glad to be away from Skylar. It didn't stop her from checking over her shoulder to make sure he hadn't followed her. She couldn't change the past. It had already transpired, but she did wonder what had happened to Clover, Essence, and the other girls. Did they ever get away from him? She hoped for their sake that they had.

Jessie searched inside her jean pockets and found several dollar bills. Was this really happening or was it all in her mind? She opened the screen and walked inside. It was reminiscent of her mother's description of her grandmother's kitchen when they looked at old pictures together. A sweet memory from Jessie's childhood was the story about her great grandmother's table, with the chrome legs shiny enough to see her face in it and the cherry red cushions on the chairs that made the kitchen so cheery. That kitchen was one of her mom's favorite places to visit. This café reminded Jessie of those photos, and this diner kept theirs bright and shiny too. *Funny how things come back around again. This retro look was popular now.*

The tiny restaurant was cozy and clean. The waitress behind the counter reminded her of Franny at the diner in Blue Cove. The pencil was tucked in her dark hair, and her blue eye shadow was a bit on the extreme side. Tears sprang into Jessie's eyes. Would she ever see Franny again? Closing the door behind her, she brushed the moisture from her cheek. She was here for a reason, and it was time to find out why.

"Sit wherever you want, darlin', and I'll be right with you. The menus are on the table."

"Thank you." Jessie sat at the lunch counter and reached for a menu. If only Reba was here. She would know what was going on. Jessie glanced around the café. Franny would look perfect in this setting.

"Don't you just love this song by the Turtles?" Her foot tapped to the beat of the song on the jukebox. 'So happy together.' " She sang the words with them. "It's great isn't it?"

"It's one of my favorites," Jessie lied because she had no idea if she liked the song, although it had a catchy tune. As for the Turtles, she had never heard of them, but the waitress didn't need that piece of information.

"I also like 'I'm a Believer' by the Monkees. It will play next. I play all my favorites when the owner isn't here. He's not a fan." She whipped out her order pad from her pocket. "What can I get you, darlin'?"

"I've heard your chocolate malts are the best. I want one and a number three." She pointed to the menu. The menu said they were the best. Jessie took her cue from it.

"They are good if I do say so myself. We use nothing but the finest ingredients, and it keeps folks from miles around coming back for more. I'm Sue Ellen by the way, and I promise you a real taste treat."

"It's nice to meet you, Sue Ellen. I'm Jessie." She smiled at her and found her foot tapping to the music.

Sue Ellen leaned her elbows on the counter and bent toward her. "I see you can't keep your feet still either. I love this place when the kids come in after school. They keep the tunes playing, and they even dance."

"I bet it's a fun time." Jessie imagined the place filled with kids.

"Are you new around here? I've never seen you in here before." Sue Ellen placed a glass of water in front of her.

"I'm passing through. I've been looking for a friend who's gone missing. I hope I can find out where she is for her parents' sake."

"A lot of kids take off these days, drifting where the feeling takes them. Do you have a picture of your friend? Maybe I've seen her around." Sue Ellen glanced around the café. "Between you and me, sweetie, sometimes I think it'd be nice to forget all my responsibilities and be a free spirit going where the wind blows me."

Jessie pulled the photo out of her pocket. "This is her."

"She's a pretty one." Sue Ellen glanced at her. "Like you are. I've seen her a few times with a blond-headed fella. I remember because they were both starry-eyed looking at each other. I always like seeing young folks in love. It does my heart good. Didn't I read that she went missing a few days ago? I'm sure she's the one."

"Yes, she's the one. Her name is Kimberly. I hope I can find out what happened to her."

"She came in a couple of weeks ago. I remember it clearly because she was with a different fella. He was an older gentleman, and she didn't look at him the same way."

"How much older?"

"I can't say exactly, but he was quite a few years older. He had a black eye, which struck a nerve in me. Something was off about him. I was bothered by the way he wouldn't let her out of his sight. Not even when she went to the ladies' room. He stood at the door until she came out. Truthfully, I wanted to help her get away from him. I probably should have called the police. It bothered me all night that I hadn't."

"Did the police ever come here to question you or anyone?"

"No, why would they? We are fifty miles away from where the girl went missing. That's why I'm bothered by the fact I didn't call them. Maybe I could've helped her."

"I didn't realize I had wandered so far. Still, she was here, and you saw her recently, which gives me hope."

Sue Ellen responded to the call, *order up*. "I'll be right there." She came back with Jessie's malt, hamburger, and fries.

"Oh my, this looks yummy. I guess I'm hungry." Jessie put ketchup on her plate to dip her fries in.

"With your tiny figure, sweetie, I'm guessing you live mostly on the green stuff." Sue Ellen patted her hand.

"That and run every day. If you think of anything

else that might help me find Kimberly, please let me know."

"There is one more thing. Not only did the man have a real shiner and a cut on his chin, but the girl had been crying. Her eyes were all red, and her skin was blotchy. You know how it gets. Enjoy your lunch, hon. Like I told you, something told me that man was up to no good."

"What makes you think that?" Jessie drizzled ketchup on her bun, studying Sue Ellen as she talked.

"He sat beside her in the booth, not across from her, keeping her blocked in against the wall. I would say the man was her father, but he wasn't very fatherly. She was afraid of him, too. I'm sure of it."

"Did you happen to see the car they left in?"

"Can't say that I did. It was lunchtime, and it gets busy. I didn't even notice when they left."

"Thank you. You've been helpful." She dipped a fry in the malt and then took a drink. *Oh wow, chocolate, creamy yumminess.* She closed her eyes and savored. She would be running tomorrow for sure. The hamburger was cooked perfectly, the fries were cut fresh and not frozen, and the malt was too good to be true.

****

Matt hung up from talking to Dylan. He gathered his stuff and got ready to leave. Walking over to the hospital bed, he gazed at her face. "Where are you, sweetheart? Please come back to me soon. We can work this case together. Just come back." His lips brushed across hers. If he hadn't been watching her closely, he would have missed it. He knew that look—he had seen it on her face many times before. "What are you tasting, sweetheart? I wish I was there to enjoy it with you.

More than once he had enjoyed seeing the look of pure pleasure on her face. Jessie was savoring the taste of something. To think he had almost left a few minutes ago. Happy for his hesitation, he was given the reassurance he needed. Pulling his chair close to her bed, he took up his vigil once again, smiling at every small expression that crossed her face. His body relaxed. He could finally breathe again.

He slipped the engagement ring from the bag the nurse had given him when he first arrived. A rainbow of colors sparkled through the stone as he held the diamond up to the light. He would take this to get it sized, and the next time he slipped it on her finger all their friends would share in the joy of it.

Matt made a few more phone calls, not wanting to leave Jessie's side yet. "Sadie, it's Matt."

"I was waiting for your call. Reba told me earlier what was going on."

"Should I call her parents?"

"No, don't call them yet. Wait a day or two. If things don't change, I'll call them myself. You don't want my son demanding answers that no one at this point can give him."

"Help me understand this strange ability that Jessie has. I don't get what's happening to her." Matt leaned closer to Jessie's face. He thought he saw her smile.

"I don't understand what she's going through right now, although Reba seemed to. I never had anything like this happen to me. Jessie seems to be more advanced than I ever was. I remember my mom telling me when I was a little girl her mom had premonitions all the time. She saw ghosts but never had an outlet to do anything with the knowledge she was given, which made her feel like she was going crazy. Jessie's are used for a reason. I'm sure, son, as soon as she is back with us, she will let you know where she's been and why."

"One can always hope. She hardly moves, but her vitals are normal. The doctors can't find any medical explanation for what is going on with her."

"After talking to Reba, I'm positive we'll know soon. I for one can't wait to hear her side of the tale and find out what she's experienced."

"Will it always be like this for her?"

"I don't have the answer to your question, but I know Jessie warned you to think seriously about what was happening to her."

"Sadie, I'm not having second thoughts. I love your granddaughter. I'm trying to figure out if I will ever get my girl back."

"Oh, she'll be back. Jessie's tough and is having quite an experience. At least Reba seems to think she is, and Reba's in the know. Did I ever tell you that Jessie looks like my grandmother? She was a beautiful and gifted woman. I think you'll have an exciting life together."

"Does Jessie's mom have this gift?" His fingers tapped on the arm of the chair.

"No, it's on my son's side of the family. My daughter-in-law would never understand any of this. She would be appalled by it."

"How about Peyton? Does she have the gift?"

"It hasn't manifested in her yet. Still, I think someday she might show signs of it. Only time will tell."

"Sadie, I will stay in touch. If you think of anything that might help, let me know."

"I will, Matt. Don't worry about Jessie. She'll be back as soon as she learns what's crucial for her to know. Whatever it is, it couldn't be learned in our time dimension."

"I'll keep working the case my way. Hopefully, we'll come to the same conclusion after we can talk again." He opened the briefcase, taking Jessie's small notebook out of it.

"I can't wait to hear Jessie's story, but if her condition changes and you think her parents need to know, call me. I want to be there too." Sadie paused. "I love you, son. She'll be back. You have to believe it."

"I'll try." He smiled at her words. "If anything changes, I'll let you know."

Matt opened Jessie's small notebook. He began reading her observations. The name Linda Cranston was underlined, and he knew he would have to find out who she was. Holding her hand, he fell asleep sitting in the chair beside her bed.

Chapter 8

The man knew she was in the café. He felt her strong presence the closer he got. Hiding behind a tree, he watched and waited. He slowly approached the diner, not wanting to arouse her suspicion or anyone else's. He shifted his weight from foot to foot. Damn. What a nuisance it was traipsing after some fool woman stupid enough to get too close to the portal. "Keep your distance," he mumbled. "Don't let that nosy waitress recognize you." He ducked back when the door to the café opened. False alarm.

The absurdity of the situation made him chuckle. One part of him wanted the fool woman, and the other side of him would love to get rid of her. What he wouldn't give to be home in his lounge chair. His fists clenched at his side. His guide told him to follow her but not to draw attention to himself. How in the hell was he supposed to do that? Damn. He had no idea who the person inside him was or what he wanted half of the time. Kicking the dirt, he frowned. All he wanted to do now was wring her pretty neck.

****

Matt invaded her thoughts when she walked out of the diner. Was he looking for her? Did he even know she was gone? Jessie had no idea how any of this worked. She only knew she didn't want to be stuck here forever. Katie would be angry if she didn't make it back in time for her party. "Darn tears." She wiped at the moisture filling her eyes. Where would she go next? She plopped down on the bench in front of the café. She sniffed, feeling sorry for herself. She sighed. All she wanted was to go home. Was that asking too much?

"Are you all right, young lady? You seem deep in thought. Maybe I can help." He handed her a tissue.

The man who sat down beside her was middleaged with gray hair at his temple, a tall man with lifeless, grayish-blue eyes. "I'm looking for a friend. Have you seen her?" Jessie showed him the picture of Kimberly. He cracked his knuckles several times. A shadow moved across his face, and pastiness took its place.

"No, no." He shook his head. "I don't believe I've ever seen her before. She's your friend, you say. And you're looking for her? Has anyone seen her?" He wiped the sweat off his forehead with his hand as he rambled on.

"A few people in town remember seeing her. I'm getting close. I know I am."

"A word to the wise. Be careful. Some people get lost because they want to. I'm not saying that's true with your friend. All I'm saying is it's possible she doesn't want to be found."

"It's possible, I guess, but unlikely. Someone else who doesn't want me to find her would be closer to the truth. In her case, I know she wants to be found. Her family is waiting for her, and so is her boyfriend. My personal belief is that something bad might have happened to her. If it has, I will find out what, and who did it." Jessie's fist clenched at her side.

"You're pretty sure of yourself for one so young. You sound like you'd be willing to take on a lot for your friend."

"I'm determined. Kimberly will be going home to her waiting family."

"Like I said, watch your step." He grabbed her wrist, giving it a twist.

She slapped at his hand. "Stop. You're hurting me. Are you threatening me?" Jessie pulled her arm free from his grasp.

"No, I'm only warning you. Sometimes things are better left alone. It may or may not be true in this case. You wouldn't want to spend all your time looking over your shoulder. Now would you?"

The way he danced around the subject was quite interesting. He knew something. "What did you say your name was?"

"I didn't say." He stood. "Keep your nose where it belongs and save yourself a lot of trouble." He walked down the road not looking back.

"That was definitely a threat." She watched him until he was out of sight. What an odd man. He fit somewhere into the picture, but how? *Kimberly, you need to help me. You brought me here. You have to show me why. I need to know soon because I want to go back. There are people waiting for me, and your story must be told.* A pen and paper were essential at this point. She wanted to write things down before she forgot.

As of now, she knew of three men who were connected to Kimberly Ryan in some way—Skylar, the man Sue Ellen saw her with a few days ago, and now this strange man. What were their connections? She stepped back into the café briefly and asked Sue Ellen for a pencil. Pulling a napkin from the holder on her way out the door, she sat outside and wrote the clues she was learning on its flimsy paper.

****

Matt hoped his time with Patrick Hamilton would prove interesting and informative. He pulled up to the place where they agreed to meet for lunch. Matt arrived first and got a booth toward the back of the café, where he waited for Hamilton.

"Patrick." Matt stood and called to him when he walked in.

"You must be Matt Parker. I've never seen you around town before." Patrick walked back to where Matt stood.

"This is my first time to the area." Matt shook his hand.

"You told me on the phone you wanted to talk me about my old girlfriend, Kimberly. I don't see how I can be of any help. It was such a long time ago." Patrick slipped into the booth across from Matt.

Matt sat after Patrick made himself comfortable. "As I told you on the phone, I'm working with Chief Macintyre. I speak from experience that even the smallest detail can be helpful sometimes." Matt handed him one of the menus the waitress had left earlier. "Let's order, and then we can talk."

"Sounds good to me. I don't like to talk about her." He glanced over the menu, making his choice. "Those were some dark days in my life. I've tried my best to forget them over the years."

After the waitress took their order, Matt spent the next ten minutes trying to put Patrick at ease with small talk. As soon as Patrick seemed comfortable, Matt wanted answers. "What do you remember about the day

Kimberly went missing?"

"Not much, truthfully. We had talked a few hours before. I told the police that when they questioned me at the time. Kimberly said she'd wait for me, but I was late. I got mad at her for not waiting." He rested his elbows on the table. "After I found out she was missing, all I felt was regret for being a jerk." He snapped his fingers. "She vanished, as if into thin air, never to be heard from or seen again. It took me a few years to get over it. I'm not sure I ever did really."

"Can you remember anything about your conversation that day?" Matt pulled out his small notebook and pen.

"I remember thinking she was trying to make me jealous." Patrick rubbed his temple. "I was always jealous of her. She didn't have to try."

"Why were you jealous if you don't mind me asking?" Matt studied the man across from him.

"She kept talking about this guy who wouldn't leave her alone. Kimberly was beautiful, stunning really." His eyes got misty. "I always worried she'd find someone better than I was. I couldn't understand why she wanted to be with a fella like me. What does that say about me?"

"You're like most of us if we're honest." Matt thanked the waitress for their drinks.

"Nice to know I'm not alone, but it doesn't help much now. I've often wondered if I had listened to her and asked more questions, if maybe that day would have ended differently." He stared out the window, a far-away look in his eyes.

"Did she mention the man's name?" Matt asked as he jotted notes.

"She might have, but if she did, I wasn't paying attention to what she was saying. I couldn't seem to get past my own jealousy issues. I've lived with a lot of regrets." Patrick took a swig of his cola.

"Were you able to recover enough to make a life for yourself?" Matt squeezed a slice of lemon in his tea.

"Sure. I moved on and got married. We had a family, but it didn't last. I divorced a few years ago. My ex told me I was emotionally distant. I get it. I am. This damn memory has been a cloud over me every single day. Kimberly was the love of my life, and I've lived with the guilt of not finding her." Patrick tapped his fingers on the table.

"Did she ever mention anyone bothering her at work?" Matt thanked the waitress when she set his lunch in front of him.

"She mentioned a hippie guy who was following her around town. Linda, her friend, started walking with her because she didn't want to be alone. I vaguely remember she also said something about some other man. No name was mentioned that I can recall. We were all young. I was obsessed with her. I could see why other guys were too."

"Are you talking about Linda Cranston? Do you know if she's still alive?" Matt asked.

"Yes, to both of your questions. She lives in a house not far from here." Patrick wrote Linda's address and phone number on a piece of paper. "Kimberly and Linda were inseparable. She was privy to some of Kimmie's deepest secrets." His hand went to his forehead. "Wow, it has been years since I called her Kimmie, my nickname for her. All her friends called her that."

They talked through lunch, and Matt asked him a few more questions. Patrick told him a lot without saying much. Matt could relate to the guilt Patrick felt. He'd been there once. Thankfully, he had met Jessie. Damn, he wanted her back. The next person he wanted to talk to was Linda Cranston.

Before going back to the hospital, he stopped by the Brass Lantern. He went up to the room still taped off by the police and slipped under the tape. "Jess, tell me what happened to you. I need you to talk to me. Kimberly was either kidnapped or murdered. I should know more soon. Thank you for the clue about Linda, by the way. I will stop by to see her tomorrow. As to what happened in this room, I know the key holds part of the answer. How do I get you back through the portal? I'm doing a bit of research on trans-dimensional portals. See how you and Jeremy are rubbing off on me. You are changing the way I approach a case, sweetheart."

Matt shook his head. "I can't believe I'm sitting here talking to an empty room and believing somehow you'll hear me. All I know is that I need to get a message to you. Since this is where you started your improbable journey, I'm hoping you might hear me from this location." Matt walked around the room, touching her belongings. He brought her up to date on the time he spent with Patrick. "Jess, he's still in a bad place. I felt sad for him in a way, and at the same time, I wondered whether he was somehow guilty in her disappearance—my thinking in every case we've ever had. You understand me. Anyone is a possible suspect and is only ruled out by the evidence."

He picked up her necklace off the dresser, letting it

slip from his fingers to the palm of his hand. The delicate chain sparkled in the light. He remembered the moment he had given it to her. The look on her face made it worth every penny he had spent on it. Would he ever see it caress her neck again? He was sure one moment that she would be back soon and just as certain in the next that it wasn't possible. He didn't want to believe she could be lost to him. "I saw the name Linda Cranston written on your notebook. Patrick told me that Kimberly and Linda were best friends. Did you know Patrick liked to call her Kimmie? I thought you might need that piece of information to help you in your search. I'm done here for today. I'll be at your side tonight and back here to talk again tomorrow. In the meantime, find a way to tell me where you are and how I can bring you home."

****

The sun felt good on her face as she lingered outside the café. She wrote on the napkin scribbling her thoughts as fast as they came. Besides, she had no idea where to go next. Jessie wanted to communicate with Matt but wasn't sure how to go about it. Was it possible for Matt to hear her? She had no notion, much less how to explain the means by which she had traveled back in time. What could she possibly do from here?

Her memory was slowly returning. The key played some part in the process, but there was no accounting for the energy that lifted her off the ground. Had Kimberly or some other strange occurrence brought her? If only she could talk to Reba. Abigail, from their second case, told her once she had concentrated her thoughts in the hope that someone could hear her. If Abbie could do it, Jessie needed to try. She cleared her mind and concentrated her thoughts, calling out to her friend.

Reba, I need to talk to you. I hope you can hear me. She concentrated, repeating the words over again. *Matt needs to know I'm okay. I have no idea how I got here, but I'm in the sixties. I'm learning about Kimberly and following where she went during the last days of her life. She's dead. I'm sure of it.* All the things Jessie had seen to this point began to play over and over in her mind. The only thing she didn't know was if Reba could hear or see anything.

"Jessie, dear, I can hear you. Research, girl. You'll find your answers in trans-dimensional portals. You're stuck in another time dimension, but I know you'll return to us when your job is done. Relax, my dear girl. You're in my heart."

The tears flowed freely down her cheeks. It worked. As for research, she didn't know if they even had computers or where she would find one if they did. The first place she would check was the library, and after that the local university. If she remembered history right, computers were still big and too expensive for private ownership. The nearest university would be the most likely place to find a computer of that size.

Chapter 9

Matt looked over the case file he had created in his notebook. He filled in the important facts he had learned so far. Every time he glanced at Jessie, it seemed strange to see her motionless. She was always full of life and energy. If he knew his girl, she was busy wherever she was at this moment. Probably running. The doctor's visit earlier had given him hope.

Two nurses came into the room. "I'm Lillie, and she's Stella. Don't you worry about your fiancée. Her vitals are all good. We are here to rotate her position on the bed and to exercise her limbs." Stella stood by Jessie's feet, and Lillie was near her shoulders. "We don't want her getting bed sores."

Stella, the smaller of the two women, said, "You're free to stay and watch. Any time you're in the room, you can massage her leg muscles and move her limbs the way we show you. We want her to be able to move them as soon as she wakes up. We don't want atrophy to set in."

Another thing to be concerned about if she didn't come back soon. He watched carefully as they showed him how to shift her. He continued to move her limbs for several minutes after they left the room. "We'll keep working your legs, and you'll be up running as soon as you wake up." He sat in the chair to answer his phone.

"Matt, this is Reba. I told you I would call if I

heard anything. Jessie contacted me today."

"I won't ask how." Matt leaned back in his chair and smiled.

"You wouldn't believe it if I told you." Reba chuckled. "She wanted you to know she is okay. The rest she showed me will be between her and me. I might tell Sadie some of it too, but no one else will be able to wrap their head around it. She's following Kimberly's trail in the sixties."

"Of course, she is." Matt rubbed his temple. "I never thought of the possibility of time travel. Why would I? Reba, it's not possible. How can that be?"

"It doesn't make sense because it falls outside the norms of logic. Trans-dimensional relates to another dimension not related to the world that we know. Jessie's body is here, but she has gone through a time portal and is hanging out in the sixties. She's walking and talking to people living well over fifty years ago. Some of those folks may still be alive, and others might have passed on. I find the whole idea utterly amazing—unlike anything I could have imagined. I can't wait to hear the stories that she will tell. You may cross paths with her without even knowing it. She'll be in one dimension and you in another." Reba paused. "How do you feel about this?"

"Hell. How am I supposed to answer you. I have no idea how I feel. I've never heard anything like this before." Matt glanced at Jessie. "Sorry, it's going to take some getting used to. I can't see it right now."

"Don't worry about what you don't understand. All you need to know is if she's okay."

"If you could see her like she is right now, you might wonder too. The doctors don't have any treatment for her because they have no idea what's going on with her. They're as perplexed as I am. The one thing that keeps me going is I was told her brain scan was problem-free and her brain is active."

"Of course, her brain is active. She's talking and observing life the same way you are. She'll be back better than ever. You mark my words. In the process, you'll save a few lives. Medical science doesn't know everything. Miracles happen every day, and they come with no explanations."

"I'll take your word for it."

"If I hear anything else from her, I'll get back with you."

Matt spent the next hour talking to Jeremy. All Jeremy could tell him was trans-dimensional portals were only a theory. He hadn't heard of anyone traveling back in time, although plenty of works of fiction had been written on the subject. Leave it to Jessie to cross the threshold into another dimension without the help of a time machine.

Matt exercised her legs and arms before he left for the night. Tomorrow, would she visit Linda Cranston as a young girl while he was talking to her as an older woman? He shook his head. This was too damn weird.

****

Jessie understood it now. Not that she could find information on the portal other than the basic fact time travel was considered pure fantasy because no known portal existed. But Kimberly had pulled her through a gateway in time, and here she was. No more wasting time. The sooner she figured this out, the sooner she could get back to Matt.

Linda was Kimberly's friend. First thing on the

agenda was to find her. Jessie had no idea where she was, but she had a feeling she would run into her soon.

Suddenly, she found herself back where her travel began. The Brass Lantern hadn't changed much over the years, at least from the outside. It still had the same beautiful gardens. Jessie walked up the stairs and through the door.The newspaper on the coffee table blared the headlines of a missing girl. She picked up the paper and began to read.

"Welcome to the Brass Lantern." The woman smiled sweetly at her. "I'm Florence Templeton. Can I help you?"

Jessie placed the paper back on the table. "It's sad about that girl."

"Yes. Kimberly worked here at the inn. She was one of our guests' favorites. Always so sweet, giving folks the time of day. If you know what I mean. Many young kids these days don't want to work, but Kimberly paid attention to folks. She was kind to them. We're all simply stunned by the news that she's missing."

"The paper says her parents reported that she never came home from work a few days ago." Gosh, was it May tenth already? She had missed some days somewhere, or did time work differently here? Confused didn't even begin to cover her emotions.

"That's right. The police have been in and out of here the past several days, asking the same questions repeatedly. I swear it felt like my head would explode. The only thing I told them about was the strange looking fella hanging around the place for several weeks before she went missing. He wouldn't leave her alone, even after she told him to go away or she'd call the police. I believe he has something to do with it, but I have no proof."

Jessie described Skylar to the woman. "Does that sound like the guy you saw?"

"It could be him or over half the young boys in the country. Heck, our town is filled with long-haired young men. If you ask me, their parents should make them get a haircut and clean up. No ands, ifs, or buts about it." The woman sniffed, her hazel eyes squinting. "But it's none of my business how some folks choose to raise their kids. In my day, my parents would have never let us get away with junk like young ones do now."

"I may be wrong, but I think each older generation says the same thing about the younger ones all the time. At least, my grandmother says they always do. As if they themselves never had any quirky behavior." Jessie smiled sweetly at the woman. "She says it's easy to forget what it's like to be young as time marches on. Fads that are unique to the times are the one constant that ties us together from one generation to the next. I was reading the other day about raccoon coats and rumble seats. That seems strange to me, but it was all the thing in its day." She knew she had hit the target. The woman glared at her.

"You can't compare the harmless fun of those days to these drug-crazy kids today. I dare you to try. You must be one of them."

"No, I can't say that I am." She smiled, wondering what the woman would think if she knew Jessie was from a different time period altogether.

"Are you going to stand here wasting my time all day, girlie? I don't suppose you're a paying customer, are you?"

Before she answered, she reached in her pocket. What she found made her know she was supposed to stay the night. "I want a room, please." This was being orchestrated, and she wasn't surprised to find herself in the room she had been in that strange night. How long ago was it? Time was mixed up for her at the moment.

"Is Linda Cranston working today?"

"Do you know our Linda?" The woman frowned. "I've never seen you around before."

"I'm not from here, but a friend told me I needed to meet Linda when I got to town." Quick thinking on her part and hopefully the lady bought it.

"She'll be here later after classes. It's her first day back. Linda was afraid to come back to work for a few days after Kimberly went missing. She'll get over it soon enough. We couldn't hold her job forever."

"I look forward to meeting Linda." Jessie took the key from Florence and climbed the stairs to her room. Florence wasn't an empathetic woman. Jessie couldn't believe the woman thought Linda could just get over the death of her friend. Having a friend die wasn't easy at any age, especially one so young.

She sat across from the strange looking dresser to wait. It was the same exact one, or at least a good replica of it. Leaning her head back against the chair, she fell asleep. *Matt was in her head again, talking to her and calling for her to come back. Where was she supposed to come back from? "I'm here, Matt. Why do you look so sad? I'm here." She waved her hands, trying to get his attention. He couldn't see her. How could that be? She was stuck inside the mirror looking out. She called to him again. Her hope rose as he approached the mirror. Was it possible he could see or hear her? He was so close she reached her hand forth to touch him. There was glass, only cold glass between them. "I'm here. Please don't walk away." The tears trickled down her eyes. "Please don't leave me."*

Jessie awakened. Her cheeks were wet with tears. And then she viewed him through the mirror sitting in the room where she was now, only he was in the future. No wonder the dream had seemed real. How long had Kimberly waited, viewing life through the mirror until Jessie had finally seen her? A cloud of depression settled over her. Would Matt take as long to see her? The room closed in on her. She needed air. Stepping out into the hall, she saw a young woman pushing a cart.

"May, I help you?" The girl with a blonde ponytail walked toward her.

"Are you Linda?" Jessie asked.

"Yes, do I know you?" The girl's brows rose with her question.

"No, you don't." Jessie went on to explain she was investigating Kimberly's disappearance.

"You seem too young to be a cop. They don't allow women to be police around here."

"I'm not a police officer. I work for a newspaper, and I'm doing a story on Kimberly. I heard you're her best friend."

"We're friends. I'm so scared for her. She'd never run away from home. Kimberly was happy. She was studying to become a teacher. There's no way she'd walk away from her studies or from Patrick. They planned on getting married someday."

"Would you like to come in and talk a little bit?" Jessie moved out of the open door and motioned her in.

"I can only stay a minute. The dragon lady will be looking for me and tell my boss. I need this job to pay for school. My parents don't have the money to send me, and they don't think a girl needs to go to college. I guess I'm supposed to get married, and that's all I'm good for, but I have dreams. Kimberly and I were alike in some ways. She was in no hurry to marry and have kids. She wanted more too. We talked all the time about burning our bras and joining the movement. Women should have rights too." She glared. "It's a man's world."

Jessie remembered reading about the bra-burning when she had researched the sixties. "Was Kimberly worried about anything in the days before she went missing?"

"There was a strange older man and some hippie dude bothering her. Kimberly didn't like the way they looked at her. She didn't want to walk anywhere in town by herself. Both were stalking her if you ask me." Linda sat on the edge of her chair. "Have you seen any pictures of Kimberly? She was beautiful. Guys followed her around like bees to honey. I liked hanging with her because once they knew they couldn't get anywhere with her, they always came to me. Truthfully, the one she worried the most about was her stepdad. He's a real loser."

"Why is that?" Jessie stood as soon as Linda did.

"He always followed her around, staring at her when he thought no one was looking. Her mom blamed her for the attention he was giving her. She has a warped view that Kimberly was trying to steal her husband. Her mom told Kimmie she wanted her out of the house."

"She kicked her out?" The piece of news bothered Jessie. She hadn't read anything about it in the papers. "None of the reports I've seen had that piece of information in it."

"Are you kidding me! Her mom wouldn't tell anyone that tidbit. It's about appearances for her. She told the police that Kimberly probably had run away." Linda went over to the dresser and ran her hand along the top.

"Do you think she ran away?"

"Nope. She had packed her stuff and was going to move in with me. You can't tell anyone, but she was living in the attic here at the inn. She'd go out the door and slip in the back when no one was watching."

"Is it possible someone found out she was living here?" Jessie asked.

"Anything is possible, I guess. She was only staying here for a few days. We were getting a place together. We were supposed to move in our new place May second."

"What do you think happened to her?"

"Truthfully, I believe my friend is dead. I have no idea who murdered her, but someone did. You'd have to stand in line if you wanted her gone." The tears flowed down her cheeks. "Her only crime was being beautiful because she was as sweet as they come."

"I'm sorry about your friend." Jessie hugged Linda. "You've given me a lot to think about."

"I'd better get back to work." She straightened the lace doily on top of the dresser. "This old piece of furniture is creepy. I don't like being in this room. Sometimes while I'm working the inn makes strange sounds. There's a lot of history in this place, and not all of it's good either."

"Were you working the day Kimberly went missing?"

"I was here, and like I told the cops I never saw her leave the place, which is strange. I still don't know how I could have missed her." Linda opened the door and walked out. "If you need anything, let the desk know and I'll bring it up to you." She waved as she walked down the hall.

Darn, she wished she had her computer. How would she learn about the history of the inn without it? Linda was right—the furniture in this room was creepy. If Linda Cranston never saw Kimberly Ryan leave, did someone murder her then wait until later to move the body? There were so many possibilities. What about the stepdad? That was a new angle. He hadn't shown up in any discussions before.

One thing for sure—she had to find out more of the history of the inn. Jessie went to the small parlor area. She picked up several brochures telling about things to see around town and a couple more on the inn. If a place had a unique history, people usually liked to advertise it. A trip to the library was the next thing on her agenda. She'd know soon enough if the Brass Lantern had secrets to divulge.

Chapter 10

Matt showed up at Linda's house on the outskirts of town precisely at noon. The small cape cod style house with clapboard siding had a welcoming front door and great curb appeal. The house was pretty, well maintained with a freshly painted white picket fence, and perfect in the New England town setting. Linda obviously loved yard work. Her flower gardens were beautiful. He couldn't help but wonder as he walked through the gate if Jessie had met Ms. Cranston yet. Of course, she had. She was the one who left the name on the notepad for him to see. If he knew his girl, they had talked, and Jessie was off on another trail tracking down a murderer. Speaking of tracking, was it possible for Radar to track Jessie into an alternate dimension or reality? Matt had watched enough sci-fi shows to understand the idea of gates and portals into another dimension, but it was fiction wasn't it? Until Jessie awakened and could tell him face to face what was going on, he would believe nothing.

He knocked on the door. "I'm Matt Parker. I called you earlier." The years had been kind to the woman opening the door. A few gray hairs were mingled among the blonde ones. Her blue eyes were bright and inquisitive. But it was the aura of kindness around her that drew Matt in.

As she unlocked the screen, she said, "Come in."

She held the screen open for him. "Please sit." She motioned him toward the chair. "I've made some tea, sandwiches, and cookies for lunch. I hope you're hungry. Having a guest to share a meal with is a rare pleasure for me." She smiled at him. "If you don't mind, we'll eat here in the parlor—it's such a cheery room. You can put your tea right there on that table." Linda pointed at the coaster as she handed him a hot cup of tea.

Matt chuckled. "When it comes to food, I seldom turn anything down. I appreciate you going to all the trouble." He took the small plate and napkin she handed him and reached for the cucumber sandwiches and hors d'oeuvres, filling his plate. Sadie and Reba would fit in perfectly in this home.

"Now that we're all settled, you can ask me your questions, and I'll do my best to answer them."

"Tell me what you can remember about Kimberly Ryan and your days working at the inn. I may think of more questions while you're talking."

She began by telling him about the woman she called the dragon lady, and about the owner at the time, who was quite strange. "Of course, at that age all adults were strange. Please eat more. There's plenty." She held the platter of sandwiches in front of him as soon as his plate was empty.

Several cups of tea and cookies later Matt walked out the door. He had learned a lot about her in the process. Linda's flowers were her pride. She knew all their names and lit up as she talked about her love of gardening. She worked in her flower beds as often as the weather permitted.

He discovered a lot more about Kimberly Ryan's

situation. Her stepfather didn't sound like a nice man, and her mom wasn't there for her either. Poor kid. Linda told him that Kimberly's mom and stepdad divorced about a year after she went missing. He also learned Kimberly's mother lived in regret until the day she died—ridden with guilt over her jealousy of her daughter and for kicking her out of the house, she couldn't forgive herself. She died a broken woman. Not much consolation for Kimberly now, who had needed her mom at the time.

Matt had no idea how he could solve this murder when some of the key players had already passed on. Still, if they could solve it, at least Kimberly would be at peace. And if Reba was right, they would save some girls living in the present too. Matt thought the case had some of the same traits of their human trafficking case, only there was a more sordid feel to it.

Linda suggested he go back to the inn and talk with Evelyn, the night clerk. She seemed to think that the woman knew more than she let on. The Brass Lantern was next on his agenda after he stopped by to see Jessie and talked to Jeremy. Had he found any new information on the inn? In his mind, the inn was central to whatever had gone on then and now. Once he got to the hospital and found out she was still doing well, he could get back to work.

****

Jessie learned in her research at the library that the inn had hiding places and tunnels built into the basement which were used during the days of the underground railroad. The original owner was a part of a network of people who hid the fugitives from slavery in their homes. They would be moved north at night into the free states, Canada, or England. Jessie found it fascinating. If the tunnels hadn't been sealed, maybe that was how Kimberly's body was removed from the inn without anyone seeing it. Were they still operational, or had someone reopened them? She would have to do some snooping around. Radar, her friend's tracking bloodhound, would be needed to help her do the snooping. What if they were still using it for something illegal? Goosebumps prickled her skin at the mere thought. Built by one man to free slaves, was it possible someone else was using it to make slaves? This part of the case she couldn't tackle alone. She needed to go back soon. Matt would have to be a part of solving this case.

If only she could talk to Matt and Jeremy. If she knew Matt, he already had Jeremy doing research. He must be totally perplexed by what was happening to her. She wasn't sure how it appeared on the other side of the mirror. Matt was in the future, and she was in the past. It was too strange to try and comprehend. On her way out of the library, she picked up a flier. Joan Baez was in concert that night not far from where she was staying. Jessie knew she was supposed to be there.

The room was packed, with standing room only, and the music blared through the night air. She forgot how loud it could get, especially near the speakers. Jessie glanced around at the crowd and smiled at their response to the music. The kids danced in wild abandonment and a freedom she had never see before. Jessie loved it. She ducked behind the large speaker when she saw a familiar face in the crowd. Skylar was surrounded by several of the girls from the commune. As she peeked out of her hiding place, there was another familiar face. The nervous man from outside the café was standing with Skylar. Humm. Interesting. What was the connection between those two? *Please don't let them see me.* She pushed farther into the crowd.

Listening to the musicians was an enlightening experience. Folk songs rang out with the words of protest and social justice. The headliners didn't just sing the songs, they led a movement. Seeing it up close, the sixties brought about great changes to the country. Revolution vibrated through the crowd along with the smell of pot. The hippie generation reshaped the culture of the country—probably more than anyone realized at the time. How many times had shifts happened with each new generation? A great subject for an article. All she knew was that there were a lot of voices that gave words to what the youth were feeling—Bob Dylan, Joni Mitchell, Joan Baez, Pete Seeger, and many more. Jessie found the whole scene interesting and wanted to learn as much about as she could before she had to go back. She loved the music and found herself dancing the night away with several strangers in the crowd.

Would she ever be able to tell her children she got to see the sixties up close and personal? Probably not, but who knows—maybe time travel would become a standard norm in a few years. From the hip-hugging, bell bottom jeans to the flowers woven through the girls' hair it was unique in every way. Heck, even she was wearing a bright colored tie-dyed tee. Katie would never believe it. Maybe Kimberly could arrange for her to bring it back to the present.

As soon as it was safe, Jessie left the concert and made her way back to the inn. Guests still occupied the small lobby area. She sat in one of the leather chairs and listened to the conversations going on around her. She wasn't ready to go to the room where it all started. Eventually, she would have to push past her fear and go up to the room again.

****

The man had caught sight of her for a moment in the crowd. She was big trouble, and he had to get rid of her before she ruined everything. As she stumbled around asking questions, it wouldn't take long for her to learn something. If she hadn't figured it out, she would soon enough. "Sky, I saw her here in the crowd. What should I do?"

"You know what you have to do. Bring her to me. I'll take care of it, and she'll never cross back again." Skylar studied the crowd but didn't see her. "Point her out, man. I don't see her."

The man searched the crowd and squeezed through the crush to where he had last seen her. Skylar was right behind him. "She's gone, dammit. She was right here a minute ago."

"Garrett, I'm not happy about this. Find her, man. Whatever it takes, don't let her go back through that portal. We can't risk it, dude."

"I'll take care of it. She's one step ahead of me, but we'll meet head on eventually. She's as good as dead. No one will be the wiser. We can bury her on the commune, and she'll simply be another missing person."

****

"I see you're back, miss." Florence walked up and tapped her on the shoulder. "Where were you all day?"

Jessie wanted to tell her none of her business, but

she chose a different approach. "I was at the library and then went to a Joan Baez concert."

"I should have known you were one of those people. You have that look, and I'm never wrong.

"Exactly what kind of people are you talking about?"

"Those crazy people trying to destroy the country as we know it. The folks who listen to that unpatriotic music."

"You don't know how wrong you are. I'm far removed from them. Truthfully, I understand what they are trying to do. I went to the concert because I wanted to see and hear what this generation is saying. I'm of the persuasion we can learn from each other if we listen. And maybe if we listen, we won't keep repeating the same mistakes of the generation before us. I'm not sure if it's possible, but it's worth a try if you ask me."

"You're exactly what I thought you were the first minute I saw you. You're a troublemaker, sticking your nose in where it doesn't belong. Telling your elders, who know better than you, what's best. I wish I could tell you to leave, but you're a paying guest. I'm keeping my eye on you."

"Wow, what have I done to her," Jessie muttered on her way up the stairs. Florence was threatened by her, and Jessie had no idea what she had done to evoke that anger. Until she was out of here, she had to be more careful.

Chapter 11

Matt spent time talking to Jeremy. Jeremy filled him in about the history of the inn. Matt wanted to search the premises if Carl agreed. The drive to the inn was pleasant enough. The temperature on the bank sign he passed said sixty-five, which was a nice start to any day. The sun was shining, a visit to the hospital earlier had assured him that Jessie was still hanging in there, and traffic was light, so he made good time.

Matt walked into the lobby and approached the front desk. "Good morning, Evelyn."

"Hello again, Mr. Parker. I see you're back. You're free to go up to the room if you like." She smiled at him.

"Is Carl in this morning? I would like to talk to him after I ask you a few questions."

"Carl is here. He's always here. The poor man doesn't get much time off. I'll let him know you want to talk." She texted him. "He said he'll be here in ten. He's fixing a water leak in one of the rooms. His work is never done. This is an old place and in constant need of repair."

"It's a beautiful inn—unique with a diverse history." Matt glanced around the inn. Now he sounded like Jess.

"There's plenty of history, which gives Carl a measure of comfort as he repairs the place."

"What do you know about the tunnels and rooms under the inn? I heard they were used by the original owner during the years of the underground railroad. Is anyone using them now?"

"No. I hope you haven't been listening to the stories around town. Those rooms were sealed off a long time ago. No one ever goes down there. I doubt most folks would know how to find them."

"What stories are those, Evelyn?" Matt quizzed her.

"People swear they've heard sounds coming from under the streets in front of the inn. The neighbors on both sides of the inn have complained. They're not hearing anything, because like I said, those tunnels aren't in use and haven't been for years."

"Are you positive?" He studied the woman's body language. Something was amiss.

"I'm fairly sure. I wouldn't go down there by myself to check, though."

"I can understand your reasoning; most people wouldn't want to." Matt smiled at her.

"Parker, what do you understand?" Carl asked as he approached them.

"I was asking about the old tunnels and rooms built under the inn that used to hide the slaves. She was telling me they were sealed years ago."

"They were. They closed them after the 1860s. Would you like to see where they were? I find the history of this place fascinating. Believe me, there would be no reason to own a building this old if there wasn't some rich history attached to it somewhere. Mostly, until I remodel the place, it's a handyman's nightmare."

"I'd love to have a tour if you have the time."

"I can't today, but I'd be happy to walk through with you tomorrow morning. Let's say at nine-thirty or ten if that works for you."

"I'll make it work." Matt shook Carl's hand. "I was reading about why the inn was originally built. The owner put himself and those he loved at peril to help those fleeing slaves."

"My grandmother, Molly Flynn, owned this place before me. She bought it precisely because of its history. A bit of a mystic in her Irish beliefs, she loved the idea of the owner opening his home and she often related it to her days in the old country."

"A great cause. I wonder how many folks passed through here."

"They say the owner kept a record of everyone who passed through, but it was never found. The night before my grandmother moved, she explained to me about hearing the cries and moaning of the slaves. She was sure the place was haunted. Her sleep had been disturbed for the last several years, and she was in a hurry to get out of here. I don't hold to the myths of the old country, and I'm a firm believer there is a logical answer to everything. Still, there are times when I wonder. Look what happened to your fiancée. I might've got in over my head in this place. I sank my life's savings into this property, so I have to make it work."

"I'm like you, Carl. I think there's a logical answer, but there might be some strange junk mixed in. I'll let you get back to work, and I'll see you in the morning." Matt climbed the stairs to the room Jessie had been found in.

If he was a betting man, he would put his money on someone having access to those tunnels and rooms again. Reba believed something illegal was going on today having to do with the inn. The neighbors around them had heard sounds according to Evelyn. Add to that Mollie Flynn's fear of a ghost, and Matt was sure something was going on. He needed Radar and Frank. Jessie may have seen Kimberly Ryan, but some of the noise and things happening had to be real people in those underground tunnels.

Matt left the inn and headed to the first neighbor to the left of the inn. He knocked at the door and was surprised when a tiny elderly woman answered. Most homes were empty in the day what with two people working in a household. The woman's smile was warm and genuine. He explained to her who he was and asked if she would be willing to answer a few questions for him.

"Of course. Come in and make yourself comfortable. My name is Ida Carver. Can I get you a cup of coffee or tea?" she asked.

"I would like a cup of coffee if it's no trouble."

"No trouble at all. I have a fresh pot in the kitchen. I always have one on in case someone drops by." She smiled again. "This big old house gets lonely when my daughter and her family are gone for the day. Do you take cream or sugar?"

"Cream would be nice," Matt replied as she disappeared into the kitchen.

She came back with his coffee and placed a plate of fresh banana bread in front of him. "Help yourself, young man. Now, what did you want to ask me? I bet it has to do with what I've been complaining to the police for weeks about."

"Why don't you fill me in. I'm new to the area, and I haven't read all the complaint reports yet."

"If you've read one, you've read them all. I always tell them the same thing, but they aren't listening to me."

"How do you know they aren't listening?" he asked.

"Because I've never seen any action. I thought maybe a few days ago they were finally going to follow up. The police were next door at the inn, but they never stopped by to see me." She frowned. "There's something going on over there. I'm sure you've heard the stories about the slaves and the history of the inn. They say the tunnels were sealed years ago and no longer in use, but they're wrong. I hear things late at night all the time, and those sounds are coming from underground."

"Are you sure?"

"Absolutely. You spend one night in my room, and you'll hear what I hear. My daughter doesn't believe me. She thinks it's all my imagination, but I'm nobody's dummy. I know what I hear, and that's all there is to it."

Matt ate a slice of banana bread and let her talk. He was sure of one thing after leaving her house—that the tiny woman knew what she was talking about. He was convinced she heard the noises coming from the tunnels. He might have to keep on eye on the inn. Something was going on, and if it was underground, it probably wasn't legal.

****

Jessie left the inn and wandered around town, not

sure what she was doing. She had learned a few new things but not much. Sensing her time here was coming to a close, she felt desperate to find out as much as she could. What troubled her the most was she hadn't come any closer to learning what happened to Kimberly. Why was she here if not to solve a cold case? Frustrated, she needed to bounce things off Matt. Every time she tried to search the inn, Florence stayed hot on her heels. She couldn't seem to get away from her prying eyes. Did the woman ever have a day off? It was quite possible she had learned all that she could and had to go back to finish solving the case. She was ready to go forward at any time. She missed Matt.

Feeling a bit sorry for herself, she found a bench in the town square to sit. "Kimberly, if you have anything else to show me, you need to hurry. I have no idea what to do next," she said under her breath."

"Do you mind if I sit here?" A youthful-sounding woman's voice startled her.

Jessie turned to look at her, and who she saw stunned her. "Kimberly," she said, her mouth dropping open. "Is it you?" she managed to ask.

"I'm not Kimberly, but that's why you're here isn't it?" She smiled.

"Yes."

"That's why I'm here, too. My cousin is dead. I know because I saw it."

"You saw her murdered?"

"No, not in the literal sense, but I knew the minute it happened. Kimmie and I are connected in a special way. She's been talking to me about you. Some folks think our connection is strange, but it was there from the time we were little. She would fall, and I would cry at home for no reason. I would get hurt, and Kimmie would cry. We always knew what was happening with each other. I guess you could say our bond was like twins. Kimmie was convinced I was her twin and that her mother gave me to my parents because she didn't want us both. I have no idea if this is true. We did look like twins and acted like them, but we were raised as cousins."

"It's unusual, but stranger things have happened, as I've found out. I'm here in the sixties talking to you. I'd call that strange." Jessie touched the woman's hand to make sure she was real.

"You have a strong energy around you, and I know you were brought to this time to hear her story. You're from the future." Her brown eyes were mesmerizing. Jessie nodded at her.

"I am. If you don't mind me asking, why didn't you meet me there and tell me?" Jessie wasn't even sure if her question made sense.

"Because in a few days I will be dead also. I know this must be strange for you, but we've been waiting for the right person to arrive, and here you are. In life, my name was Hope Ryan.

Jessie tried to grasp what she was saying. "You're alive at this moment, but..." Her voice trailed off.

"This situation must be strange for you. You were summoned to this time period by Kimmie so we could meet today. You don't have much time left before you must return. To keep you too long would put your life in jeopardy."

Hope began to tell their story.

Jessie wrote as fast as she could, asked questions where she could, and was amazed by what she heard.

She looked away for a moment and then turned to ask another question. Hope was gone. Was any of what she had witnessed real or in her mind?

Jessie returned to the inn, climbed the stairs to the room, and waited. She had no idea what would happen next.

****

Matt bent over the bed and gave Jessie a quick kiss. He told her about his talk with Ida. "She reminded me of Sadie, Jess—a little spitfire. I want you to meet her, and Linda Cranston too. I enjoyed my talk with her. I think both of those ladies are lonely. Maybe before we leave we can get them connected. Matt opened his briefcase to add a few notes from his conversations earlier. His hand pulled out the odd-looking key. Without thinking about it he placed it on the top of her hands and settled into work. Glancing occasionally at her quiet, still form, he thought he saw her move out of the corner of his eye. Moving closer to the bed, he noticed she clutched the key in her hand. "Come back to me, sweetheart," he whispered in her ear. Was she moaning? He bent closer to listen; her lips appeared to be moving. Still, she remained quiet. Wishful thinking on his part.

Chapter 12

The sound of weeping awakened Jessie. Kimberly was there in the mirror again, beckoning for her to come. Jessie knew it was time to go back to Matt. Hope had told her when she found Kimmie's killer, she would find hers as well. Armed with a few facts of the murderer in her mind, Jessie approached the mirror. What was next?

She placed her hand on Kimberly's from her side of the mirror, palm to palm and fingers to fingers. Energy shot through her hand and up her arm. The whirling, spinning sensation began lifting her off her feet, and she was pulled through the mirror. The force was extreme. She felt her body reshaping as she passed through another energy field. The speed changed suddenly, and thankfully she blacked out.

Opening her eyes, she had no idea where she was, but she knew he was there. "Where am I?" were the first words out of her mouth followed by, "hi."

"Welcome back, sweetheart." He leaned over and kissed her. His hand held tightly to hers. "Are you okay? I wasn't sure I'd ever see you like this again." He shuddered and wiped the moisture from his cheek.

"How long have I been here?" She ran her hand down his cheek tenderly. "I'm glad to be back with you." She struggled to sit up.

"Wait, let me help." He moved the bed up and

adjusted the pillows behind her head. "You've been here several days." He squeezed her hand again. "I can't wait to hear about your travels, but I'm afraid it will have to wait until the doctors try to get answers for what you've gone through. After Evelyn found you unresponsive at the inn, you were brought to the hospital." Matt pushed the call button. The nurse came in to check and then ran out of the room. She came back, followed by several doctors. After several tests, the consensus was that she was fine, but they wanted to keep her overnight for observation.

Jessie started to argue, but Matt kept pressing her hand to keep her quiet. As far as she was concerned, they were wasting time.

"Why wouldn't you let me tell them I wanted out?" She glared at him.

"Because you had folks worried for several days, including me. I want to make sure you're okay before we do anything else. The case will still be there in the morning."

"I know you're right. You'll never believe the story when I tell you. I'm still a bit foggy. I probably could use the rest." She closed her eyes and drifted off to sleep while Matt held her hand.

****

Watching her toss and turn reminded him she was really back. Matt found it hard to take his eyes off her for fear she would suddenly be gone again. He called Reba, who reminded him more than once she had told him Jessie would be back. Sadie was jubilant, and Jeremy couldn't wait to hear all about her time travel, if that's what it was. As the word got out in Blue Cove, Matt had several calls from friends to check on her.

Jessie slept through them all. Eventually, he closed his eyes and slept too.

She was watching him when he opened his eyes. "I thought you'd never wake up. Did you miss me?" Jessie sat on the edge of the bed, ready to get going.

"What do you think?" He grinned at her, reaching for her hand. "It's hard to put into words what the last few days felt like to me."

"How do you feel now?" Her thumb stroked the palm of his hand.

"Right now? I'm damn happy to see you." He moved closer and kissed her. "I've missed the gorgeous blue eyes of yours and seeing those dimples when you smile.

"Are you ready to hear where I've been?"

"You know I am. Probably, away from here where we can't be bothered."

"While you were sleeping the doctor said I was good to go. All we need is the paperwork and my clothes, then I'm out of here. I want coffee and something gooey to eat."

"Gooey sounds good to me. Being with you sounds even better." He squeezed her hand clasped in his. "I know where your clothes are if you want to get dressed." He went to a small closet and pulled out the bag with her personal belongings in it. "Here you go." He handed it to her. "I'll step outside the door. You have ten minutes tops to get dressed. I'm not letting you out of my sight for any longer than that."

"Matt, I'm sorry our weekend was ruined," she called after him. "I really did try not to get involved." She laughed. "Like that's even possible."

He stopped on his way out the door. "It's not your

fault. There'll be other weekends and a lifetime of days to be together. Now get moving because ten minutes is all you're getting." He grinned. "I'll poke my head back in here in ten, ready or not."

Jessie smiled as he closed the door. She loved that man. Taking her jeans out of the bag, she slipped into them and pulled the tie-dyed tee over her bra. "Thanks, Kimmie." She ran the brush through wild curls, sweeping her hair into a ponytail. When Matt knocked and opened the door a few minutes later, she waited in the chair.

The nurse came through the open door. "You're free to go." She handed her the release papers. "We're all so happy to see you doing so well. You're a mystery to us. No one had any idea what was going on in your body. Your brain scan told us you were active and humming, but your body was unresponsive. You'll be a case study for these doctors for a while. It would be good to have your own doctor check you out when you get back home. You can see it is recommended by the doctors here. If you should feel strange, come right back. We have no idea what caused it or if it will happen again."

And neither did she. Jessie looked at Matt's frowning face. She was ready to talk to him. She took the papers and handed them to Matt to put in his briefcase. Grabbing her bag, she took Matt's hand, pulling him toward the door. They didn't have a minute to lose. The case was waiting to be solved.

"Where did that shirt come from? It wasn't in the bag of clothes I brought to the hospital."

"Let's call it a souvenir from my travels. I love it." She tugged on his hand to get him moving.

Iona Morrison

"Slow down." Matt slipped his hand free. He gathered his files, stuffing them in his briefcase, and grabbed his glasses from the phone stand.

"Sorry, but I'm in a hurry to get out of here. I have a lot to tell you, and we have no time to lose." She reached for his hand again.

Matt took another look around the room before he was out in the hall. "We have plenty of time to do this right, Jess, so take it easy."

"I know. I want to get out of the hospital room before they change their minds and make me go back." She walked a more leisurely pace once she neared the elevator.

Matt opened the car door for her. He drove to the local coffee shop where he had spent several hours over the past few days. "First things first. You said coffee and something gooey, and I know firsthand this is the place."

"Thank you. I'm not sure what it says about me that I wanted something sweet the minute I got back." She took a sip of coffee followed by a bite of a heavenly sticky bun.

"Now that your sweet tooth is being satisfied, can you please tell me where the hell you've been."

She patted his hand. "There, there. No need to be testy."

"I'm not, but I've been worried for several days if I would ever see you again. Questions are in order if you ask me."

"If you want a technical explanation, I'm not sure I have one." She took another bite, closing her eyes and savoring the moment.

"The look on your face right now—I saw it once

96

while you lay motionless. I knew you were tasting something that you liked."

Jessie laughed. "I don't hide my pleasure for good food, do I?"

"I love that about you." Matt's fingers drummed on the table. "I want to know where you were and what you were doing even if it blows up my logic. Impatience is getting the best of me."

"Don't get all spacey on me. I had a groovy time where I went. Peace out, brother." She chuckled at the look on his face. "I'm trying out a few of the words I heard people say." She paused to gather her thoughts. "I have no idea how it worked. You saw me unresponsive here, but I was alive and well in 1967. I talked to people, tasted the food, and even had money when I needed it. Don't ask me how because I have no clue. I went to a Joan Baez concert."

"I don't get it." Matt frowned, shaking his head. "How the hell is that possible?"

"I have no idea, but it was as real to me as you are sitting there."

"Reba said you were in two dimensions and that you had gone through a portal or gateway into another time dimension."

"She told me to research trans-dimensional portals or time travel. I went in search of a computer. I found a gigantic one at the university. Way too complicated for me to use but the operator asked the questions for me. Gateways into another time is a sci-fi concept. Few scientists in the sixties believed it was possible, and only a few fringe folks entertained the idea. I could find no proof of it then, and I have no idea what I would find now."

"Not much, if Jeremy is correct. There is more scientific data that supports that it's a possibility now than at any other time, and plenty of movies are built around the idea." He pursed his lips. "Tell me what happened."

"I told you about the argument going on in the closet. The next morning, I got locked in the closet when I reached for my dress. After the mirror and the closet incidents, Carl changed my room. The new room had strange energy in it. I knew it the moment I walked in. The energy got stronger before I went to sleep. I awakened to weeping. Kimberly was looking out at me through the mirror. I was mesmerized by the light coming from the mirror and was drawn to it. When I picked up the key on the dresser, a strange electrical sensation went through my hand and shot up my arm. I was lifted off my feet, spinning in circles, faster and faster, until I was pulled through the mirror. I returned the same way—at least I think I did. How I ended up at the hospital I have no idea. The energy took me out of my body. I guess it could put me back in it no matter where it found me." Seeing his expression, she added. "I know, it's all too weird."

Matt shook his head. "It's not possible as far as I understand. Yet I know your body was in the hospital, but you were gone."

She told him about Rainbow Ridge Commune, Skylar, and his girls; what she knew about Kimberly to this point; and most important of all the meeting with Hope Ryan. "It was eerie how much she looked like Kimberly. I think those girls are identical twins. They may have been raised as cousins, but they're twins. No doubt about it."

"Why would a mother give up her daughter? I don't get it."

"I've been thinking about that. What is worse than being jealous of your daughter's beauty but to have two girls prettier than you?"

"Linda Cranston told me her mother blamed Kimberly for her new husband's roving eye." Matt shook his head. "How crazy is that?"

"I'm beginning to think nothing is strange anymore. I'm not sure what is true and what isn't."

"Where do we begin? A lot of the key players are dead now." Matt sipped his coffee.

"I want to see the tunnels and rooms under the inn. I believe they've been reopened and that someone is using them. That's how Kimmie's body was taken out of the inn without being seen, or she's still hidden somewhere in the inn."

"What makes you think that?" he asked.

"I saw it flash through my mind. Hope believes that's what happened too. No one saw Kimberly leave the inn after work that day."

"Which reminds me. I'm supposed to meet Carl in thirty minutes to get a tour of those tunnels, and you're going with me. I'm not letting you out of my sight anytime soon. Your computer is in the trunk if you want it."

"Do I! It'll be dope to have it again. You can't image how I've missed being able to look up information online. Hope Ryan is at the top of my list to check out."

"What's your theory?" Matt glanced at her while taking the last bite of his bagel.

"If what she told me is true, and I have no reason to

doubt her, when I find Kimmie's killer, I'll find hers. Can you imagine I was talking to her in the park? She was alive—I even touched her to make sure—and then she told me in a few days she would be dead." The look on Matt's face was enough to let her know he was struggling with it the same way she had.

"You're blowing my mind. I can't wrap my head around any of this." Matt reached for her hand. "We need to go, but before we do, I want to know what you were tasting." He squeezed her hand.

Pulling her hand away, she stood. "Only the best chocolate malt ever, with fries, and a great burger to top it off." She was headed to the door, waving for him to hurry.

"You have much more to tell me, and I need to fill you in on what I've found so far. How close do you think we are to solving this crime? We can't miss Dylan's and Katie's engagement party. They'd never forgive us."

"We won't." Jessie looked at the spot on her finger where her ring should be. "We need to include our friends in our happiness."

"I could have told you that. Oh, I did." He chuckled.

"Yes, you did, and you were right." Her voice was barely audible.

"Let me savor this moment. I never thought I'd hear you say that I'm right and you're not. Can you say the word 'monumental?'" He emphasized the word, drawing out every syllable.

She glanced at Matt with a shocked look on her face. "What happened to my ring?"

"I took your ring to the jewelers to have it sized.

He had to send it off." He grinned at her. "Still, this a moment to enjoy."

"There's no need to go overboard. It won't happen again if you're not careful." She swatted his arm playfully.

"Aw, Jess, I missed you." He leaned toward her and kissed her. "Welcome home, sweetheart." He deepened the kiss and hugged her tight.

Chapter 13

Matt parked the car in front of the Brass Lantern. "Let's see what this place holds for us today."

"I don't see my rental car in the space where I parked it." Jessie's head turned back and forth looking for the car.

"I returned it. I had no idea how long you'd be gone." Matt shut off the engine.

"Good idea." She squeezed his arm. "I'm a bit nervous about going in this place again. The night that I went through the portal or whatever ensued was a bit scary. I don't want to experience that again anytime soon. Please stay with me. Don't leave my side."

"Don't worry. I'm not letting you out of my sight." He patted her hand on his arm. "We have a case to solve, and I still want to know what happened to you. Can it happen again?"

"Anything is possible, I guess. Let's hope not, or we'll never be able to have a normal life. We could go home together at night, and I'd be gone in the morning."

"Don't like the sound of that, but I love you, and this stuff seems to come with you. Getting used to it might be on my fiancé job description list." Doubtful he could ever get used to the idea of her suddenly disappearing again, he pushed the thought away. He would wait to examine his feelings on the subject another day.

"Everyone says relationships have a learning curve. Ours seems to be a tad larger and stranger than most. I hope you understand how much I appreciate you hanging in there with me despite all the weird things I seem to hand you from one month to the next."

"Love is funny that way. I'm determined to make this work because as I learned once again over the past few days my life would be empty without you." He opened the car door and stepped out. She appeared nervous, and that bothered him.

She reached for his extended hand. "Not many men would put up with all this nonsense. You're a keeper."

"You are too." He smiled at her. "I loved seeing my ring on your finger. I can't wait to put it back on. Once in its rightful place, there'll be no more taking it off. I want the whole world to know you're my woman." He grinned playfully, beating his chest. "I know technically you'll never be mine, but I still like to think of you that way."

"How astute of you. I think you're catching on." Jessie laughed quietly.

"Nope, I think it's more like you've told me often enough, and it's getting through my thick head. You belong to you." He tapped his forehead playfully.

"Sounds perfect to me." She stopped. "I think it's only fair that I tell you if I had lived in the sixties, I probably would've been one of those bra-burning women. Maybe that's why I find myself in all this trouble. I'll fight for the rights of women, dead or alive. The message must have gotten out in the spirit world." She shuddered at her memory of Clover and Essence.

"Someone needs to fight for women. They have

been suppressed for too long. It's past time. You'll always be my sweet little feminist." He stroked the palm of her hand, and it drove her nuts.

"Women had few rights in the sixties. I'm happy I'm alive now. I'm especially glad that you let me be who I am and encourage me to be as strong as I can be. Sadie was that voice in my head growing up. I feel blessed to have those in my life who never tried to force me into a mold I wouldn't fit." She stopped walking, and so did he. "Kimberly had no one fighting for her. No one to encourage her. Her stepdad is a suspect at best, her mother abandoned her, and men exploited her. We must solve this case. It's the right thing to do. I want to believe someone would do it for me or our daughter if she needs it." She reached for his hand. "This is important to me, and I wanted you to know."

"One of many things I love about you." He laced his fingers through hers as they strolled into the inn.

"Welcome back, Ms. Reynolds. Should you be out and about this soon? Are you feeling okay?" Evelyn took her arm, leading her to a chair.

"I'm fine. Thank you for your concern." She sat in the chair where Evelyn pointed. "We're here to see Carl. We have an appointment."

"I'll get him. Are you going to stay here tonight? I'd be happy to move your things to a new room." Evelyn sat on the arm of Jessie's chair.

"I'm not sure what my fiancé wants to do. Either way, we'll get my stuff out of that room."

"I wouldn't want to stay there either." Evelyn rubbed her arms and shuddered. "Carl wants to remodel that room completely and get rid of the strange furniture pieces in there. I'm sorry I put you in that room. I had no idea the room was haunted."

"What makes you think the room is haunted?" Jessie asked.

"If you could've seen the look on your face when we found you lying on the floor—" Evelyn folded her arms. "—There wouldn't be a doubt in your mind either."

"I don't remember much about that night. Maybe it's better my memory is faulty if what you say is true."

"You sit here and relax, sweetie." Evelyn patted Jessie's knees. "I'll go get Carl. Between you and me, Carl is afraid you're going to sue."

"He has nothing to worry about. I'm not suing anyone," Jessie assured her. "Besides Carl doesn't even believe in ghosts."

"He's a believer now." Evelyn spoke softly so only Jessie could hear.

"What was that all about?" Matt sat on the chair next to her.

"Evelyn told me she would move us to another room if we wanted to stay here." Jessie grimaced. "The room holds no appeal for me. I'm not sure I want to stay in there."

"Can I make a suggestion?"

"Of course."

"We should stay here tonight. This isn't the romantic weekend that I planned, but plans can be rescheduled. We're in this case like it or not, and we need to solve it." He held her gaze. "What do you think?"

"I'm in as long as you're with me." Her fingers tapped nervously on the edge of the chair.

"If that's how you feel, let's stay in the room you

105

were in. You can sleep, and I'll keep watch. I'm ready to find out why the hell you had to go through this stuff. I'm still not sure how the experience has affected you. Remember I saw you for several days in the hospital. I want to make sure you're okay." Matt stood as Carl walked into the room.

"Are you ready for your tour?" Carl asked. His size made Matt seem small.

Matt stood and reached his hand out to Jessie, helping her out of the chair. "We're ready."

"Ms. Reynolds, it's good to see you looking well. The last time I saw you I wasn't sure if you'd make it. I imagine you're ready to put your stay at the Brass Lantern behind you and shake the dust of this sleepy town off your feet."

Jessie smiled at Carl to ease his discomfort. "As hard as this might be to believe, I'm okay, and I have a few more things to do before I go home." She leaned close to Matt. "You might have to describe how bad I looked. This is the second person to say those words to me." She saw him nod.

"I'm sorry you missed your spa day and spent it in the hospital instead. I feel bad about your experience here at the inn. Did the doctors have any answers for what happened to you that night?"

"I didn't get any. Did you?" She glanced at Matt.

"Not one. They were as stumped as the rest of us." He frowned and held her hand a tad tighter.

"As much as you don't want to hear this, I think Evelyn might be right about your ghost." Jessie squeezed Matt's hand hoping he'd get the message. He loosened his grip, which was a relief. She felt safe when he was near her, but he didn't know his own strength.

"You're right. I don't want to hear it, but it hasn't stopped me from thinking about the possibility the last few days." Carl shuffled his feet.

"Here's the thing—this isn't my first run-in with strange manifestations. If we do our job the way we should, then maybe your ghost will be happy and leave your inn in peace." She smiled at Carl and crossed her fingers. "Lead the way. I, for one, want to see these tunnels. I've been reading about the history of this place, and I think you've made a great investment."

"Nice of you to say. After the past few days, I may be a bit skeptical. I'll take a wait and see approach." Carl motioned for them to follow.

"Suit yourself, but it'll pay off. You'll see." She leaned closer to Matt, and they followed Carl.

Carl led them to the library at the center of the main floor. He closed the door and locked it. With Matt's help, he shifted the furniture around and rolled back a large throw rug in the center of the room. Once the rug was moved, it revealed the secret door hidden underneath it.

"This is the first room the fleeing slaves were put in." Carl stepped down the ladder, followed by Matt, who turned to help Jessie.

The room was large. "How many people would come at a time?" Matt asked.

"The number varied. This safehouse was farther north than a lot of the others. Those who made it this far were often on their way to Canada or leaving for England. Over the years the family who lived in this house helped many slaves find their freedom."

"It would be great to read the stories of those who made it." Jessie's imagination took over. She could see

107

the room packed with weary humans trying to save their families from slavery. History was one of her favorite subjects—people simply amazed her. "Where are the tunnels?"

Carl pointed to a large set of shelves at one end of the room. "This where the family stored their food. This unit acted as a cover for what I'm about to show you. He pushed a small lever behind one of the shelves, and the wall slid open. "What the hell?" Carl frowned. "This was sealed off years ago."

"You may have a problem then." Matt stepped through the opening in the wall. "Look. It's a fake wall. Whoever is using this forgot to close it." He pointed at the door that was designed to look like the sealed wall.

"One of the owners sealed the area off because the tunnels were becoming too dangerous." Carl grabbed a flashlight. They made their way through the tunnels. Everywhere they looked the walls and ceilings had been shored up to protect their structural integrity.

"Where do the tunnels lead?" Jessie asked. She hoped they'd continue to walk through the tunnel to the end.

"When it was time to move the people, they would walk this way to the wagons waiting in an area that used to be on the outside of town. You'll see in a moment if the other end is opened." Carl pointed to shovels and picks leaning against the wall.

"Do you mind if I take one to see if they can pull some prints?" Mat asked.

"Not at all. We'll grab it on our way back. We are nearing the end." Carl pointed to the makeshift ladder leaning against the wall. He reached up and pushed at the other end. The door gave way and sprung open. "I'll be damned. This is all open. We won't go out. I don't want anyone to see us, but take a quick peek. You'll be able to see where the tunnel leads."

"Isn't this the park down from the inn?" Jessie recognized the area—she had run through the park a few times before she went through the portal.

"Yes. You can imagine what it was like for those folks coming out of these tunnels into, what was at the time, an open field protected by trees and the cover of night. Fearful of being caught, they made their way to the waiting wagons." Carl leaned against the tunnel wall.

"Was this place ever discovered or any of the slaves captured?" Jessie asked him.

"No, several families worked together, and they were never discovered, and none of the slaves were ever taken back to their owners."

"People like this family who opened their home are heroes to me. All the lives that were saved and changed because of their risky decision to get involved." She glanced around the tunnel, which seemed to be alive with the history of the people who passed through it. "This inspires me. It makes you wonder how those once freed went on to live their lives." Her hand rubbed over the plastered walls. "If these walls could talk."

"Speaking of walls talking—" Matt smiled at her. "—Flynn, did you know your neighbors have made complaints to the police about hearing sounds coming from the tunnel area?"

"No, I didn't. I wonder why the police never checked it out. I'm going to have them sealed from this end again." Carl tugged to make sure the exit door was shut.

"Wait a few days. Maybe we'll catch them in the act. I'm curious as to what they're being used for now." Matt moved the ladder back to where they found it. "We don't want to tip them off."

"I'll wait until you give me the all clear before I do anything. This is a part of history and should be preserved, but not used or it will be destroyed." They started back through the tunnel.

"Hey, Carl, what is this?" Matt pointed to a strange looking wall.

"Damned if I know. It looks like a door. It shouldn't be here as far as I know."

Matt pushed against the door, and it opened to another series of tunnels. "Where does this go? I want to follow it." Matt led the way with Carl and Jessie following close behind him.

They followed through a maze of tunnels and found a large room filled with sleeping bags and a door. It was locked from the outside. "We went a fair distance down here. I have no idea where the door takes you outside. We might have to check some of the abandoned buildings in the area. If they're doing something illegal, they wouldn't want to be coming out in the park. There are always people hanging out there."

"Matt, look at what I found." Jessie picked up a woman's compact from the floor. "Maybe we should check this room." They found several other items including a flip flop, lipstick, and a piece of paper with several cryptic words written on it.

"I know what you're thinking. Let's keep it to ourselves for now," he whispered in her ear. Matt grabbed one of the shovels on the way back through the tunnel.

The library was restored to how it looked when they first came in the room. Jessie watched Matt and Carl as they talked about the tunnels, the new addition, and how to find out who might be using them. She checked out the shelves of books. One of her theories was looking more possible as she stood there—Kimberly was murdered in the inn, and her body was moved at night through the tunnel or remained somewhere close by. Hope gave her a few suggestions, and what she needed now was proof. A body would help. If Kimberly was buried anywhere near the inn, Radar could find her. She would remind Matt about that fact. If she knew Matt, he had already thought of Frank and his bloodhound. A small bird hopping on the branch outside caught her attention.

"Are you ready for lunch?" Matt slipped his arm around her waist.

"I'd like to have lunch with you any day." She turned her head to see him.

"I think my pick-up lines are getting better. What do you think?" Matt grinned at her.

"I see a definite improvement." Amusement tinged her voice. "But my responses have gotten better too.

"Hell, yes they have. The key to a good response, I've learned, is to remember to always put food in it somewhere." He turned his head to hide his smile.

"Are you saying I like to eat?" she asked. Her voice sounded sharp.

"Not me. I'm saying you enjoy what you eat. There's a difference, and I love that about you."

"Smooth recovery, but then everything about you is suave." She ran her hand across his cheek.

"See you both later. I can't believe you want to

stay in that room, but I'm glad you're going to be around to keep on eye on this place. I'll let Evelyn know," Carl called to them as he left the room.

Jessie walked beside Matt out of the inn. There was no way she would stay in the room again without him. She might feel differently tomorrow, but not today.

Chapter 14

As soon as Matt got in the car, he turned in his seat. "I called Frank. He'll be here tomorrow. Reba told me she thought something was still going on, and I thought I could use his help."

"I was hoping you had called him. Kimberly was murdered somewhere in the inn, and if her body is nearby Radar can find where the bones are buried. Remember Grace Walters in our last case? He found her. He can also track those who are working underground in the tunnels. We think alike, and I'm glad."

"How are you feeling?" He glanced at her.

"I'm fine and want to get this case solved. I'm ready to go home." She latched her seat belt.

"I know you haven't told me everything yet, and I want to hear it all."

"Processing it all may take a while. The crime didn't start with Kimberly. She may have stumbled into an ongoing plot. She wouldn't cooperate, so they killed her, and eventually her cousin Hope. Or maybe her death was only the beginning. I have no idea, but it links the past and the present together somehow."

"What are you thinking?" he asked while starting the car.

"We may be looking at a smuggling ring, only more sordid. What we found in that room tells me they've been holding girls in there—they're being transported for something. I saw Skylar operate as a spiritual guru for those wanting to be cared for and protected, all the while exploiting them." Jessie adjusted the belt rubbing against the curve of her neck. "Kimberly had one thing against her. She was beautiful. Skylar wanted her for one of his wives, her stepfather was obsessed by her, and there was another man that I learned about while I was there. None of them are probably alive anymore. Skylar could be. He'd be fairly old, and I'd have no idea how to find him."

"You may be right. I was thinking more along the lines of drug smuggling. It could be both. We'll find out soon enough I guess." Matt drove to the restaurant.

After lunch, Matt made calls to Dylan, Jeremy, and Tom. He wanted information on any ongoing investigations in the area. What Jessie had told him at lunch made him a believer in her theory. At the same time, he wasn't ready to give his idea up, either. Jessie was convinced that Kimberly was murdered. She had seen some part of it.

Matt dropped Jessie off at the library to spend some time on her computer. He was hesitant to let her out of his sight, but she convinced him she needed to have space, and so did he. His next stop was the local police station where he spent time with Chief Macintyre. Matt wanted to see the police reports from the neighbors who lived near the inn. Sam said he had sent out officers, but they thought it was the fantasies of some old women. "Ida Carver, one of the women your officers dismissed, knew exactly what she had heard. She was right." Matt explained to him what they found in the tunnels.

"I asked several times, sent different officers out to the houses, and they all reported the same thing."

"Ida told me no one had checked on her complaint."

"I'll have to look into it. If they didn't go, then they've falsified a report."

"If they had searched her complaint out you might have discovered what was going on a few years ago. All this is connected to what happened to Ms. Reynolds. You might have missed a chance to prevent this from happening in the first place."

After listening to excuses for a while, Matt was frustrated. The chief, as a small-town cop, had found it too easy to get complacent. He would have to make sure his department stayed sharp in the future. Crime had no respect for the size of a town. It showed up everywhere.

****

Jessie felt at home among all the books. She loved having her computer and racing from one article to another. There was plenty of interesting information that began to paint a picture for her.

Kimberly had been right. Hope was her twin sister. Jessie found the truth among the live-birth records. The girls were born minutes apart. A couple of months after they were born the Ryans divorced. Each one of them took one of the girls. She also found the adoption record for Hope. Hope's father gave her to his brother and his wife to raise as their own. They were childless. Information was limited until later in the girls' lives. She found some of their school records. The sisters went to different high schools, but both were cheerleaders and good students. It was strange how closely their lives paralleled each other—down to the clubs they joined and the offices they held in the student body. Out of sight didn't mean out of mind as far as those two were concerned. Hope went missing a few weeks after Kimberly disappeared. Her body was also never found.

What a sad story. None of the adults considered the consequences of their actions and what it might do in the lives of their daughters. No wonder Kimmie and Hope were drawn to each other. They found a way to be together even when their parents tried to keep them apart. Jessie shut her computer off and went outside to wait for Matt.

She had some calls to make. "Grams, this is Jessie. I wanted to tell you I'm okay and we'll be home soon."

She could hear grandmother's sniffles. "I tried not to worry. Reba kept telling me you'd be okay. But as the days wore on, I wasn't sure. It's good to hear your voice, dear girl. I want to hear all about your travels, but not today. It's enough to know you're back with us." She paused. "Matt called right away, of course, but hearing your voice is sweet music to my ears."

Jessie told her a small portion of what had happened to her. "Grams, did the women really burn their bras?"

"Not all of them, of course—it was symbolic of our activism. I burned one of mine." Sadie chuckled. "Not the one I wore, though."

"I'm sure I would have done the same thing. Do you know who I got to see?"

"Who, dear?"

"Joan Baez. I went to one of her concerts. I admit I loved her and found myself dancing along with the crowd, feeling a freedom I've never felt before."

"She was one of my favorites at the time. I was fresh out of high school when I went to one of her concerts, and I was hooked." Sadie chuckled. "It was a unique time, and there were many changes happening. I can't help thinking…" She paused.

"About what, Grams?"

"I was thinking you and I have both been alive in the sixties, and it has to be our sweet secret. You get me. Not many grandparents can say that."

"And you get me, too. I can't wait to spend time telling you everything. I'm still processing it all. We'll be home in time for Katie's engagement party. Love you."

"Right back at you. Don't forget to call Reba. She's waiting. Your parents don't know. None of us knew how to explain it to them."

"Good to know. I'll call Reba next. I'm glad I don't have to explain it to Mom and Dad—they would never understand." Jessie clicked off her phone, and it started ringing.

"Hello, this is Jessie."

"Hi, sweet girl, I couldn't stand to wait a minute longer. I can't wait to hear all about your great adventure when you get back to town. Right now, I have something to tell you. You're closing in on a dark secret, and someone knows about it. While you were in the past, you encountered someone from the present who is aware of who you are. Be on guard."

"How can I have met someone in the past who is from the present? The whole idea doesn't make any sense." Jessie shook her head in disbelief.

"Neither does traveling to the past through a portal

in an altered state. You were here while you were there. This case is unusual all the way around. You have already learned truths which you will find to be odd. I'm right, aren't I?'

"Of course, you are. Truthfully, everything about the case is unusual. I'm still not sure how I got pulled into the middle of the madness."

"Jessie, you know how this works. Write about the murdered sisters and watch the vermin scatter out of their holes."

"How did you know about the sisters?" Jessie asked.

"I hear and see a few things myself." She chuckled. "This story has a few sordid twists before it's done, and the guilty will come out swinging with the stroke of your pen. Get busy writing, dear girl. No more delays."

"Okay, I'll write." She waved at Matt, who parked in front of the library.

"I'll be waiting to hear how this case is solved. It may take you longer than you think and follow you home."

"Matt's here. We'll talk later," Jessie told her.

"Sounds good. Stay alert."

Jessie grabbed her computer case and walked toward Matt. "How did your time go at the station?"

He kissed her cheek. "Honestly, Jess, it frustrates me how inept police departments are at seeing the bigger picture." He held the door open, and she slid into the front seat.

"Don't you think it's a human condition and not partial to any one group? I mean, I wouldn't know anything about this case nor would I have looked for it had it not been for a ghost. Maybe going through life blissfully unaware might not be bad." She latched her seat belt.

"You don't really believe that, do you?" Matt glanced at her.

"To be truthful, no. It might be nice to try for a while though." She grinned at him.

"What's up? That doesn't sound like the girl I know." His fingers drummed on the steering wheel.

"You're right. Reba told me I need to write a story about the murders of the sisters. She said it would break everything open. I don't know if there would be anyone who'd print the article in their paper. I'm unknown in this area."

"Max could contact someone at the Globe and pass the article on to them. I'll call him. He'll do it once he knows how important this is to the case." Matt pulled away from the curb. "You can write, and I'll keep watch. We need to shake the tree. I wouldn't doubt we're dealing with a few different crimes and suspects."

Once they pulled into a parking space at the inn, Matt placed the call to Max. "He said to send it to him as soon as you're done. He has a friend at the Globe. He's going to call and ask him to save space for your article."

They spent a little time after lunch with Ida Carver and Linda Cranston. Linda was positive she had seen Jessie somewhere before. Was it possible Linda remembered their meeting from the past? It was all so confusing.

Jessie's afternoon was spent on the computer. A troubling picture emerged of the twins forced to believe they were cousins, but in their hearts, they knew they were sisters. Writing every chance she got, she made Kimberly and Hope come to life in her article. *"Do your job."* She felt relief when she typed the last words in the story after Sadie edited it. Jessie sent the pages to Max in an email. *"Let me know if I need to make changes."* All that was left to do was wait.

Chapter 15

After dinner at the inn, they climbed the stairs to their room. Matt said, "I want you to rest."

"I will." She sat in one of the chairs and watched Matt go over to the dresser, studying it from every angle. "It's kind of creepy isn't it?"

"I wouldn't want it in my house." Matt leaned his hip against the odd-looking furniture piece. "Tell me exactly what you remember from that night." His arms folded across his chest, with a perplexed look on his face. "I don't understand how it's even possible."

"I don't either." Jessie retold him the events. "As I approached the mirror, I was in awe of light flowing from it. I remember thinking I saw an angel behind Kimberly which drew me closer. I picked up the key and dropped it almost immediately, but it was too late. The minute I touched it, the electricity shot from my hand up my arm. I felt the light lift me off my feet, and I began spinning around faster and faster until I blacked out. I awakened at the commune." Jessie closed her eyes, reliving the moment. Her body tensed. Shivers crept up and down her back.

"Was it painful?" Matt struggled with what she told him. "Could there be side effects?"

"Not that I can remember, but coming back was weird. The force felt as though it was reshaping my body. It's hard to rationalize. I went through the mirror coming and going." She shook her head. "I have no idea how I was able to get to the hospital when I returned. I worried that I might be stuck there for good. One time I saw you sitting in this room, but you couldn't see me."

"What was that like?" he asked. "I felt sick every time I came in this room and wondered if I would ever see you again." Matt paused. "I was scared, and I rarely am."

Tears stung her eyes. "I know the feeling. I wasn't sure if I would make it back to you. I called you, but you couldn't hear me." She scooted to the edge of her chair. Her emotions were too raw. She changed the subject. "Besides, I didn't want to be stuck in the sixties. I'm a modern woman." She laughed hitting her forehead with the palm of her hand. "Imagine me not being able to get a loan without a man signing for me."

Matt grinned, shaking his head. "I wouldn't want to be the loan officer who told you no. But then again I wouldn't want you stuck in the sixties either. I'd miss moments like this." He took her hand and tugged her out of the chair as he walked by. He sat, easing her down onto his lap.

"How are things in Blue Cove?" She leaned back against him.

"Dylan says things have been quiet and swears it's because you're here. My guys seem to think cases find you."

"It doesn't take a rocket scientist to figure it out— they do find me, or at least their ghosts do. But in a way, I'm glad because we've solved some big crimes that were going undetected. I think we've helped a few people along the way too."

"Helping people is important to you isn't it?" He stroked her back. She relaxed in his arms and curled into his side.

"At the top of my list. Our only way to be happy in this life is to help others. We are meant to rise above ourselves and care for others. At least that's what Reba has helped me to see. It's worked for me to get through all these strange things, and I'm not going to change now. I'm helpless." She yawned.

"You're perfect—a dream come true." He continued to rub her back. "I can't imagine you any other way."

"I can be a pain. My mom can fill in the details if you need them. I do tend to get stubborn occasionally, and I've been known to dig in my heels if I see injustice. Of course, you've already seen this character flaw. I believe you have been on the receiving end. I don't take well to men treating me as a subordinate. You're fully aware of this side of my personality also."

"This chin of yours is inclined to rise as a witness to your stubborn streak." He tapped her chin gently. "I've seen it on more than one occasion. I've also been chewed out a few times for lecturing you instead of treating you as an equal. I'm walking into this relationship with my eyes wide open, and I love who you are. Even the wacky, strange side of you, which I have no clue how or why it comes about."

"I'm glad." She yawned again. She lay her head against his chest, and her eyes closed.

"Rest, sweetheart. I'm not going anywhere." Matt knew the moment she fell asleep. Her body softened against him. Her breathing was even and steady. He didn't know what to expect, but he wasn't letting her go. If it was possible to stop her from going through another portal or dimension, he would do anything within his power.

Matt eased her off his lap and onto the chair. He pulled back the covers and carried her to the bed, trying hard not to wake her. She stirred as he laid her down. "It's okay sweetheart. You'll be more comfortable. I'm not going anywhere," he said softly while stroking her cheek. Moving the chair next to the bed, he kept watch over her sleeping form. Not that he would admit it—this one had scared him. Glancing at her, he wondered how moving through the portal had affected her physically and mentally. She seemed okay, but Matt wanted to make sure. Grabbing the notes he had made on the case, he read over them, searching for anything that would jump the case forward.

An incoming text told him that Max's friend at the Globe was running Kimberly's and Hope's story tomorrow on the front page. Jessie's story was bound to stir up trouble. One aspect he found troubling today was Linda Cranston, who kept saying to Jessie she looked familiar. He wrote it down in his notes. Was it possible she could remember Jessie interviewing her in the past? Too weird for him to consider.

****

She was trapped in the tunnel with no way out. Pushed from the back, she couldn't see his face. Only his voice and the smell of him stuck with her, and he promised he'd return. It was dark and damp, and she huddled in the corner. She needed to get out soon. Suddenly the darkness was filled with light. Kimberly's face came before her, followed by Hope's and other young women too numerous to count. One scream of anguish turned into tens, then hundreds and thousands. Their faces were of every ethnic background from all around the world. Each one clamored to tell their story and witness against those who had hurt them.

One woman's voice called out louder than the others. "Who will speak for those of us who no longer have a voice?"

Jessie buried her head in her hands and sealed her lips tight. Why was this happening? The anguished cries became louder, and the light diminished. The woman called again, and Jessie plugged her ears. The light retreated until the room was almost dark again. The third time the voice called to her, Jessie couldn't take it anymore. "I will tell your stories," she shouted. The cries stopped, the light flooded the room, and she knew this was the purpose of her life. Names popped into her mind. She had to write them down.

"I'll do it. I will…" she moaned, repeating the words again.

"Jess, sweetheart, are you okay?" Matt patted her hand when she opened her eyes. She lifted to a sitting position. "Where's my notebook? I need it quick. I have to write this down."

"Are you okay? Was it a nightmare?"

She waved him off and started writing. "I have to write this down before I forget." The list of names grew until she could write no more. She grabbed her laptop and began searching for them in missing persons sites. "I can't believe they're all here. I don't know what to think."

"What's going on, Jess? You've got me worried."

"With all the unconventional things I've gone through lately, I have another to add to the list." Jessie told him about her dream and the woman calling to her. "I tried hard to ignore her. I don't want to open myself to anything else. Each time I ignored her the room got darker. In the end, I said I would give voice to their stories."

"What happened next, and what were you writing?" Matt sat on the bed beside her.

"All these names filled my mind. I wrote them as fast as I could, but I'm sure I forgot some." She pointed at her laptop. "They are all here among the unsolved cases and missing persons. Tell me, what am I supposed to do with all of this? I could be busy twenty-four-seven and not be able to help all of these women."

"I don't know how this works, but I think it's more about knowing there are many who need help and then helping those who you can. You might not be able to come to the aid of everyone, but you can do your part to assist a few."

"Of course, you're right. Why me?" Jessie glanced at him and waited for his answer.

"That's easy, sweetheart—you care." He took her laptop from her side and the notebook out of her hand. "I want you to rest. I want you at full strength tomorrow. Your article will be in the Globe tomorrow, and you know what that means. We're in for a wild ride." He kissed her good night.

Chapter 16

Matt whistled. Walking down the stairs, he couldn't be happier they had made it through the night without any incident. He picked up a Boston Globe on his way to breakfast. The Brass Lantern was known for its gourmet breakfast menu, and he couldn't wait to try something. He wanted to see Jessie's face when she saw her article on the front page. She had gone down a few minutes before him to get a cup of tea and to talk to Evelyn before the night clerk left for the day. At least someone had a good night's rest. He was tired, but glad to see her perky and almost back to normal.

He found her in the dining room sipping her tea. Coming up behind her, he placed the open newspaper in front of her. "Did you see your story? The Globe put it on the front page."

"Are you kidding me?" Her eyes scanned the page. "Oh my, you're not. Wow, I will need to buy a few copies of this. Awesome." Her smile broadened.

"I'm proud of you." He kissed her cheek, enjoying the pinkish tinge that followed.

"This is you, Ms. Reynolds, isn't it?" Evelyn sat in the chair next to Jessie.

"Yes," Jessie answered.

"I read the whole thing. You didn't know this girl, but it's like you knew her personally. How do you do that?" Evelyn leaned forward in the chair.

"I was an investigative reporter. I researched her life." Jessie took a sip of her tea.

"I never had any idea Kimberly had a twin sister named Hope. Everyone in town is talking about it. I even clipped out your article." Evelyn pulled it out of her purse to show her. "If you don't mind me asking, why did you write about her? Most folks stopped thinking about her years ago."

Matt smiled at her. "I can tell you one reason she wrote the piece, Evelyn—she cares."

"Over fifty years and no one still knows what happened to her. It seemed wrong to me. Sometimes if people are reminded, they will remember some small detail that will make a difference in a case being solved."

Evelyn leaned close to Jessie and lowered her voice. "Our ghost was here because she wanted your help. I'm right, aren't I?" She looked at Jessie over the top of her glasses.

Matt grinned at Jessie. "You can tell her, sweetheart."

Jessie nodded. "Yes."

"I knew we had a ghost. I knew it." She shook her head. "I knew it. Carl will have to believe me now." She stood. "I'll leave you to your breakfast. This is our secret. Word of our ghost can't get out, or it will ruin the inn's reputation." Evelyn put her finger to her lip. "Not a word."

"And so, it begins. I wonder what else will surface today." Matt looked over the menu. "I was told the Eggs Benedict is good, as are the fresh scones. What looks good to you?"

"The crustless quiche sounds wonderful, along

with a blueberry muffin." Jessie gave the waitress her order.

"How did Evelyn know about the ghost?" Matt rubbed his chin.

"She told Carl every time one of the mirrors fell off the wall that the inn was haunted. He didn't appreciate being told there was a ghost." Jessie thanked the waitress as she filled their water glasses. "Matt, I wish you could have seen the mirror. The anchors were still in the wall, and the wires were firmly attached and hadn't broken. It was like someone threw them down to the ground. But they were heavy, and no woman without supernatural strength could have lifted it off the wall much less throw it." Jessie poured cream into her fresh cup of decaf.

"As we now know, the mirror had help in getting your attention." Matt reached for her hand. "Did you get any sleep last night?"

"You know I did, but you look like you could use some sleep yourself. You can't stay awake every night watching to make sure I don't go through a portal. You'll be a wreck in a few days. As you told me last night, I need you to be at full strength because the ride is about to begin."

"You're right." He tugged at his shirt collar.

"As soon as we eat, you are going to the room to take a nap, and I'll watch you to make sure you don't go anywhere without me." She chuckled.

"I get the point." He placed the napkin on his lap. "Let's eat while it's hot."

"My, oh my, this melts in your mouth. Taste this." She placed a slice of the quiche on his plate. "It's not a pie crust, but it tastes like there's a crust. I'd love the recipe. This would be great for Katie's inn."

"You have to try this. Give me your spoon." He filled her spoon with some of the Eggs Benedict.

"Wow, another keeper. I can see why the locals say this is the best place around for breakfast. Look at the blueberries in this muffin. I'm sold. I would come back here if only to eat again. I'll have to think about whether I would stay overnight though."

"You won't come near this place unless I'm with you." Matt thanked the waitress as soon as she refilled his coffee.

"I need to run today. Will you run with me later? The park might be an interesting place to run and watch for anyone who might be coming or going if you catch my drift." She tilted her head, her brows rising as she talked.

"I'm way ahead of you. We'll run in the park and around the area to see if we can see where the new tunnel might come out." Matt charged the bill to their room. "I'll take a nap, but I want you to wake me in an hour. No longer." They walked out of the dining room and climbed the stairs to their room. "Remember, sweetheart, one hour." He stretched out on the bed and fell asleep.

****

She listened to his deep breathing for a few minutes. If she hurried, she would be back before it was time to wake him. He would be upset if he found out, and she would get a lecture which was probably deserved, but sitting idle was not in her playbook. Hope had told her the name of a man she thought might have the information she needed. While she was waiting for Matt to go to sleep, she searched for him online. He was still alive, and she had the address in her pocket. The house, according to GPS, was a few blocks from the inn. Jessie grabbed her purse and opened the door.

"Where do you think you're going?" Matt lifted his head off the pillow.

"Would you believe me if I said I was going to get some tea?" She closed the door again.

"No, because you wouldn't be telling me the truth. Jess, you're not good at deception or hiding your emotions on your face." He yawned.

"I thought I could check out this address and be back in time to wake you." She plopped down in the chair. "I'm used to doing some things myself, and you did promise me I could continue working as we have been."

"Unless what?" The muscles in his face tightened.

"My life was in danger. But as you can see, there's no danger here. I haven't been threatened, and no one has sent me any creepy notes. This is probably the safest case I've been on in a while. I can check on this while you rest and be back before you know it."

"Not alone." Matt shook his head, pushing up into a sitting position on the edge of the bed. "You've returned from a place only you have been—and God knows where. We have criminal activity going on right now in this inn, and you've written an article linking Kimberly and Hope as twin sisters and not cousins. You've stirred up memories that some folks would prefer to leave buried. We'll check the address out together. Give me a few minutes." Matt walked into the bathroom.

"I'll wait for you in the hall." She started to stand.

"No, Jess, you'll wait right here. Until I believe

you aren't in danger, we do this my way…please." Matt smiled at her.

"You knew you'd get me with 'please.' You're not playing fair." Jessie sighed, sitting down again. "Hurry. Time's a-wasting, please," she said through gritted teeth. "I want to go on record that I'm sure I could do this on my own." Her foot tapped in rhythm under the chair.

"Duly noted." He shut the bathroom door with a chuckle.

Mumbling under her breath, she said, "I could do this without your help. It's no big deal."

"I'm ready. Let's go." Matt grabbed her hand, tugging her out of the chair.

"Here's the name and address. Hope gave me his name, and I checked to see if he was still around. He lives close to the inn." She handed him the paper she had written on after her chat with Hope.

"Put on your running shoes. We are going to be a couple out for a jog. I don't want to draw attention to us right now."

Jessie changed into her running clothes when Matt stepped into the hall to answer a call. She wanted to be outside with him. Jogging was the perfect cover. All the inactivity was driving her up the wall. If they could solve this case soon, she could be back in Blue Cove and put this whole bizarre experience behind her. She missed her friends, her store, and her cottage. The sooner she got there, the better. Jessie laced her shoes.

Chapter 17

"We'll work our way to this address in a while. Let's go through the park first. I'm curious to see if we can find where the tunnel comes out." Matt held the inn door open for her. He started jogging when he got out to the main sidewalk, and she kept pace with him.

The day was perfect for running—pleasant, but not hot. She loved running beside her guy. "We should do this more often."

"You'll make a runner out of me yet." He smiled at her. "I have to admit I almost like jogging when I'm with you. The conditional word is 'almost.' "

"You love it. You know you do." She smiled back at him. "Was your call important?"

"Routine station stuff. The guys said to tell you hi, and welcome back." Matt kept a steady, even pace.

"It's good to be outside. You have to admit the day is gorgeous and perfect for a bit of outdoor sleuthing." She took a deep breath. "I needed this." She picked up the pace, and he kept up. "I'll race you to the park." She took off fast, laughing at the surprised look on his face. "Last one there buys dinner," she called, looking over her shoulder.

She stood by the park entrance. He exhaled a deep breath as he slowly came to a stop in front of her. "You win. I'll be happy to buy dinner for the pleasure of your company." They walked the circumference of the park.

"You let me win, didn't you?"

"Who me?" He winked at her.

"You're guilty, but I don't mind." She glanced coyly at him.

"It was for a good cause." He stopped and faced her. "Do you remember what you saw as you surveyed the park from the tunnel door yesterday?"

"I do." Jessie moved to the area that appeared familiar. "Matt, over here. Is this crazy or what?" The door was marked with a historical plaque, and a thick padlock kept it from being opened.

"That's interesting. Either they have a key to the lock and it was left open that day, or they have created another door." Matt pivoted, scanning the park.

"I wonder what they're moving in and out of those tunnels."

Matt glanced at the text on his phone. "We should go by the address you wanted to check out. Frank is close to town and will be here soon. I found a motel that will let him have his dog. Radar can help us find out what our suspects are involved in."

"Is the police chief okay with all of this?" she asked.

"I'm working with Macintyre, but I don't seem to see him much. I can't figure him out."

Their run took them by the address on Jessie's paper. They ran past the house and back again, but they didn't see anyone. "We might have to stake out this house tonight. We can do it after dinner with Frank. I heard about a great Italian restaurant not far from the inn." Matt grabbed her hand. "We'll come back later."

They rounded the corner on the way back to the inn when a car careened toward them from the opposite direction. The driver's speed increased, propelling the vehicle like a rocket toward them. The car's tires squealed on the asphalt. Matt shoved her out of the way in the nick of time. He fell on top of her, shielding her from harm with his body. The car quickly turned around to pass them again. "Geeze, are they drunk or crazy?" Jessie tried to get up, but Matt shoved her down again, right before she heard a popping sound. "Are you kidding me?"

"Nope, I'd say they're sane and mean business. We're the targets." Matt led her through several fenced yards, staying away from the streets so they wouldn't be seen.

"This changes the nature of the case." More than once she was pressed up against the side of a house while Matt checked to make sure it was safe to cross over the next street.

"We have to keep moving. We're sitting ducks out in the open like this." He called Macintyre to let him know what was happening.

"Did you get a look at the car?" the chief asked.

"A dark colored large SUV, but other than that I hardly had time to avoid being hit." Matt checked before they ran to the other side of the street and hid by the side of another house.

"The sooner you get out of sight, the better."

"We're working on it. What the hell is going on around here?" Matt's free hand clenched at his side. What was he thinking when he left his gun in the room?

"I'm on my way. I'll be at the inn soon."

Matt shoved Jessie against the exteriors of at least two more houses to keep them from being seen by the people in the slow-moving SUV who looked for them.

The vehicle moved at a slow enough speed for Matt to clearly see the make and the first few letters of the license plate. He would give it to the chief and let him deal with them. He was relieved when he and Jessie made it in one piece to the shelter of the inn.

"This is one time I'm glad I didn't follow my own plan to go by that house alone." Jessie passed through the door Matt held open for her.

"Are you okay? I didn't mean to shove you to ground that hard. I reacted as fast as I could. At times, I don't know my own strength. The main thing was to get you out of the line of fire and away from the car barreling down on us. I didn't want to get hit, either."

"I'm fine. As much as I appreciate you trying to save me, I don't want anything to happen to you either. It's been a strange few days, and I don't want to have any do-overs. I'll sit right here in this chair and not move. How much can one person handle before it all goes wrong? A simple cold case from over fifty years ago has turned into a much bigger problem. Me and my stupid articles. I have to quit stirring up trouble as Katie always tells me."

"You think." He grinned at her. "It happens every time you open your computer to type. Macintyre is here, and I want to have a word with him. Stay where I can see you." Matt walked over to where Sam stood.

****

Jessie watched Matt and Macintyre talk for the next several minutes. Matt's clenched jaw, wide stance, and the throbbing vein in his neck told the story, and he was letting Sam know exactly how he felt. From where she sat, his voice grew more intense when he demanded to know where the town's officers were and why they weren't investigating any of the neighbors' complaints. Before he calmed down, Matt filled Sam in about the tunnels, the articles they had found in the underground room, and the car that had almost run them down. Jessie was sure she had heard him call the town's investigation inept.

Matt was used to his guys listening to what he said. She could tell he didn't appreciate Sam's excuses for why his men hadn't done their jobs. The two of them would have to work it out.

Her thoughts returned to the dream from last night. She had made a commitment to tell the victims' stories whenever she could. There would be a price for bringing their stories before the public. She had learned the lesson repeatedly in the last year. The sheer number of these cases could be overwhelming. Had she been sleepwalking through most of her life? Yes, she had Stuart Adler, her own stalker from the past, to contend with, but she had no idea there were so many women around the world who were suffering in the same way. Most of them were not as lucky as she had been to escape. Kimberly and Hope hadn't been.

No wonder there were all these restless spirits who couldn't find peace and rest. There were also males among those restless ones. Amir Baz and the other college students came to mind. Gina, her first experience with a ghost, had opened her eyes to a side of life that she hadn't known existed. Maybe the address she had shown Matt was hitting too close to home for someone. The rats were coming out of their holes.

"Are you ready to leave? Sam is coming with us to meet Frank. We'll ride with him." Matt interrupted her train of thought.

"I need to change before I go anywhere." She glanced at her grass-stained running clothes.

"You head up and change, and I'll be up in a few minutes."

Jessie changed her clothes and ran a brush through hair. "Kimmie, we want your help. I have no idea what we've gotten into. I'm pretty sure you do though. Were these tunnels open while you worked here?"

"Jess, who are you talking to?" Matt walked in the door.

"Kimmie and I were having a chat. I wished she could tell me what I can't understand. We must be getting close. Yet it seems like we've only begun to scratch the surface. We're running out of time." She latched the necklace at her neck. It was a gift from Matt when he flew her to San Diego.

"This may be all Sam's case soon. I have to get back to town soon. I've been gone too long as it is." He grabbed his clothes on his way to the bathroom.

"You know how this works. It doesn't matter who else is involved. We will solve the case. The ghosts choose us, and that's the way it is."

"Well, they'd better get busy because our time here is coming to a close."

"I'm ready. You'd better hurry. Macintyre is waiting for us." She sat in the chair to wait. It didn't take long, and they were in Sam's car on their way to meet Frank.

"Stay close tonight, Jess. I don't believe these guys will let up. They may be following us now. I have no idea if we'll have another run-in with them yet tonight. A cornered animal is always the meanest and hardest to figure out."

"I will."

They arrived at Frank's motel. After introductions, they were on their way to dinner. As the men talked, Jessie watched the cars behind them to make sure they weren't being followed. She was on edge, and even their arrival at the restaurant didn't help calm her. The host seated them at a table near the window. The dark SUV passed by the restaurant, slowing down right in front. She saw him at the same moment he saw her and raised his gun to point it at them. "Duck," she screamed right before the bullet hit the window, putting a hole the in the glass and grazing the waiter walking by. The vehicle sped off.

"Is everyone all right?" Macintyre asked the patrons while Matt tended the waiter on the ground.

"It was the same car," she told Matt. "The man who shot at us looks familiar to me. I have no idea how he could be, though. Yet I'm sure I've seen him before. Whether around town, at the game the other night, or God forbid back in the sixties, I've seen him. Please don't ask me how that's possible. I couldn't begin to tell you." She put her finger to her lip as if to zip it shut.

After the waiter was taken to the hospital and the restaurant and its staff were settled, Sam took Frank back to his motel and them back to the inn. Arrangements were made for Frank to meet them in the morning at the inn, where the track would begin. Jessie wished she could remember where she had seen the man before. *Think, girl.*

Chapter 18

"Jess, Sam seems to have no idea who or why these guys are shooting at us. We're on our own figuring this one out. I like Macintyre—he's a nice man, but he doesn't run a tight ship."

"What's new? It usually comes down to us, Matt. Our cases have worked the same way every time. Let's do our job, then we can go home and celebrate with our friends. We'll watch each other's backs, like the great partners that we are." She flashed a smile at him. "Don't look so shocked, I've listened to some of what you've told me."

"I love you, Jess. You manage to make the unusual almost palatable." He walked upstairs with her and unlocked the door. "Please, stay put, stay away from the key, and keep the door locked. I want to check around and don't want to worry about you."

"Do you want me to go with you? I'd be happy to. I'm not thrilled about the prospect of staying alone in this room."

"I want you to do a couple of things for me."

"Anything." She squeezed his hand.

"Call Jeremy to find out what he's found out. I hope he has something for me about this inn. You should talk to Reba too. I'll call Tom. I won't be gone long, and after I get back, we'll plan. Right now, I need to tie up some loose ends." He kissed her and hugged her tight. "Promise me not to touch that key."

"I promise. Hurry back." She followed him to the door, pulled him back, and kissed him. She locked the door after he closed it. Reaching for the computer, she sent Jeremy an email to call her when he got a chance. She changed into something more comfortable and called Reba.

"Jessie girl, I'm always happy to hear from you. I hope you're not suffering any side effects from your recent adventure. You can tell me all about it when you get home. I only hope I can wait that long. First things first though—how are you feeling today?"

"I'm fine as far as I can tell, but I'm not sure what my body went through when I passed through the portal," Jessie paused to take a breath. "I can't wait to tell you about the places I went to and all the stuff I saw. The whole encounter was cool. I did bring back one keepsake, and I can't wait to show Sadie."

"When will you be coming home? Are you wrapping things up there?" Reba asked.

"Hopefully, soon." Jessie told her about being almost run over and shot at. "Other than that, things are no further along than when we started."

"You know better than that, Jessie. You're getting close, and someone feels the law closing in on them. Seeing it all come together is a matter of timing and using your wits. You have work to do. Don't let fear paralyze you. New and strange experiences are never easy, girl, but I've never known you to be a quitter."

"I'm not quitting, but call me cautious and I might have to agree. This was supposed to be our weekend together, which has come and gone. Matt has to be back to work soon, and here we are in the middle of something we weren't looking for."

"You know these things are messy and never convenient. It is what it is. No time to feel sorry for yourself. If I know that man of yours, he's already planning your special time together. It's only delayed, not forgotten."

"When you're right, you're right." Jessie smiled to herself.

"The people involved in this are hurting thousands of people by what they're doing. They must be stopped, and you two are the ones to take them on."

"Reba, you're the only person I know who can slap me upside of my head and make me smile while you're doing it."

"Everyone should have a person like that in their life. I'm happy to be yours. My husband, Lawrence, is mine."

"I guess I should go. Jeremy should be calling me soon."

"Before you go, I have to warn you. I already told Matt. There is someone in this case who has dabbled in the dark arts. Like Irwin, whom you contended within Palm Springs, this person is stronger than you think. Remember what you learned—you'll be fighting on that front while Matt fights on another. Where you'll be taken is completely new. You'll find it hard to believe, but it's still true. I'll see you at Katie's engagement party a stronger, wiser woman. You can take on the world, my dear. Don't overthink this."

"I'll try not to." Jessie shut off the call. She fell asleep waiting for Jeremy's call.

****

Matt had a few things he wanted to take care of. He

didn't want to leave Jessie alone, but he had to allow for it or neither one of them would get anything done in the future. He spent some time working out logistics with Carl for the track in the morning. Carl would be there to open the tunnels and was fine with the dog going through the rooms if the guests were gone.

"Do you have anything else you require for tomorrow?" Carl asked. "I'll be around all day. All you have to do is ask for me."

"I appreciate you being open to this. Macintyre will be here with the search warrant in the morning. We must do this by the book. Do you have any idea what these guys might be moving through those tunnels?"

"I wish I knew. I'm still grappling with the idea the tunnels are open and being used. I spoke to my grandmother, and she told me she wasn't surprised. She told me she heard strange noises all the time, but she thought it was ghosts. I asked her why she never told me, and she told me she had, but I scoffed at it. She's right. I would have done exactly that." He took off his cap and then plunked it back on his head. "I don't want to believe in this stuff, and she wants me to understand it's real." Carl scowled and shook his head. "With what happened to your fiancée I have to rethink everything. My grandma used to tell me Irish tales. I quit listening with each passing year."

"If you had to make an educated guess, what are they moving through the tunnels?" Matt leaned his hip against the wall, his hand at his side.

"I'd say drugs because that's where the money is. Big money to be exact." Carl rubbed the red stubble on his chin. "Addiction seems to be at crisis levels in this area, and if someone can make a buck off another's misery, they will."

"That's for damn sure." Matt pushed away from the wall. "How long have you lived here?"

"For a couple of years before I bought the place."

"Have you noticed anyone spending lots of money? You know what I mean. A police officer who suddenly buys a hundred-thousand-dollar sports car or a factory worker who buys a big house?" Matt asked.

"I'll have to think about it. I haven't moved in those circles, but my friends might know of someone. I'll be discreet and ask around. Truthfully, I haven't interacted much with the town folks until recently."

"Thanks. I'd appreciate it if you'd check. I'll talk to Macintyre in the morning about it too. We need to catch a couple of breaks to get to the truth." Matt frowned. "Time is something I don't have much of. Right now, I need to get back to Blue Cove and my job."

"I'll keep my eyes and ears open." Carl shook Matt's hand. "I'm happy your fiancée is better."

"I am too, but we had another close call. I'll get to the bottom of this, and when I do people will be going to jail." Matt's hand clenched at his side.

"I wouldn't want to be on your bad side." Carl whacked Matt on his back. "If she were my fiancée and someone had hurt her, I'd be angry too."

"It's not only her, but lots of folks are getting hurt. If they're smuggling what I think they are, people are dying because of them." Matt followed Carl into the dining room. "I'm done for tonight. I've been gone long enough."

"Are you ready for what you arranged earlier?" Carl smiled at him.

"I'm ready. Give me time to get to the room." One of his plans was going to work if he had any say in the matter. Matt took the stairs two at a time. Unlocking the door, he saw her sleeping on the small loveseat. She hadn't touched the key, and she was still here. He could breathe again.

"Hi, sweetheart." He rubbed his lips across hers and watched her stir.

"Hi back at you. Where did you go?" her sleepy voice asked him.

"I had a few things to take care of, and one of them was to let you out of my sight without feeling panicked. I made it for a good hour. It was my gift to you. You'd get sick of me hovering over you every moment."

"As much as I love you, that would get tiring fast, for both of us."

"I'm growing. I knew you'd feel that way." Matt went to answer the knock at the door. "This was the other reason." He opened the door. Carl wheeled in a cart. The bouquet of roses in the center was surrounded by champagne chilling on ice, two glasses, a small chocolate cake with the words "I love you, Jess" written on it, and two cups of hot tea.

"Have a nice evening, you two." Carl left the room.

Chapter 19

"What's all this?" Jessie pushed her hair out of her face.

"We might not have had the weekend I had planned, and we will be in the thick of things in the morning, but you and I are going to have our own moment to celebrate our engagement before we share the news with any of our family or friends." He popped the champagne cork and poured some into each of the goblets.

"The roses are beautiful." She stood to see them more closely and sniff their beautiful fragrance. "Thank you." She took the glass he handed to her.

He patted the space beside him. "To us, and to our love. May it last a lifetime."

"I'll drink to that with pleasure." She clinked her glass to his. "Cheers."

"Before we talk, I have something I want to give to you. When you were gone, I stood in this room looking at this necklace." He held the sapphire and diamond necklace up to the light, watching it twinkle. "I wondered if I ever would see it again on your beautiful neck. I bought these to go with it, and I can't wait to see you wear them too." He handed her a small box with the matching sapphire and diamond earrings in it.

"They're beautiful. Thank you." She leaned her head against his shoulder.

"The blue reminds me of the color of your eyes—beautiful, like you. I want to know everything I can about you. Your likes and dislikes, your favorite color, ice cream, and anything else I can discover about the woman I love. We have these moments, and I want to make good use of them."

"You always surprise me. I had no idea when I first met you that my hunky cop would turn out to be the romantic guy my heart always longed for." She sipped the champagne from her glass and wrinkled her nose. "The bubbles always tickle." She sighed and leaned back into his arms.

He gazed at the beautiful woman in his arms. As they sat, he learned details about her life, and her esteem grew in his heart—her favorite color, red. Her car should have told him that secret. Mint chocolate chip ice cream was her go-to flavor, and roses topped her list of favorite flowers, although daises were a close second. Chocolate anything could win her heart, and she ran because she loved it. He told her some of his own stories, including the crazy things that he did with his brothers growing up. Her laughter made him smile as he thought of it. Not once did they mention the case. They were for a moment simply a couple in love discovering each other. It was a thoroughly wonderful evening in Matt's estimation. Now, holding her while she slept beside him, was the perfect ending.

Opening his eyes, he reached for her, but she was gone. "Jess," Matt called, feeling the panic rising inside him. Jumping out of bed, he reached for his pants while pushing his arms through a shirt. He was going for the shoes when she walked in carrying two cups of steaming coffee. Limp but relieved, he sat on the edge of the bed. "Where were you?" he asked louder than he intended to.

"I didn't mean to alarm you. I thought I could make it back before you got up." She handed him a coffee the way he liked—strong with a little cream. "Frank will be here in thirty minutes, and I thought you might like coffee and a scone before you got to work."

"Right. Thanks, babe." He went into the bathroom.

"While you're in there, you might want to rethink your shirt. It's wrong side out." She laughed inwardly.

****

Frank and Carl were there to meet them when they came downstairs. Jessie petted Radar and gave him the treat that Frank handed her. "Hey, big fella, are you ready to get to work?"

"He's ready, and guess what I saw on my drive over here."

"I bet you saw a hawk." She remembered the story Frank had told her on one of their cases. The appearance of the hawk would mean a successful track. "Am I right?" Jessie glanced at him.

"You're right." Frank nodded and smiled.

"We need all the help we can get. Right now, there are lots of pieces and no way of knowing how they fit together."

"By the way, it's nice to have you back among us. Matt told me the story of what happened to you. I don't believe even Radar could track you through a dimensional time portal." He laughed, tapping her shoulder.

"Seems ridiculous to hear you say it aloud," Jessie said, her hands planted on her hips. "I was the one who went through the portal, and it was as wild as it sounds."

"There's never a dull moment with you, and that's a fact." Frank walked over to Matt. "Where are we going to start?"

"We're looking for any sign of Kimberly's body around the area or in the inn. This case is decades old, and I'm not holding out much hope, but we have to try." Matt patted Radar's head.

"When it comes to bones and decomp, he's pretty good at finding it." Frank put on Radar's harness with the skull and bones on it. As soon as you're ready, I'll let him scent off this human decomp that I carry in this vial." Frank held up the small tube with pieces of human bone in it. With any luck, we'll bring closure for those wondering where she's been all these years."

"I think Kimberly was murdered in the inn. No one saw her leave the day she went missing. I could be wrong, but they murdered her and carried her body out later, or she could still be in the inn." Jessie joined the conversation as the men talked.

"Gads, that's a grizzly thought." Carl frowned. "How is that possible without the smell overwhelming everybody who was here at the time?"

"You'd be surprised what people come up with to cover their crimes," Frank answered.

"I'm game if you are, Frank. We can try inside or outside first. I'll leave that up to you." Matt patted the top of Radar's head.

"The chief is here with the warrant, so we can start when you're ready." Carl pointed at Sam walking toward them with the papers in his hand.

"We're inside. We may as well try while we're here and go out if he leads us." Frank knelt beside

Radar, holding the small vial of decomp in front of his nose. "Find the grim reaper. Let's get to work." The dog sniffed the air, and his head went down. Radar started up the stairs. Bypassing the rooms, he proceeded to a door with another set of stairs leading up to an attic. Smelling box after box, Radar made his way to a large trunk at the back of the attic. He pawed at it, sniffing around the trunk, and sat. Frank tried to open the closed lid, but it was locked tight.

"Do you have a key?" Matt asked Carl.

"I have no idea. I wouldn't know where to even begin to search for something this old." Bending down, he inspected the lock more closely. "Ms. Reynolds, do you still have that strange looking key? The keyhole looks similar to the shape of the key that I saw in your room. It might be worth a try."

Jessie's heart began to race. "Of course, it makes total sense. The key will fit." She raced down the stairs to their room and reluctantly grabbed the key, bringing it back with her. She kneeled beside Carl as she tried the key in the hole—it was a perfect fit. She turned the key, the lock moved, and the trunk lid shifted and groaned. Jessie knew Kimberly was in there the moment she saw the light flooding out around the key. She jumped up. "I can't look, Matt." She moved away to let him open the trunk.

As Matt opened the lid, the light filled the room. "We have a body."

"Damn." Sam rubbed his temple. "She's been here all this time."

Kimberly stood in front of her, totally whole and surrounded by light, interacting with her. Jessie said, "It's Kimberly. I'm sure of it. Hope has to be somewhere nearby."

Matt stood. "Sam, do you have a team in place to work this, or do you want me to call the FBI?"

"Under the circumstances, after what we talked about the other day, I think we need to get someone from the outside in here."

Matt called Tom, and he hooked him up with the agency in the Boston area. "Agent Bartlett and a team are on their way."

"My dog is restless. I don't think he's done." Frank gave him the command again, and Radar was on the move. They followed him through the kitchen and to the backdoor. As soon as Matt opened the door, the dog moved out the door, down the steps, and made his way to the garden. where he began digging around the roses.

"Obviously, something is buried in this spot too." Carl shook his head. "What did I get myself into with this place?"

"This is only the beginning. We will have Radar do the tunnels as soon as Agent Bartlett and his team gets here." Matt went to stand by Jessie. "What are you thinking?"

"The whole case is starting to make sense to me. Kimberly used the key that locked her burial place for the past fifty-some years to take me through the portal. I followed the last few weeks of her life. The same light I saw in the mirror was in the trunk as you opened it. Soon she'll be able to rest in peace and be free from this place." Jessie swiped at the tears filling her eyes. "What a terrible way for her life to end, and yet here she was waiting to be found all these years."

"She's not lost anymore because of you." Matt squeezed her hand.

"She chose me. Even though I don't always understand the whys of this stuff, it's orchestrated in a way that I can't take credit for the success. I know there is a body in this garden. They will find Hope. I'm sure of it. She told me when we talked that if I found Kimberly, I would find her as well." She sat on the garden bench. "There's a good feeling associated with finding them and giving them a final resting place."

As soon as Agent Bartlett arrived, his team went to work. It wouldn't be long now. "Love always finds a way to triumph, even in the darkest of circumstance," Jessie whispered to the ghost standing by her side.

Chapter 20

"How's your dog holding up?" Matt asked Frank. "Do you think he has another track in him?" Matt watched one of the agents begin to carefully turn dirt. As he worked, he tried not to disturb any possible remains.

"Radar's resting. This was a short track but with a depressing ending for him, Matt. What else are you looking for?"

"Drug residue or anything that might tell us what our suspects are moving through the tunnels. We have no idea what we'll find—if anything. I have the lab checking for prints on a shovel we found in one of the tunnels."

"I remember you mention that you were concerned about drugs. I brought my dog trained to find drugs along this time. If drugs are being moved in the tunnel, Kilo will find them. I'll put Radar in his crate and get Kilo when you're ready."

"I can't wait to see another one of your dogs in action. What's the breed?"

"A Belgian Malinois. He's not as open with people as Radar is, but he's good at his job. He saved my life once, and he's my buddy."

"I'm sure he'll do a good job. Your dogs work well for you."

"Is she okay?" Frank pointed at Jessie.

"You know how she wrestles with all the strange things happening around each case but finds peace in bringing each victim home. Solving their murders, to her way of thinking, allows them to rest in peace." Matt folded his arms across his chest. He smiled at Jessie when she glanced at him.

"I feel the same way. It's the only way you deal with all the sadness. What we humans are capable of isn't always humane if you ask me. That's why I like my four-legged friends best. We'll be ready as soon as you are." Frank started toward his vehicle to get Kilo out and put Radar in his crate to rest.

"Sounds great, Frank. We'll start in ten minutes." He walked over to Carl and told him what they wanted to do next. "How are you with all of this?"

"Never mind a body in the attic and them digging up the roses, which are bad enough. Now the tunnels. What did I get myself into? I wonder if my grandmother knew all this was going on. I understand why she wanted to get out of here. I'm not far behind her in my thinking.

"We're ready, Frank." Matt motioned to him.

They went into the library and locked the door. Moving the furniture and rug, Carl lifted the door into the secret room down below. Matt went first and turned to help Jessie.

Kilo and Frank went down next, followed by Carl and Macintyre. "This day has been a bit of bummer for you, Carl, but it's awesome to think of the slaves on their way to freedom who hid here. You've got a cool place." Frank patted Carl's shoulder as he walked by him.

"Thanks. I might be able to make it work. I have

to. I sank all I own into it."

Frank let Kilo smell the small bag with drugs in it that he had brought. "Find the drugs, fella." The dog began methodically moving through the tunnels. Picking up a scent, he came to one area which seemed to be a dead end, and he moved in circles pawing at the ground and sitting.

Jessie went over to where he was sitting. Running her hand up and down the wall, she hit an odd patch with a bulge in it. She played with it and moved her fingers back and forth over the bump. The wall moved, sliding into another section like a pocket door, opening into another room. "Would you look at this." She stepped cautiously into the next room.

Hundreds of boxes were stacked in the room. Matt opened one. "We've got enough opioids to keep the addiction problem going for a long time. We need to have these tested. If they're smuggling drugs in from another country, the batch could be contaminated."

"I'll be damned. Those neighbors knew what they heard all right." Sam looked in another box. "I wonder how long they've been in operation and who's buying the stuff."

"So far this is the second room like this that we've found. I'm wondering if there are more. I don't want them to know we're on to them. Let's seal these boxes and take this sample to the lab to be checked." Matt handed Sam one bottle. "Bartlett will be interested in this find. I'll bring him down here as soon as we're done."

"Do you want me to close the door? We should leave it the way we found it." Jessie asked.

"Not yet. Bartlett needs to see this." Matt walked

over to Frank. "There's a new tunnel and another room I want him to check out. This room was hidden. I'm curious if there are other new tunnels down here."

"We'll give it our best shot." Kilo got back to work. He led the way to the room they had found a few days before. Picking up the human scent around the room, he followed the trail down through the new tunnel, coming to another area where he pawed the ground.

"Shh," Jessie said, placing her finger to her lips. "I hear voices." She stopped, putting her ear against the wall. "The sound is coming from behind this wall."

Jessie ran her hand along the wall. There was nothing. "It must open from the outside. I can't find a latch or lever. This wall is smooth."

"Hold tight. I'll be right back." Matt walked out of sight.

"Do you think they're in there now?" Frank asked her.

"I can't make out if they're male or female. The voices aren't clear." Jessie leaned against the wall, placing her ear against the surface.

Matt returned with a couple of agents, and they began to work at getting through the wall. "Jess and Frank, move out of range. Sam, keep your gun ready." The first agent's pick pierced a hole through the wall. The voices Jessie heard suddenly became screams.

Several young women huddled together in the corner of the room. "Be careful—they're scared," Jessie said. She moved into the room before Matt—reassuring them was at the top of her list.

"Jess, you talk to them." Matt got out of the way and let her handle the situation.

Jessie squatted down beside one of the women. "Don't be afraid. No one will hurt you. I promise. What's your name?" she asked the petite, dark-haired woman to the right of her. Her dark eyes warily stared at Jessie.

"Crystal," the tiny woman answered, stroking the back of a younger woman who cried uncontrollably.

"How'd you get in here?" Jessie reached over and patted the hand of the crying young woman.

"They locked us in this room a few hours ago. They promised they'd be back, but I pray they never do."

"Who locked you in here and why, for heaven's sake?" Jessie glanced at the women. Anger rose inside of her at what she could sense had been done to them.

"It's a long story. Our experience is the same." The women in the circle all nodded in agreement. "A lady approached each of us and invited us to be a part of a women's mentorship group. We were told it was an all-woman organization created to help women overcome their social fears and be strong. Something I've always wanted to be." The woman sniffed.

"What happened next?" Jessie felt the knot in her stomach growing. She had a sick feeling she knew what was coming next.

"She wouldn't take no for an answer, and we all found ourselves in a strange group. First, we learned they wouldn't let us go. They exploited us both sexually and for our labor. The leader became our owner—we weren't free to come and go. We could only do what he told us to do. You wouldn't believe me even if I could explain it right."

"Who are they?"

"If we tell you, we're as good as dead." The woman rubbed her arms. "We've seen too much, and they're powerful people."

How many other women are in the group?" Jessie squeezed the tiny woman's hand. Tears welled up in her eyes.

"More than I know, I'm sorry to say. This group operates freely in several countries in the world. I feel gullible. I should have been able to see through it."

"It's possible for anyone to be taken in." Jessie's chin edged up. Possible mind control, she thought. "Matt, we can't leave them here for those men to come back and find."

He squatted beside Jessie. "We won't leave them. You know me better than that. Their safety comes first." He grabbed her hand. "Are they okay?"

"No, and I'm angry." Her face was red and her chin tight. "Trafficking in opioids and enslaving humans both in a place where slaves once hid making their way to freedom. It's ironic if you ask me."

"You feel that way. This is my inn, and I'm ashamed this is taking place right under my nose," Carl said.

"How are we going to get them out of here?" Sam asked. "If one of my officers has looked the other way, I don't want them to know what we've found, or our suspects might scatter."

"I'll get Bartlett. He'll know what to do." One of the agents went to get his boss.

"For now, we guard these women until we get them to safety. No one comes in this place."

"They'll protect you." She sat beside Crystal again. "I'm sorry this has happened to you. My name is Jessie.

158

I forgot to introduce myself earlier."

"Are you really going to help us?" Crystal wiped her dripping nose on her sleeve.

"Besides tissues, is there anything I can get you? Are you hungry?" Jessie hugged each of the women.

"They said they were coming right back. There is no restroom, and we've had no food or water."

"How long have you've been here?"

"A few hours. Our master was sending us to another master, but they said the heat was on and they would move us later."

"Why do you call him master?" Jessie asked. Skylar came to mind.

"Because he made us his slaves."

"Are there more women being recruited?"

"Yes, the woman who talked me into joining used to be an actress. She was famous, and that's why I thought it would be okay."

"What they're doing isn't legal. The FBI will track this down and give Interpol a heads up."

"Why are you down here? The men told us no one knew about the tunnels and we'd never be found if they left us," Crystal asked.

"We knew, and my friend's dog found you. Right now, we need to get you to a restroom and find you some food." Jessie stood.

"There's a small bathroom right off the library. You won't have to open the door into the lobby area. I'll go to the kitchen to get some food." Carl led the way to the room and showed them the restroom. "Keep this door locked until we are done here, Jessie."

"I will." Jessie spent time chatting with the ladies. Her dream became more vivid in her mind the more she talked to them. She had no idea the night she wrote those names on the list that these five women's names would be among them. This was one wild ride that she was on.

Chapter 21

Bartlett knocked on the door to the library, and Jessie let him in. "Matt is in the room downstairs." She pointed the way.

"Thanks." He disappeared down the stairs into the tunnel.

Jessie got as close to the stairs as she could without falling to listen to them talk. The agent and Matt were formulating a plan which involved removing the women and the drugs in a matter of a few hours, taking them out through the tunnel by way of the park. The room would be restocked with sealed boxes weighted to feel like the bottles of opioids. The words "sting operation" came up several times. The idea was to make the area appear like the women had escaped. Bartlett hoped to buy some time and keep the suspects in the area looking for the women.

Debriefing would take place at the agency in Boston. Music to her ears was what Matt said next. "If you don't mind a suggestion, it would be smart if you were to let Jessie sit in as you question them. She has a way of understanding what these women are going through and can get them to open up."

"Arrangements can be made for that," she heard Bartlett reply.

"She's already learned some information about how they were recruited and how the group functions.

Let's just say it's a strange cult and women come out on the bad end of it."

"Damn, we live in crazy times. Here we are digging up a body from decades ago, and we have a strange case staring us in the face today."

"We should have these drugs tested too," Matt suggested.

There was another knock at the door. Jessie checked before she opened it to one of the agents working outside. She pointed the way down the stairs and followed him.

"Sir, I think you need to see what we found. There's a body."

"Damn, a corpse could mean anything. Possibly it's one of the slaves who died legitimately and was buried outside. I doubt it, but it's a theory." Bartlett walked upstairs followed by the others.

"I take it you heard what the agent said—they found a body." Matt came up behind Jessie.

"It's got to be Hope. I told you if we found Kimberly, we would find her." The women were eating. "How long were they going to leave the women in the room with no resources?"

"I doubt they even thought about the women's needs." Matt frowned, glancing at the women.

"Cruelty comes in many forms." Jessie shook her head. "Our suspects should be locked up with no food or restrooms to see how they like it. Of course, I know we must treat them better, or we'll become like them."

"How can we ever thank you all?" Crystal asked. "We never thought we'd ever see our homes again. Thank you, from all of us." The women nodded in agreement.

"Don't thank us yet. We need to get you to safety and arrest those responsible. We are going to do everything in our power to get you home to your families as soon as possible." Matt's hand brushed against Jessie's.

She knew he would, too. Lord, how she loved this man.

****

The rescue operation went off without a hitch. Once Crystal and the others were out of reach in Boston, around the clock surveillance of the tunnel area began. Yet, even with Radar's help, they hadn't found the other entrance to the underground area—the one their suspects were most likely using. Jessie knew that it bothered Matt. His frustration came through in his voice each time she talked to him.

After being in Boston with the women for a couple of days, Jessie learned more than she ever wanted to know about the cult that had trapped and confined the women. The FBI was building a case against the leader and several of his followers. It reminded her of an earlier case at Lizzy's family compound. How was it that people could get ensnared in these strange groups? Clover and Essence followed Skylar the same way, with blind devotion.

She would have to research and write an article on the subject. There always seemed to be some new want-to-be authoritarian waiting in the wing to take the place of a despot taken out of commission. It was job security for those investigating the crimes. Finally, she was back at the inn and with Matt.

"Hello, Ms. Reynolds. We missed you the last couple of days. Did you enjoy the fair city of Boston?"

Evelyn asked when she walked in the lobby of the inn.

"I didn't see much, but I learned a lot. Probably more than I wanted," she added under her breath.

"You missed a lot happening around here. Bodies in the attic and gardens, and people in the tunnels. What's the world coming to?" Evelyn sniffed. "I know you were here for some of it, but the action hasn't stopped while you were gone. Have they identified the bodies yet?"

"We're still waiting to hear." Jessie leaned against the front desk.

"Between you and me, one of them is Kimberly." Evelyn lowered her voice. "What do you think?"

"You could be right. We'll know soon enough," Jessie assured her.

"That's a fact. I can't imagine what this will do to Carl's business."

"People can surprise you. Sometimes what we think will turn them away becomes the very thing that will draw them. Let's hope it works that way for the Brass Lantern." She crossed her fingers and smiled at Evelyn. "Do you know where Matt is?"

"He was in the dining room the last time I saw him. That man of yours sure takes his job seriously. I wished Macintyre was more like him. Sam needs a fire lit under him to get him to move."

"Speaking of my man, I can't wait to see him. I'll talk to you later." She was on a mission to find Matt. He sat at a table by the window. Absorbed by the paperwork in front of him, he didn't see her until she squeezed his shoulder. "I missed you, but I think you might have been too busy to miss me."

"Never." He stood and hugged her.

"I'm curious to know what you were thinking about. You didn't see me, your own loving fiancée, when I walked in the room." She grinned at him.

"You mean other than the fact you snuck up behind my back. Case notes are the culprit." He pulled out a chair for her.

"Whew, I'm glad it was the case." She put her hand dramatically to her forehead. "I was afraid I was beginning to lose my appeal."

"You? Not possible," he whispered in her ear and placed his hand on her shoulder. "You've got my heart."

"Nice to know. Maybe you should put on your glasses." She tilted her head to see him better. "I wouldn't want you to miss me altogether."

"You know me, Jess. A case can consume me."

"I love that about you. You always work hard for every victim." Her hand brushed against his where it lay on her shoulder. "I'll quit teasing you." She waited until he was seated again. "What have you got at this point?"

"Illegal contraband, two unidentified bodies, five women, and zero suspects. Reba told me this had been going on for a while, and I know she's right on the mark." Matt drummed the pen on the table. "Do you have anything to add?"

"Crystal and the other women talked. What they were ensnared in is odd to the point of being almost unbelievable. I'm still thinking about what I learned. As for the bodies, I know one of them is Kimberly. I saw her watching as you opened the trunk. All of it seems to resemble what I saw in the commune in the sixties— Skylar and the man that Crystal named as Orin Corbitt.

Orin had a woman he promoted to a slave master who recruited the women into the group. The women were branded with Orin's initials in their pelvic area—a painful and humiliating experience for each of them. It was a bizarre pyramid scam from which there was no escape for the women they were trafficking in."

"Did money exchange hands?"

"Naturally, the recruiter was paid for every woman she brought to Corbitt. Camilla Browning was the out of work actress Crystal told us about. Browning hadn't had a great part in years. Who thinks up this junk?" Jessie shook her head. "Skylar had gathered Clover and the other girls under the guise of protecting them from men who would hurt them. What did he do? Kept and used them himself. You can't make this stuff up. Crystal couldn't understand why she was unable to resist Camilla or Corbitt."

"I wonder if the woman might be a part of the group operating out of here. What were those five doing in that room? Why did they leave them?" Matt asked.

"Crystal said that Orin had given them to Camilla Browning. She had recruited enough to become a slave owner in the pyramid structure. The FBI will be sorting this out for a while, but they're building a strong case against Corbitt and Browning."

"Frank and I have been searching for the opening to the new section of tunnels. We haven't had any luck yet. I keep thinking today is the day."

"Let's go back to the room where we found Crystal and the other women. Maybe we're missing something. It can't be long now." Her voice was filled with optimism.

"We've combed over the room and worked our

way out from there and still haven't found anything."

"Let's try again, keeping in mind that this is the day." She reached for his hand, lacing her fingers through his.

"Now that you're here I can see our luck changing in a good way." Matt closed the folder with his free hand.

"Have our friends in the SUV been back for another visit?"

"If they have, I haven't seen them." Matt stood beside her and tugged on her hand as he started to walk. "Are you ready to search with me?"

"I'd do most anything with you." She smiled at him.

Chapter 22

Back in the room where they had discovered the women, Kilo moved restlessly around the room. "I can't imagine what's wrong with him," Frank said.

"Is it possible he senses something we can't see or hear?" Jessie asked.

"Of course. Dogs hear things long before we do and are far more aware of danger than we are."

"Danger is the perfect word. We should be careful—our friends might be getting close," Jessie told Frank as she went to the area where they had found the women. Down on her hands and knees, she moved across the area searching for an abnormality. She ran her hand at the base of the wall from the corner outward. Her hand found a small button and pushed it. The door sprang open.

Kilo took off before Frank could stop him, and Matt raced after them with his gun drawn. Jessie moved up the tunnel behind them. Barking mixed with growls grew louder, then the popping sound of gunshots and the squeal of tires stopped her progress forward. "Matt, is everyone okay?" she called out.

"We're good. Guess what we found?" He paused. "The other entry, and we surprised them as much as they surprised us."

She reached them. Matt leaned against the wall with blood dripping down his arm. "You've been hit."

She ripped his shirt to see how bad it was. "I thought you said you were okay. This doesn't seem fine to me." Matt grinned at her. "What are you smiling at?"

"She cares." He glanced over her head at Frank and winked at him. "Honey, it grazed me. I'm fine, but our suspects got away, dammit."

"What I want to know is how you found the way to open the door? From this side, it's easy enough, but from the inside, I couldn't find it." Frank showed her the way to open the door from the outside of the room in the tunnel where they were.

She put her hand on Matt's arm. "We're going to have that arm checked. No arguments."

"I'll let you have your way, but first I've got to get some back-up to watch this area." Matt made a call. The door led to an abandoned factory.

"Two can play this game." She called Sam and told him to bring a doctor with him, filling him in on the details.

****

Matt kept her in his sight, waiting until he could get her alone. He liked how she took charge when it came to him. He was tired, and his arm hurt like hell. Five stitches and a lecture later, he was ready to sleep. They had a few days before they needed to go back to Blue Cove, and he'd had one night alone with her. Life wasn't fair. New plans for another getaway would be in the works as soon as he could arrange it.

"I told you it wasn't a scratch. Honestly, Matt, you'd better take care of yourself. If I remember right, you always lecture me to be careful."

"Yes, I do, and now you know how I felt when you told Valentine the porn king to shoot you. At least I was trying to protect Kilo and not antagonize a known criminal." He patted her arm. Her face grew red. "I'll try to be more careful in the future, sweetheart. I want to marry you and spend my life loving you, not make you a widow."

"You're good at smooth recoveries." She fanned her face and kissed his cheek. "According to Frank, Kilo is one tough customer. He would have taken them down. It was better that he was the dog in the room rather than Radar." She glanced at Matt's face. "You're tired. Why don't you go to the room and sleep?"

"Are you trying to get rid of me?"

"Not at all. You have enough officers and agents here to watch every entry of this place, including the windows."

"I promise I'll go to our room soon. We're having dinner with Bartlett. He's on his way here now from Boston."

"Are you sure you're up to it?"

"I'll live. He says he has news for us. Most likely it's confirmation for you that Kimberly and Hope have been found. I can't miss you gloating because you were right all along."

"I don't gloat, and you know it." She swatted his good arm.

"Whoa, I hit a nerve." He moved wrong and grimaced. "I'm teasing you, sweetheart. I should know by now to trust what you see. It's accurate every time."

"Thank you." She smiled sweetly at him. "Support has arrived. Let's get this over with. I want you to rest."

****

"Parker, how are you doing?"

"I'll survive." Matt stood to shake the agent's

hand.

"Sounds to me like you're trying to be a tough guy. Hurts like a son of a gun, doesn't it?" Bartlett sat in the chair across from Matt. "Carl said his chef made something for dinner for us. I'm ready to eat. How about you?"

"How's the case going on your end?" Matt asked.

"Jessie knows how strange the stories we've heard the last few days are." He turned to face her. "You were good with Crystal and the others."

"Thank you."

"You have a damn good partner. Parker, you're one lucky man." He picked up his water glass.

"I couldn't agree more." Matt nodded. "She's mighty fine."

"I wanted to have dinner with you both. Jessie was right—one of the bodies is Kimberly Ryan, and the other is Hope. We are looking for family or friends to notify. Linda Cranston was helpful with a few names, and so was Patrick Hamilton. Both friends were relieved to know the girls' bodies had been found. Both were murdered with the same instrument. We know because it made the same pattern on both of their skulls. Bones can talk long after most forensic evidence is gone. Blunt force trauma to the base of the skull fractured the skull bones in two places. I wonder if their killer is still alive at this point."

"Any idea what the item was that made the distinct pattern?" Matt asked.

"The lab is still working on it. They're running tests on the drugs and tracking any codes or lot numbers they've found on the bottles One of the lab technicians lifted a couple of prints off the shovel, and they're running them through the system."

"I guess this is one time we hope they have a record. Something has been bothering me since our run-in with the suspects. They weren't driving the SUV, but rather an old white van. I'm wondering if there's someone else behind the scene bankrolling the operation." Matt swallowed the pill the doctor had given him with a gulp of water.

"Could be. Did Macintyre run the plates?" Bartlett wanted to know.

"I only had the first three numbers. They were eliminating everything that wasn't the make of the vehicle in question. I should have info on it soon."

"Jessie, you're quiet tonight. You can jump in at any time." The agent smiled at her.

"Kimberly and Hope were twins. To have them murdered with the same instrument means most likely the same person murdered them both. I'm wondering if the murderer thought Hope was Kimberly, as odd as that might seem. Few people around here knew Kimberly had a twin. I might have to think more about this." She thanked the waitress who set their dinner in front of them. "What's next?"

"We wait, build the case against our suspects, and hope they'll slip up sooner rather than later." Matt reached for her hand. "Wait for the break. You know how it goes."

Frank joined the group, and they ate the great meal prepared by the inn's chef. Matt was concerned the incident earlier might have spooked the suspects and that they were running scared. Leaving the opioids was the same as losing millions of dollars. They might come back, but not without more firepower. They couldn't be taken by surprise again. Kilo or Frank could have easily been shot. It was damn near a catastrophe. The only thing that had saved them was that the suspects were as surprised as they had been. As the evening wore on, his arm bothered him, and he wanted to take something more for the pain, but he had to wait.

"Matt, you could use some rest. My men will be on guard tonight, and I'll see you in the morning, with more. Hopefully, they won't be back tonight." Agent Bartlett stood. "Frank, you have a damn fine dog there. I'm impressed with his work and will highly recommend you for any cases."

"Thank you, sir. I'm proud of him myself." Frank stood to shake the agent's hand before he left.

"Frank, with the suspects still on the loose, do you want a police escort back to the motel?" Matt stretched his legs and stood.

"Not necessary. Carl said I could stay here tonight, and my dogs are welcome. I'm headed up to bed if you don't need me for anything else." Frank grabbed Radar's leash for the sleepy dog, who rested at his feet. "Kilo is in the crate in the room. He doesn't like people, but he'll do everything to protect me. He's a great partner too."

"I'm headed there myself. See you in the morning." Matt reached for Jessie's hand, holding it. "Are you ready, sweetheart?"

"I'm ready." She paused at the desk to say goodnight to Evelyn.

He refused to go to the room until she was by his side. Carl stopped them next.

"I don't know how to thank you for all you've done. I will have the new tunnels sealed as soon as this case is over. No one will be able to get in them again. My grandmother was stunned to hear about everything going on here. There's no way she could have dealt with all this at her age. I'm glad she's far away from the Brass Lantern."

"You might want to consider leaving the old ones open and restored. People will be fascinated with the history of slaves staying there on their way to a free life. You could do tours and sell souvenirs." She smiled at him. "Thank you for a great meal."

"The least I could do after the day you all had. Sleep well. Parker, you look like you could use it."

Relief filled Matt once the key unlocked the door. His legs felt heavy, and he lay on the bed with his hands stacked behind his head. Within a few minutes, he was asleep.

Chapter 23

Jessie checked to make sure Matt was breathing. His quiet stillness concerned her. Something that Reba had mentioned about someone from the past would be in the future kept going through her mind. She had no idea at the time what she had meant, but she was beginning to get a picture that made sense to her. She would tell Matt in the morning.

Placing her computer on her lap, she began to write about Crystal and the other women's stories. Nothing could be printed until the investigation was over, but she wanted to write down the notes she had while they were fresh in her mind. While she was at it, she'd write about her journey to the past. It was her secret for now. Reba and Sadie would enjoy reading it, and she was excited to share it with someone who would understand.

This case was changing her. Amazed with each unusual thing she experienced, she felt a new strength grow within her to accept the challenges and to change with them. Her career would have grown in New York, but she couldn't believe for a minute she would have grown as a person the way she had since moving to Blue Cove. Gina and the Harvest Club was the start of a whole new life for her. She checked on Matt again. Before she could move away, he had her hand held tight in his grip. "Stay beside me."

"If you don't mind my computer coming with me. I want you to sleep." Jessie grabbed her computer from the table.

"I want you close. I need to know you're all right too." He sounded groggy.

Jessie plumped up the pillows and climbed in bed beside him with her computer next to her. She reached for his hand, holding it tight in hers until he was once again asleep. She carefully let go of his hand and continued to write the story of her time in the past. As she remembered Skylar and the strange little man, a picture formed in her mind and a possible answer to who might be responsible. Now all she had to do was figure out if it was even possible. She shut off her computer, turned off the light beside the bed, and stared into the dark room, her mind refusing to shut down. "Kimmie, show me, and we'll get him," she whispered into the quiet room. She cuddled close beside Matt's sleeping form and fell into a restful sleep.

****

The morning took off running when Matt got a call from Agent Bartlett, who was in the dining room waiting for them. "Jess, it's time to wake up. Bartlett is here with some news."

She focused on the fact he was dressed and ready to go and rubbed her eyes. "You go ahead. I'll be down in a while. I have to get ready." She reached for his hand. "How's your arm?"

"Grouchy, a little like me for sleeping the night away with you beside me. I wonder if we'll ever have a normal time together."

"I'm betting my money on you finding a way." She smiled at him. "You're awful good at what you do, Mr.

Chief of Police."

"Is that right?" He leaned close, balancing against the bed with his good arm, and kissed her. "I'm glad you have faith in me because I'm beginning to wonder."

"I'll be down as soon as I can. Don't wait for me. You know it takes me longer to be presentable than it does you." She struggled to sit up, still dressed in her clothes from last night. She hadn't intended to fall asleep in them. But a shower and some clean clothes sounded nice. Her grumbling stomach reminded her food would be great too.

"Don't take too long." He waved as he walked out the door.

Jessie jumped out of bed and went about her morning routine. As she walked out of the room, she felt a hundred percent better. Funny how feeling fresh and clean made a difference in one's outlook. "Good morning, Evelyn, how's your morning going?

"Did you hear that the bodies were those of Kimberly and her sister?" Evelyn pushed her slipping glasses back up her nose.

"Yes, the agent told us last night. Why are you here? Don't you usually work at night?" Jessie asked.

"I'm taking extra shifts in the day while our morning lady is on vacation. Carl works overnight when I go home." She straightened the guestbook. "The crashing mirrors and all the strange stuff happening around the inn make perfect sense to me now. We've had ghosts. You had a run in with them, didn't you? That's what happened to you that night." Evelyn grabbed the feather duster as she chatted.

"Yes." In this case, Jessie figured the simplest

answer was the best.

"Someday I'd love to hear about it. That ghost show should interview you," Evelyn mused. "It's right up their alley."

"I'd rather not. The fewer who know about it, the better I think." Jessie leaned close to her. "We have to protect the inn."

"I suppose you're right. Still, I think it's kind of cool myself." She paused. "I have no idea what else is happening, but Carl is in a foul mood and ready to dump this place."

"I hope not. This is a beautiful old inn with a terrific history. My friend Katie owns an inn too. She's good at what she does, and many of her guests return every year. They love the place with its relaxing gardens, and I do too."

"Where do you live?" Evelyn asked.

"I live in one of the guest cottages on the property. It has a beautiful view of the cove, and I like to think of it as my small piece of heaven on earth." Jessie smiled wistfully. She missed the peace of her cottage. "I guess I'd better get into the dining room before Matt sends out a search party."

"I still think you should tell your story of what happened that night on one of those TV episodes. You could make some money and be famous." Evelyn straightened the guestbook and shifted the pen. "I would do it in a heartbeat."

"I'd rather not be famous. My life is almost perfect the way it is. A few tweaks here and there, and I might even say it couldn't get much better." She turned to leave. "I'll talk to you later."

****

Where was she anyway? Bartlett wouldn't tell him anything until Jessie got there, and she was taking longer than was necessary. Boy, he was grumpy. Any personal time she spent on herself was always worth it. Focusing on the small talk around the table wasn't working. He glanced at the door. Finally, he stood as soon as she walked into the room.

He pulled out her chair. "What took you so long?" he said in her ear. The look she gave in return he deserved—and more.

"Wouldn't you like to know?" she whispered, smiling at the men around the table. "Good morning. I trust I didn't keep you waiting too long. I told Matt earlier to go ahead without me. I required a bit more time this morning."

"Not a problem, Jessie. We've had a chance to relax with our morning coffee. I consider it a luxury. Now that you've arrived let's order, and I'll fill you in on what we've learned since last night." Bartlett motioned to the waitress.

"I'm sorry. I told you I was grumpy." Matt leaned toward her as he spoke.

"You're hurting, and I know your plans were ruined by all this. I'm sorry." She put cream in the decaf the waitress had just poured.

"No excuse for my rudeness. I'm anxious to get back home and put this behind us, but we're no closer to solving the case." He squeezed her hand.

"They don't need us to work it." Jessie looked over the menu.

"Aren't you the one who always says others may get involved, but we'll be the ones to solve it because the ghosts chose us," Matt grumbled at her and felt lower than a snake.

"I'm the girl, but here's the thing—if we leave now this case will probably follow us home. At least we'll be on our home turf that way." She smiled at him.

He had to hand it to her—she made the possibility sound almost promising. The food placed in front of him smelled great. Besides being a grouch, he was hungry. Maybe breakfast would put him in a better mood. She didn't deserve his mood. "What's new since last night, Bartlett?"

"We found out who owns the SUV. When we went to his house, his wife said she hadn't seen him in a few days. He's a respected doctor in the area which means he could write prescriptions and make some kickbacks on the opioids. The fingerprints belong to a local guy with an extensive record of misdemeanors and felonies. I think our guy just graduated to the big time. We're no closer to solving the twins' deaths, but we'll keep working on it. You both are the reason this case opened at all. I think it's safe to say our suspects aren't going to come back here with all the police presence. You're free to go home, back to your jobs, and we'll take over the case and work with Sam Macintyre."

"Sounds good to me. How about you, sweetheart?" Matt was ready to get back to Blue Cove.

"Fine with me. You know how I feel about it." Jessie tilted her head to see his face.

He nodded. "If it's all right with you we'll leave today?"

"If you're leaving, I'm out of here too." Frank approached the table.

"You're free to leave, Frank." Bartlett picked up his fork and knife. "If you ever want to work for the agency, let me know. Your dogs did their jobs like pros, and so did you. I would be happy to write you a report and a bureau recommendation to add to your resume."

"I'd appreciate that. Anytime I find myself working with a new unit it's great to have those recommendations in my file." Frank took a bite of a blueberry scone.

"No reason for any of you to delay. If I were you, after what you've been through, I'd be out of here as soon as I could. I'll keep you informed on where the case is headed." Bartlett tapped the table in front of Jessie's hand. "You, young lady, will have to come back and testify. Crystal told you a lot, and you might be used to corroborate the witnesses' testimony. I was impressed with the way you got each of those women to talk. If you ever want a job with the agency, I'll give you a favorable recommendation. It was a real pleasure to work with each of you."

After they finished their meal, they went to their room. "How do you feel about leaving the case without a resolution?" Matt unlocked the door.

"I'm okay. If we are supposed to solve it, we will. If not, I might think it odd, but I'm getting used to new experiences. Besides, I'm ready to be home. Dylan and Katie's engagement party is this Friday, and if we missed it I could never face her again."

"Never sounds like a long time. I'm sure she'd understand."

"Oh, she might understand, although I'm not sure about if she would forgive me. I'd never hear the end of it." Jessie laughed and patted his arm. "Katie may be small, but she can make you feel guilty for a long time."

He nudged her shoulder playfully. "I'm sorry for being a jerk earlier. This case has too many loose ends to my way of thinking. I don't like walking away with it not finished. Have we failed Kimberly? This isn't my jurisdiction, but still, I'm invested."

"I get it. I am too. I even traveled back in time searching for answers. Talking about time travel, Reba said something to me that I've been thinking about. What if the person who I met in the past and is tied to the present is a child of one of the killers? I have no idea why, but I think it's possible. I mean, if Skylar had a son or grandson that was anything like him, he'd be Orin Corbett. From what Crystal told me, his teachings sounded like what I heard Skylar say at the commune while I was there. Or maybe in some bizarre way Skylar found a way to cross through the portal too."

"Whew, I didn't see that coming. How could that happen?" Matt found himself shaking his head like a bobble doll.

"It happened to me, and I have no idea how. There are many things which have no simple explanation."

"I'll take your word for it. I'm ready to be out of here. Case unsolved or not, I've been concerned you'd go back through some portal, and I'd never get you back." Matt helped her pack her remaining items. Once the suitcases were packed, he carried them downstairs.

Carl helped Matt carry cases out to the car. "I'll miss you both. I hope they get this figured out soon and my place can return to normal, whatever that means at this point."

They exchanged business cards. "Let me know if they arrest any suspects in the case. I've never left in the middle of an unsolved case before, but you have a lot of good folks on the job. I'm sure arrests are imminent." Matt put the suitcases in the trunk.

"I'd be happy to give you a free weekend on me. The first thing I'm doing is get rid of that peculiar dresser and redo a few of the things in the room you were staying in."

"Thanks, Carl. I might take you up on the weekend. If I can ever get away from the crazy stuff that seems to dog us." Matt closed the trunk of the car. "Jessie must have stopped to talk to Evelyn." He walked into the inn with Carl. He reached his fiancée's side, and his hand brushed against hers.

"Are you ready to leave?" She smiled at him.

"Anytime you are. The sooner we leave, the earlier we get home. I'll let Dylan know we're on our way." He sent a text to Dylan.

"I'm sure we'll see each other again. Goodbye," Jessie told Evelyn, waving as she followed Matt out the door.

"I can't say I'm sad to leave." Matt turned on the engine. "Nothing about the past several days is logical at all. I can't make sense of any of it."

"Sorry about all of it. I seem to attract this weirdness. If you remember, I did try to warn you to think long and hard about staying with me. This doesn't seem to be going away."

"Jess, you don't need to apologize. I'm not upset with you. If anything, I'm angry at myself and the way I handled everything. I should have known the dog was on to something the way he was acting. I should have listened more carefully to what you were saying to me the night before all this happened, and I certainly wasn't listening to my own training."

"Before you go any further, I think you're taking way too much guilt on. You're not a superhero after all. As amazing as you are, you don't know everything, you can't prevent things from happening, and you can't protect everyone all the time. Lighten up."

"I think you were right about keeping our engagement quiet for now. There's too much going on, and we don't want to upstage our friends."

Jessie realized for the first time how close she was to losing him because of all the odd events happening in her life. Everything together was depressing.

The car was quiet for most of the drive home.

Chapter 24

She stood in one of her favorite spots. The cove was beautiful, and she never tired of watching the changing scene before her. The ocean was her come-to spot to ease the trouble in her mind. The window in her cottage was the perfect spot to take it all in.

Matt came up behind her, wrapped his arms around her, and pulled her back into his chest. "Your suitcase is in your bedroom, sweetheart. Are you okay?"

"What was the purpose of the last several days and our lost weekend if there are still no answers in this case?" She rested her head against his shoulder.

"I wish I had the answer to your question because it's the same question that I have." He stroked her arm. "Dylan told me I have a stack of paperwork waiting for me. I'm headed to the station. What's on your agenda?"

"My store is calling to me. I want to implement a few of the suggestions I learned the first few days of the conference and, of course, see my cousin and Audrey." She turned in his arms. "I wish I understood the purpose. I'm still attached to it and don't know how to find closure for me if I can't bring it to Kimberly and her sister."

"Bartlett will keep in touch. Maybe that will help." He kissed her goodbye. "I'll call you later."

"Okay." She grabbed her purse. "Wait. I'll walk out with you."

He reached for her hand, holding it until they got to her car. Kissing her again, he opened the door for her. "See you later."

Her drive to the store took little time and was always a pleasant one. The thrill of owning her own business hadn't worn off. She loved the place. Feeling a sense of pride every time, she walked through the door. Reba, Peyton, Audrey, and Sadie all waited for her. She had barely closed the door when the questions started flying her way. The next twenty minutes she told and retold the story of Boston, Kimberly, and Crystal.

"Wow." Molly shook her head as she strolled in after seeing Jessie talking to the others. "You all are having a great time in here."

"Pull up a chair and listen to Jessie's story. She's had an eventful and exciting time in Boston." Sadie patted the empty chair beside her.

"An amazing story, dear, but you've left out the point we all want to hear about. Tell us, dear, how did you travel back in time? We are all curious and want to hear." Reba squeezed her hand.

"Hear what?" Molly and Peyton said at the same time.

"You heard me. Our Jessie managed to travel through a gateway into the past. I can't wait to hear all the details."

"I hope you won't be disappointed. I'm still trying to figure out what the purpose was for me to go back in the first place."

Taking the next twenty minutes, she told them what she knew. There were interruptions, of course, but the questions kept coming, and she could tell her friends were interested in what she had to say. The more she shared with them, the more the disappointment she had felt earlier settled over her.

"You know, my dear girl, there are reasons for every experience even if we don't see them at the time. Past and present often collide until their secrets are revealed. This case is not done with you, and you're not done with it either." Reba patted her hand. "Everything will be fine in the end, but there is a rocky road ahead for you and for Matt.

Sadie added, "You'll know soon enough how this all ends. I'm sure of it."

Glancing around the circle of the women in her life who loved her and were trying hard to encourage her, Jessie was grateful. Her heart lighter, she enjoyed the coffee Molly brought her, the laughter of Reba and Sadie, and serving customers who wandered through the door. Her day seemed a few shades brighter.

****

Matt tackled the mounds of paper on his desk. His mind wandered to the gray car that seemed to be following them from Boston. A fluke, possibly, but his gut told him the occupants were tailing them. He would have to keep his eyes open. If the car was in town, he would have to let Jessie know.

"Hey, glad to see you back. Katie was starting to worry Jessie wouldn't be here on Friday. Without her best friend, it wouldn't be a celebration." Dylan sat in the chair in front of Matt's desk.

"There was no way she would have missed it unless she was incapacitated. I find their loyalty to each other refreshing." Matt shifted the stack of papers he had gone over.

"How's she doing? The last several days couldn't

have been easy for her."

"The hardest part for her seems to be leaving without the case concluded. It's hard on both of us. We're not used to unfinished business. It's a strange feeling." Matt scowled. "Between you and me, I haven't told Jessie yet, but I'm sure we were being tailed on the way home."

"What you're saying is the case isn't finished with you yet. Her name was on the article in the Globe. It would be nothing for someone to figure out where she lived. Add to that you guys messed with an obviously profitable business and you could say you'll probably see this case to its completion."

"You might be right. I was thinking more along the line they're sending someone to get rid of us."

"Sorry about your weekend, man. I know how you were looking forward to it."

"There'll be other weekends and more plans if I have anything to do with it." His words showed his frustration level even to himself. "Sorry. This time with Jessie took it to a whole new level of strange. I wasn't sure if I'd ever see her again. All the talk of two dimensions, trans-dimensional portals, and time-travel messed with my logical brain. She actually went back in time, and I have no tidy explanation for how. I may never know, but it doesn't change the fact that it happened. I hated to walk away from the case with no conclusion. Let's just say it didn't help."

"How are you and Jessie as a couple?"

"We're solid, but the rest of this can be taxing. I've got some thinking to do. Jessie asked me several times to think this through seriously because this seems to be her life. I've handled it all well up to now. This time it shook me."

"What are you going to do?" Dylan paused. "Please tell me you guys aren't breaking up."

"I love Jess—more than ever—but I have to figure out if I can live every day with the abnormal stuff happening." Saying the words aloud made him cringe inside. He couldn't think of life without her, but would this be any kind of life? "I'm not going anywhere, but I can't be cavalier about it. She challenged me to think this over seriously, and that's what I'm going to do. I want our decision to get married to be one we've both thought about, based on our love, with both of us determined to make it work in the face of some of the strangest odds ever."

"You've got me worried, friend. Jessie is your match in every way. Can I be honest with you?" Dylan leaned forward in the chair.

"Of course. We're friends."

"You're running, man. I get it she was there but out of reach for days. You had to be scared. But before you throw the greatest gift you've had in a long time away, remember what you were like before she came. I can fill in a lot of details if you need help. You were no fun to be around."

"What would you do if it was Katie going through all this? We can't even have one damn weekend together without some supernatural interference."

"Katie has other issues that make our lives less than perfect. Doesn't everyone? You're not an easy guy when you're focused on a case. You can be a grouch when things don't go your way. It's the truth, and you know it."

"What's your point?"

"You'd be a fool not to put a ring on her finger as soon as possible. For once don't overthink what's going on with your heart. Step in—the water is fine."

"We'll see." Matt opened one of the files on his desk. "I have work to get done."

Dylan stood to leave. "I'm saying this as your friend—don't be an ass. You give her up now, and she'll be gone to you forever. There are plenty of guys willing to take your place in her heart." He walked out before Matt had time to respond.

He couldn't help it, at least not yet. This week had frustrated him personally and professionally. It wasn't Jessie's fault, but she hadn't helped either. For now, he'd give himself a break and not think about it too much. He worked the rest of the afternoon and drove home to his empty house, sat in his favorite chair, and turned on the TV. Mindless entertainment was what he wanted. Okay, he was feeling sorry for himself. He could live with it.

Chapter 25

Jessie waited all last evening, but he never called and so far, not today either. Was it possible this was the end of them as a couple? If it was, there was nothing she could do about it. This was her life for now. She had even found her purpose and grown during this case, and there was no turning back for now. To this point, he had handled all the weird stuff happening to her. From ghosts to dragons he stood strong, but this time felt different to her. She was frustrated that he had been upset several times, which was not like him. She would give him the space he desired and hang out with Katie.

Jessie walked over to the inn to see her friend. Dinner time was the perfect time to go. Something smelled delicious when she walked through the kitchen door.

"Are you getting excited about your party?" Jessie called out to her friend.

Katie turned around squealing. "You're back. It wouldn't have been a celebration without my best friend to party with me." She scrutinized Jessie's face. "Are you okay? I heard all sorts of rumors about the weird things happening to you. I want to hear the truth straight from your mouth. As soon as I put the food out for my guests, we're going to eat here in the kitchen. You'll tell me all."

"Yes, ma'am." Jessie fought back the tears. Katie

was the one person she could share her fears with about losing Matt. She wanted to tell somebody. The weight of it pressed in on her. The possibility became more real and depressing to her every hour she didn't hear from him.

She talked, cried, and talked some more, and by the time she finished Katie was indignant. If Jessie hadn't restrained her, Matt would have got an earful. Katie was angry. For a change, it was nice to have someone baby her and be on her side. She was having a pity party, and she was okay with it. A person could only be strong for so long.

****

Matt awakened feeling better. After two days of wrestling and most of the night, he had made a big decision, and all was right in his world. He left the house and was halfway down the street when he noticed the gray car in the mirror. Without a doubt, he had a tail. He should let Jessie know right away. She would have to keep her eyes open, and he would too.

He stopped by the store on his way to the station. She opened the door when he knocked. "Good morning." He went to kiss her, and she turned her face away. "Is everything all right?"

"What do you think?" She frowned with her hands planted firmly on her hips.

"Why don't you tell me, Jess. You seem to have something on your mind." His good mood slipped away fast as he raked his hand through his hair.

"I understand you're having doubts. Be honest about it, will you? You said you would call, and you didn't. Then you waltz in here like nothing has happened. If you're over me at least man up about it."

"Sweetheart, I don't waltz anywhere. I walk like a man." He grinned, but seeing her expression his voice took on a serious note. "Yes, I've had a doubt or two, but never about you—only the unusual folks that seemed to have attached themselves to you. This time shook me. If you could have seen yourself as I saw you all those days... I believed you'd be back one minute and then lost to me for good in the next. We shared a night of pure magic, but I worried you would be gone when I woke up. I'll admit, it's hard to think of a lifetime this way. But the alternative is worse."

"Did you even consider I was afraid too?"

"I was feeling sorry for myself. I can't say that I did. I wouldn't be truthful if I said I had." Matt looked away from her.

"I wasn't sure I would find my way back. The one thought that kept me going was I knew you'd find a way if there was one to bring me home." She took a step toward him and stopped. "Will I have to worry with each new phenomenon that comes my way that you'll want to leave? I don't think I can handle the emotions of it."

"There are no guarantees how I might respond in the heat of the battle, but I know I want you in my life always. I'm sorry I put you through this."

"Where do we go from here?" she asked.

If you care to hear what I think, I'd be happy to tell you." Matt placed his hands on her shoulders to keep her from walking away.

"I'm listening." Her hands were still on her hips.

"We announce our engagement as soon as your ring is back, and like any couple in love we take life one day at a time. We celebrate with our friends and party. That is if I'm forgiven." An awkward silence followed, leaving him unsure.

She studied him for a moment before she answered. "I forgive you for not calling me and not trusting me enough to share your fears with me. As for being afraid, that's a human emotion we all know. I'll excuse you for that." She lifted his hand off her shoulder. "I worried for the past few days that you were breaking it off with me. I might have talked to my friend." She smiled at him for the first time since he had walked in. "I'm sure after Katie gets through yelling at you, I'll be asking forgiveness for talking to her instead of calling you too."

"Not to worry. Dylan called me an ass, and he was right. Katie can give me her best shot. I deserve no less. Are we okay?" He reached for her hand.

"I believe we are."

"Will you be my date tomorrow night?" he asked.

"You know I will." She squeezed his hand.

"The other reason I came in here—on our way home the other day I thought we had a tail. Today the same car followed me and continued down Main Street when I stopped in front of the store. You were right when you said the case would follow us here. I'm not sure what part the occupants of the car play in this, but I guess we'll know soon enough."

"Closure would be nice, and if this is how we get it then bring it on."

"Ah, my fearless dragon slayer has returned." He leaned in to kiss her. "Thank you, sweetheart." His lips touched hers, and they were lost in the moment. She wasn't lost to him—he had lost sight of her, but she was back where she belonged. The sound of the bullet hitting the window startled them both. Matt pushed her to the ground and fell on top of her to shield her.

He called for backup, and the car took off as the police cruisers raced down Main with lights and sirens. They were planted firmly back in the game. Matt called Bartlett to let him know at least some of the suspects had followed them to Blue Cove.

Chapter 26

The bullet hole in the window and the bullet lodged in the bookshelf told her if the shot had been slightly to the right one of them would be having surgery at this moment—or would be dead. A wake-up call wasn't pleasant, but in this case it was vital to keep them alert. She recalled Kimberly's not so gentle reminder that her murderer was still out there, and Crystal's traffickers still had to be caught. This was by no means over, and life couldn't be normal until it was. Watching Matt spring into action did her heart good. She never loved him more than when he was every inch the professional acting in the heat of the moment.

Matt's team worked on extracting the bullet, but the car and its occupants got away. Jessie figured the car would be disposed of and a new one would replace it, which meant they would have to be more on guard than ever. Sadie wouldn't be allowed near the store until she knew it was safe for her to return.

"Jessie, can I talk to you for a minute?" Peyton came in the back door. "Wow, what's going on? Why all the police?"

She told her about the drive-by shooting. "Thankfully, the store wasn't open yet, and no one was hurt."

"Cousin, you live one crazy life." Peyton paced in front of the counter.

'There's never a dull moment." Jessie gave a nervous laugh in response.

"Dull moments. You've described my life, I'm sad to say. I may have jumped from the frying pan into the fire though, and I wanted to run something by you." Peyton stopped suddenly and then began moving again.

Peyton walked three steps forward and four back. Jessie counted each one of Peyton's steps, trying to keep up with her. "I'm listening, but I doubt you're in any trouble. You're the most disciplined person I know."

"I didn't think I could sound any duller, but the word discipline is a perfect depiction of boring. My friend talked me into doing something totally out of character. In fact, the more I think about it, the more I want to back out of it." Peyton stopped in front of her.

"My interest is piqued. Tell me more." Jessie grabbed her arm to hold her in place.

"I don't want to get in their way." Peyton pointed at the officers.

"We aren't in their way. There's Evan. I wonder what he's doing here." Jessie waved as Evan walked in the door.

"He's taking pictures for the station while Marcy is out of town this week. At least, that's what Evan told me," Peyton said.

Interesting. Jessie smiled. Evan and Peyton are talking. "Now, what is it that you're about to do that has you worried?" Jessie asked her.

"You remember my friend Destiny?"

"I could never forget Destiny. She's the one you followed more than once into trouble." Jessie chuckled as the image of Destiny traipsed through her mind.

Eclectic and bohemian chic, she was Peyton's wild child friend.

"Yes, but she is my best friend—like Katie is yours."

"We sure know how to pick them, or they knew how to pick us because we made it easy for them to. Having said that, Katie has been at the center of every fun thing I've ever done."

"The same is true with Destiny. Only now, I committed myself to a trip to Arizona to ride the trails, sleep in the great outdoors, and relive history around and near the town of Tombstone. You know how I hate camping. What am I going to do?"

"Destiny knew how to play you to get you to say yes to that plan." Jessie laughed outright when she thought of Peyton in the desert heat and sleeping under the stars.

"To my defense, I held out against her pleas for several minutes. She wore me down." Peyton shook her head, a perplexed look on her face. "Darn, she's good."

"Cous, I think you should do it. Sounds like the perfect plan to take you out of your boring life and into a brand-new adventure. Safe and routine are highly overrated. But you're talking to someone whose life was turned completely upside down since moving here. I might not be the best person to listen to."

"The question is, do you like your life? Are you happy with it?" Peyton started pacing again, this time at a faster speed.

"I love it. Maybe not all the bullets and stuff. But I don't think I'd change a thing." Jessie grabbed her arm again. "Please, you're making me dizzy."

"Sorry." Peyton leaned against the counter. "It does

seem to have worked out quite nicely for you all the way around. You're with your best friend, you met a great man who's a bit of a hunk, and you're different. I mean different in a good way. Stronger, and surer of yourself than you were growing up." Peyton grinned. "It appears I'm on my way to Arizona in a month. I wonder what awaits me there."

"Cactus, heat, and bugs to name a few things," Jessie teased her cousin. "Maybe if you're lucky a hot cowboy and not an old one will lead your adventure. I can't wait to hear every detail."

"You forgot to mention snakes. I'm almost sure I should cancel." Peyton grimaced. "I hate the slithering creatures."

"You'd better not cancel! You don't want to miss out on the hot cowboy, do you?"

"Are you talking about hot as in heat, or hot as in hunk?" Peyton asked.

"We're talking about Arizona in the summer, so maybe he's a sweltering, sweaty hunk."

"What do I have to lose?" Peyton shrugged her shoulders.

"At the most a few weeks, but quite possibly a boring life." Jessie smiled at her.

"You talked me into it. I'm going to do it. Arizona, here I come." Peyton laughed.

"I mean, what could go wrong? Destiny and you together in all that heat, with only one hot cowboy." It wasn't that funny, but they laughed as though it was.

****

Matt had been off his game. There was no way they should have got off a round. The car had followed him home—he knew the danger, and even this morning he hadn't followed them. He came into her store instead. Knowing the danger, he let his guard down, and she was in the line of fire. Bartlett was busy in Boston, building the case against Orin Corbett. They had the identities of two people involved with the drug smuggling, but Bartlett wasn't handing out the info yet. For now, Matt's department would work this end of the case. One thing he knew was sure—they wanted Jessie out of the way so she couldn't testify against them when they were caught.

How could she be laughing after being shot at only minutes ago? He smiled. Her laughter was like music to his ears. Whatever Peyton was saying Jessie was enjoying herself.

"Chief, we're about to wrap up here. Did you happen to get any of the numbers on the plate?" Dylan stood beside him. "They're having a good time. It's as if she has no cares at all." Dylan smiled when they laughed.

"I know." Matt handed him the numbers he wrote down earlier. "I imagine they'll dump the car and get another one. Still, if it's a rental, we might find something. These guys are never as smart as they think they are."

"We'll keep you safe at the party tomorrow night. I've already hired some off-duty cops from Rocky Pointe. Katie made me promise. I hope you're ready for a tongue lashing from her. She seems to think you're in need of a few reminders about how lucky you are to have Jessie in your life."

"She can lash away. She won't say anything that I haven't already said to myself. Besides, it was your friendly pep talk that kept me thinking most of last night. Thanks, man."

Dylan slapped him on the back. "Hell, what are friends for? Are you guys okay?"

"We're better than okay. It was a discussion that was past due and essential for us to have. All the tension of a case can take its toll on us."

Dylan heard Jessie laugh again. "She seems to take it all in stride. That girl is good for you." Dylan grinned. "You know what they say—all work and no play…"

"I get it." Matt glanced at Jessie. "These guys mean business, and we're going to have to be on our toes. A different car might present a camouflage until we recognize we're being followed. I'm not sure Jessie will pay that close of attention to her surroundings."

"You know what I think? You're going to have to marry the girl soon to keep her safe. She walks in places must of us would fear to go."

"You've got that right. She seems to enjoy dragging me along with her."

"More like you follow in her wake." Dylan laughed and gave Matt a smack on the back.

"Yeah, and that too."

Chapter 27

She dressed with care for Katie's engagement party. Sadie had bought her a new dress that fit perfectly. At least that's how Katie described it when she saw it on her. Tonight was about celebrating Dylan and Katie, and Jessie couldn't be more excited. From the time they were little girls, they had talked about their weddings. The reality was even better than the dreams of young girls. The sapphire necklace and the matching earrings from Matt were perfect with the blue of her dress that shimmered with silver threads running through it. "Tonight, this girl feels like a princess ready to dance the night away with her prince." The mirror didn't answer her back, only smiled the same way she did.

She sat in the chair waiting for him to come, and he didn't disappoint. He arrived looking more handsome than ever.

"Have I ever told you I love you in that color?" She gazed into his gorgeous blue eyes. The dark sexy blue smoldered as he held her gaze.

He shook his head. "Nice to know. I love you in blue, but this dress takes the color to a whole new level. You're stunning." He turned her around, dipped her, and slowly brought her up tight against his body. "You ready to dance the night away?"

"With you, always." She pushed back to see his

face. "Have you seen our friends around today?"

"No. And tonight we have a police escort compliments of Dylan and the guys. Dylan hired off-duty cops to guard the party. Katie's idea. At least for tonight, we should be able to celebrate with our friends in peace."

"Wow, I've never had a police escort before. Sounds kind of sexy to me."

"You might not think it is after you see what's waiting outside the door. But right now, I can kiss you without anyone watching, and I'm not wasting any more time talking about it." He claimed her lips. "A mere sample of what the night holds for us."

"I like the way you think, Mr. Parker. I might have to spend the evening with you."

"I'll hold you to that. We should go. Dylan warned me to be on time with you because Katie was mad enough at me already for making her friend cry. I didn't know I made you cry. I think we'd better be on time or she might tell her big brother to have at me. I'm sure Liam wouldn't mind giving me a few good punches for hurting you."

"You're probably right, but I'll protect you." She grabbed his hand as they walked out the door.

Matt wasn't kidding. The officers formed a guard all around them with their guns drawn. Slight over-kill to her, but it seemed like something men would do. The whole boys and their toys idea came to mind, but she had to admit she did feel safe.

"Your chariot awaits." Matt opened the back door for her. The officer driving started the car, and their escort lined up in front of and behind them.

"They won't let you drive?" she leaned over and

asked.

"Not tonight. This is odd if you ask me."

"I was thinking the same thing."

"Another thing we see eye to eye on. We'll do fine together, mark my words." He laced his fingers through hers.

"I'm sure we will."

Liam's and Connor's joint pulsated with the sounds of the celebration when they arrived. The sign on the front door said closed tonight for a private party. The music, cranked up extra loud, spilled out to the parking lot every time the door opened. She was happy to have made it through the door without tripping over one of the men guarding them. Katie squealed in excitement the minute she saw Jessie, which brought several men with guns drawn to the source of the noise. It was going to be a long and strange night if this continued. Before she could stop Katie, she had Matt in the corner, her finger jabbing him in the chest. Matt was a big boy, and he could handle Katie. She would keep her eye on Katie and lend him a hand if necessary.

Matt came up behind her. "Whew, my ears are still ringing. Your tiny friend's opinion can pack a punch. Not that I didn't deserve some of it. Please dance with me and rescue me from any further tongue lashing. A man's pride can only take so much."

"My friend has been known to have extremely strong views on many subjects."

"You can say that again. Right now, I've fallen a few pegs in her estimation. I'll have to find a way to get back in her good graces." Matt maneuvered her on to the dance floor.

"The wonderful thing about Katie is that she says

what she wants and then it's like it never happened. Ten minutes later she won't even remember what she said."

The night included many toasts to Dylan and Katie's happiness. The music was great, and she hadn't danced this much in years. Liam and Connor wouldn't let her sit down. Katie had put them up to dancing with her to make Matt jealous. If the scowl on his face was an indication, it had worked. Liam grabbed her hand again. She shook it off. "No more. I'm dancing with Matt on this one." She walked over to where he sat. "Dance with me."

"Finally remembered me, huh?" The frown lines on his forehead deepened.

"This was Katie's payback. You should know her by now. She let you have it and then got her brother involved to make you jealous. My sweet friend thinks she's looking out for me."

"I got played. Is that what you're saying?" Matt stood and took her hand.

"Yes, you did, and they enjoyed the fact they made you suffer. Let's enjoy the rest of our night together. In a few weeks, all these folks will be celebrating with us."

"I couldn't ask for anything better." Matt pulled her tight as the band played one of their favorite songs.

"Matt—" She closed her mouth as soon as he put his fingers to her lips.

"We aren't going to talk about the case, or anything else. It'll all still be here after the song is finished, as an amazing woman has told me often enough. Right now, all I want to do is hold you in my arms and dance what's left of the night with the love of my life."

"I can live with that." She moved closer to him as his hand tightened around her waist. The words and the melody carried her away.

****

He held her hand in his as they walked to the car surrounded by the officers there to protect them. Reality was sinking in, fast.

"Chief, it's been quiet tonight. I'd like to keep it that way. Let's get you into the car and home as soon as we can," Kip said as he opened the door for Jessie.

"Sounds good. Be sure you watch for any car that appears to be tailing us," Matt reminded them.

"We'll keep our eyes open, sir. Was it a nice party?"

"Yes. Don't you think it was, Jess?" He turned to ask her.

"Liam did a great job planning every detail. Dylan and Katie enjoyed themselves, and that's the most important part." She reached across the seat for his hand and squeezed it.

"Were you able to trace the car's plates?" Matt asked.

"Gary did. It was rental, like you thought. They had a card on file which turned out to belong to a Doctor Ethan Gibbs. Bartlett went to the guy's house again, and there is still no sign of him. The FBI has put him on their list of suspects. We returned the car to the company. Agents are checking other car dealers in the area to see if he might have tried to rent another car."

"Nice job. All useful info. It was the doctor's SUV used in the drive-by. The good doc must be getting some kickback on opioid prescriptions."

Jessie glanced at him. "I'm surprised he'd put his

practice in jeopardy. Makes me wonder if someone is setting him up as a fall guy. Blackmailing him because he wrote the prescriptions. Does it sound feasible?"

"An angle we should consider. Most people get started on painkillers legitimately. Once addicted, they need to have someone who keeps writing the prescriptions. Gibbs could be mass producing prescriptions or selling black-market pills to his patients. I'm sure there's money involved."

Kip checked the mirror, watching the cars around him, and said, "Ideas that Bartlett talked to Gary about earlier. You guys are on the same page. Jessie, he also told Gary to let you know they're building a case against Corbett and his actress recruiter. They still have no idea why the women were dumped and left at the tunnels."

"I've been thinking about that myself. It doesn't make sense, especially after not returning for them. Unless someone else was coming to move them. Maybe there's more than one group involved."

"A question to ask Crystal." Matt took out his small notebook from his jacket and jotted a reminder to himself.

"Which brings us to more questions and why I got mixed up in this—to begin with, who murdered Kimberly and Hope. How do their murders play into what's happening now?" Jessie asked.

"The key to the whole case must lay in the answer. You're right. There was no reason for us to be involved otherwise. Finding out how Kimberly's death intersects is paramount to solving it."

Kip pulled the cruiser in beside Jessie's car. He wouldn't let them get out until everyone was in place.

Matt got out first and bent over to take Jessie's hand. That simple gesture saved his life. The bullet flew over the roof of the car into the darkness. The next several shots hit all around them. Officers returned fire while a few made their way into the wooded area around the inn and Jessie's cottage.

The gunfire went on for what seemed like hours to Matt but was only minutes in duration. He wanted to be out there with the others. Moments like this made him mad as hell. He couldn't even take her out for a simple date. "Sorry, sweetheart, I'm sorry the night had to end this way."

"What about Katie and Dylan? If they arrive now, they could get shot." He could hear the panic in her voice.

Kip answered. "Don't worry, Jessie. The road is blocked off. They can't drive to the inn." He listened in on the radio. "They haven't found anyone, sir."

"Too many places to hide and get away. With the cover of night and all those damn trees, we're targets."

"As soon as we can get you out of here, we will. Your house would be easier to watch over you both, Matt. There are no wooded areas. Jessie, I'm sorry, but you're going to be uprooted again. These guys mean business." Kip waited for the all clear. "Even with all the police presence, they almost had you dead to rights, Matt. If you hadn't bent over, you would be dead."

"Not a pleasant thought." He frowned, determined to find the guys and get them off the streets as soon as possible.

Chapter 28

Jessie couldn't believe she was back at his house with officers inside and out. The open suitcase on the bed told the story. This madness had to stop. Matt was asleep in his chair. There was no way she could sleep. She was sick of it. Their lives were constantly interrupted by anyone who got the idea to shoot at them.

Answers were what she wanted, and Kimberly and Hope had better have a few. Her mind raced back and forth. Somewhere in all the bizarre happenings, there was something to unlock the case. *Think, Jessie!* She tapped her fingers against her forehead. *What am I missing?*

Jessie leaned her head against the pillow and closed her eyes. Suddenly Kimberly was there, leading her through the maze in her mind, weaving the people and the places she had seen into a clear picture in her thoughts. Was this a dream or happening to her in reality? Jessie had no idea, but she couldn't move. Her body remained immobile, still and in place. Kimberly's demeanor suddenly changed as the vision moved forward. Wide eyed, Kimmie's fear was palpable, as the darkness enclosed her. She was shut into the small dark space alone. Her breathing became labored in time. What was she listening for? Jessie watched as death quietly suffocated the breath from her body. Then she heard Hope calling out Kimberly's name and frantically searching for her. Out of the darkness, Jessie saw an odd-looking stick with a strange configuration at the base raise. Hope was struck from behind and never knew who had killed her. The weapon was turned on Kimmie's lifeless form, which made no sense at all. Tears rolled down Jessie's cheeks. The trance-like sensation lifted, and she could move her limbs once again. The sisters' mother, their father, or who murdered the twins? *Reason it out, Jessie.* She frowned. The emotion of the vision remained, swirling around her. Kimberly had been betrayed, but why? The more she thought about it, the less she could understand the logic of it. Murder rarely seemed logical, but still there had to be a reason. In this case, it seemed more like a crime of passion. But who, and why kill Hope too? Unless—no way. Even the thought of it was preposterous. She went over the possible suspects from her travels forward, and only one person made any sense. But no shred of evidence collaborated her theory. Intuition said she knew the killer, but facts said she didn't.

****

Matt couldn't believe he slept through the entire night. With everything going on he hadn't thought about the case at all. Kip must have started the coffee because he could smell the aroma the closer he got to the kitchen. Jess leaned against the island. "Good morning, sweetheart. How'd you sleep?"

"Not too bad considering our night." She turned to face him when he walked in.

"What's on your agenda for today?" he asked.

"I gave Audrey the day off. I have to open the store

and work today. I don't want Sadie near the store until this is over, and Peyton is staying with Sadie and away from my house and store too."

"I can take my files and work at the store. I don't go in on Saturdays. I'm sure a couple of the officers will be going with us, or new ones will take their place. Dylan told me we will be shadowed for the next couple of days."

"Usually, I would say it wasn't necessary, but this time it is. Those goons weren't afraid to come after us with all the police around. We've seen this kind of desperation before, and I don't want to underestimate them."

"Proves my theory that you're growing and evolving with every case. I'm impressed, sweetheart." Matt poured coffee into a travel mug. "Do you want a cup of decaf? Kip made a fresh pot with you in mind." He pointed to a separate carafe on a hot pad.

"Sounds good." She put cream in another mug before he poured the coffee in it.

"Are you ready to go?" Kip walked into the kitchen to refill the cup he held in his hand.

"Thanks for making the coffee, by the way." Matt poured the dark brew into the cup Kip placed on the counter.

"It's the first thing I do every morning if I want to face the day. A bad habit I guess, but I'm not giving it up." Kip smiled.

"We're both going to Jessie's store. I'll do my paperwork while I'm there."

"It'll make our job easier. We won't have to be two places at once." Kip drank the coffee Matt handed him. "I'm ready anytime you are."

"Jess, did you need anything from home?"

"I grabbed it last night. I'm ready to go when you are." Jessie walked into the bedroom to get her purse and laptop.

"Kip, give me five." Matt lifted five fingers. "I hope you have someone to relieve you. You've been on duty long enough. You need to get home and sleep."

"Dylan is changing with me. I'll leave as soon as he gets to the store." Kip pulled the keys out of his pocket. "I'll be out in the car. I want to check with the guys outside to make sure things are tight before we have you both come out."

****

The drive to the store was uneventful, a good thing in her opinion. Happy to be back into her routine, she straightened the book display table giving attention to how the books were arranged. No more broken glass or bullet holes. She glanced at the church across the street. Matt called in a favor and had the glass replaced overnight. The fact that Matt and Dylan were underfoot meant things weren't completely normal, but it didn't matter. Humming a song, she got busy putting many of the new ideas she had learned in place. Independent bookstores were doing well across the country even though some of the bigger companies weren't. Good news for her. She had several orders coming in the next week or two, all thanks to the conference.

At nine o'clock, she glanced at her watch. Time to open. She flipped the sign around at the front door and unlocked the doors into the coffee shop—the same practice she had every morning, except today an uneasy feeling nagged at her. Customers strolled in from Joe's like any other day. But the sensation didn't go away and seemed to grow stronger as the morning progressed. Having no idea what or who might be the issue, she kept checking out everyone who walked through the doors. She hoped something or someone would tip her off.

"You've told me to let you know if I have one of my premonitions." She spoke quietly to Matt, not wanting to alarm the customers.

He placed the file down on the table. "Yes. What's up?"

"I'm not sure, but we need to be alert." Her gaze strayed again to the coffee shop. "Does Bartlett have a picture of the Gibbs? I would like to know if he is anywhere in the area. Knowing how someone looks could make a difference in a matter of life and death."

"I'll call him and tell him to email me what he has." He turned to fill Dylan in on what she told him.

She waited on two customers, and the impression remained. If only she knew who she was looking for. There were several men in Java Joe's this morning, but none of them troubled her. Only a woman with her back toward the doors seemed problematic. Logic told Jessie to let it go. The woman was only having coffee, but when had she ever listened to reason?

She waved at Molly through the open doors. She kept one eye on the woman to see if she moved or if Jessie could catch a glimpse of her face. Molly brought over some goodies for Dylan and Matt. She stayed to talk about the party. A new customer came into the bookstore a few minutes later. Jessie's hands clenched at her side. She didn't want anything to happen to her friend or the newcomer looking at the book table, an older woman whose sweet smile made Jessie want to shoo her out the door as soon as possible. Jessie remained where she stood, the atmosphere charged with apprehension.

Unexpectedly, the woman in the coffee shop shifted in her chair, and her sweater lifted enough for Jessie to see the gun. Goosebumps moved down her back in a wave. Was she an officer or was this the lady Crystal told her about? Darn, she needed a photo. She couldn't jump a stranger drinking coffee for heaven sakes.

Jessie lifted her phone and snapped a picture of the back of the woman's head. Her haircut was unique, and maybe Crystal or one of the other women would remember it. She sent the photo to Crystal in a quick text and waited for Crystal to respond. Just in case, she patted her jacket to make sure her gun was in the holster, reassuring herself she had put it on before she left. Matt wouldn't need to lecture her, after all, for forgetting to carry it during a case.

"Jess, come here. I want you to check this out." Matt walked over to the counter with his computer in his hand.

She hunched over the computer to see the photos, her head next to Matt's. Warning bells went off inside her. She quickly maneuvered the gun out of the holster and gripped the handle tight in her hand. Out of the corner of her eye, she saw the woman pull her gun and attempt to take aim at them. As she had practiced for the past several months, she pulled her gun out, shoved him out of the way, and shot at the woman before she pulled the trigger. The first bullet grazed the woman's arm, stunning her long enough for Jessie to shoot again. Bullet two ricocheted off the floor, hitting the woman in the leg. What happened next reminded her of a slow-motion scene out of a movie. The woman screamed, dropping her gun to the ground as she fell beside it. The coffee shop customers scrambled under tables or went running out of the store. The older woman who had come into her store was in a dead faint on the floor. Dylan jumped into action, kicking the gun out of the woman's reach. Kenny ran out from behind the counter in the coffee shop to help Dylan tend to the woman's gunshot wound. Matt simply stood there watching with a shocked expression on his face.

"Damn, Jess. Sweetheart, how did you know? One shot to the head could've taken me out. I'm impressed." He sat shakily in the chair next to where the woman fell when she passed out. Calmly he called for an ambulance and backup, belying what she knew was going on inside his gut.

She couldn't answer him even if she wanted to. Her body shook too hard to put two words together. "I had to do it," she said breathily. "You could've been killed. She was going to shoot you, Matt. I had to do it." She fanned the sweet lady's face as she rambled on making no sense whatsoever.

"Damn, you were good. Where did you learn to move and shoot like that? You almost knocked me off my feet and still managed to get off a couple of rounds." Matt held her trembling hand in his. "Adrenaline. We'll be calm in a little bit." He placed her hand on his chest, where she could feel his racing heart. "It may take a while." He shook his head. "I'm proud of you, sweetheart," he whispered, rubbing her shoulders.

"What happened?" The lady on the floor struggled

to sit up. Matt helped her into the chair.

"You fainted. There's an ambulance on the way, and I want them to check you over before you move around anymore." Jessie jumped up and paced back and forth.

"Are you okay, young lady?" Her head followed Jessie's movement. "Did I see you shoot a gun or was I dreaming?"

"You weren't dreaming. This woman just saved my life." Matt pointed at Jessie.

"I had to shoot her when I saw the gun. I'm sorry to have scared you. You'll probably never want to come to my store again, and I wouldn't blame you." Jessie swiped at the tears forming in her eyes with a hand that still trembled no matter how many breaths she took.

"I know this young man, and if our chief of police says you saved his life that's good enough in my book to call you a heroine. I'll be proud to shop here as soon as I can stop shaking." She smiled her sweet smile at Jessie.

Jessie held out her trembling hand showing how unsteady her hand was. "You and me both."

The ambulance arrived, and more police, followed by Reba and Molly, who sat in the chair dumbfounded by what had happened.

"How did she know?" Molly asked Matt.

Reba took Jessie into her arms and soothed her like a mother would. "Okay, sweet girl, breathe and relax. You don't have to say anything. Matt's telling everyone who'll listen. He couldn't be prouder."

"Why are you here?" Jessie asked. Reba always came for a reason.

"I felt I had to get over here. This is the beginning

and not the end. Don't relax yet—you still have work to do. There are more to come. Kimberly's murder will be solved, but a town will be shocked when they see how many people are tied to a crime that has been passed from father to son for generations."

"Strange. I was thinking of the father-son angle when it came to what you said before. Now all I have left is to figure out is what father, and who is the son? Somehow it's all connected."

"Of course it is, dear. That's how all of this works. Bask for a while in the glow of Matt's praise. That man is so in love with you it will make all the ladies around you green with envy. I couldn't be more pleased. While you finish your task, I will go sit with Irma Masters. I think this morning might have shaken her a bit. Bless her heart."

"Yes, she fainted, and the medics need to check her out before she leaves."

"I'll make sure they do." Reba went into the coffee shop to talk to the ambulance crew.

"Wow, Jessie, you were terrific. I couldn't believe my eyes, and I know the chief is still stunned." Kenny shook her hand. "The lady isn't too happy with you, though." He glanced at the woman on the gurney. "I'd say you made a new enemy."

Jessie heard the injured woman calling her names. "Kenny, are all your customers okay? No one else was hurt?" She started pacing again.

"They're all fine and telling Gary and Dylan what they saw. I don't think you have to worry. The folks in there are on your side. You saved the chief of police. How did you know?" Kenny asked.

"I was concerned about the woman when I first

saw her. When she shifted in the chair, I noticed the gun. I knew then to keep my eye on her. There is no way I would have fired my gun inside if she hadn't pulled hers first." Jessie's whole body still shook inside. What she needed was a good cry.

"Don't worry, sweetheart, it's all good." Matt put his arm around her waist and pulled her into his side.

The text she was waiting for from Crystal confirmed what Jessie already knew—this was the woman who had recruited them. In too deep, she wanted to save her own skin. If she was running scared and willing to act on her own, then the others might be too. It was only a matter of time before they showed up. If they weren't here already. Now if she could only calm down, she might be able to tell Matt about Camilla Browning.

Chapter 29

By the end of the day, Jessie was thoroughly embarrassed by all the attention. All she wanted to do was to get away from the store and have a few moments of solitude. A warm bubble bath, a glass of wine, and a good cry might be nice too. Between the police asking her questions and Matt's recounting to anyone who would listen about how she had saved his life, she was exhausted. Add to the fact Max from the paper was interviewing her and eyewitnesses for his front-page story. If she didn't get out of here soon, she'd lose her mind.

Still, it was kind of sweet how Matt kept reaching for her hand, glancing at her warmly, and praising her repeatedly with her acts of bravery. She plopped onto one of the leather chairs, willing herself to calm down. Her hand still wasn't that steady. She really didn't like shooting people. What could she have done differently?

The store was closed to customers as the police worked back and forth between Joe's and Idle Time. It didn't stop the people trying to get a look at her and inside the store, wanting to see where it all had gone down. If she could get away from their prying eyes, she would.

"We can leave soon if you want. You look like you're ready to bolt out the door." Matt sat in the chair across from her.

"I'm not comfortable being the center of attention. I can't believe you picked up on my discomfort. I'm usually able to manage my emotions." She lifted her head. "What was my give away?" She glanced at him.

"First of all, sweetheart, you don't hide your feelings well. I love that about you. There's no games or nonsense with you. Besides the deer in the headlights look on your face, if you twist the hair around your finger any faster, it will be tied in knots." Matt chuckled. "Take a deep breath. You're a heroine, and the locals will be talking about this day until something else comes along to take its place. One good thing is it'll bring more customers into your store, who might have to buy an item or two while they're here to stare at you." He patted her hand.

"Great. That's comforting. I don't know if you've noticed or not, but I'm a bit of an introvert, especially in new and uncomfortable situations."

"I've noticed. You're the kind of woman content to be in the background, chilling with your friends, and letting them shine. The problem is, Jess, you're hard to ignore. Believe me, every man notices you the moment you walk into the room. It's a reality. I know you don't want to hear that, but it's true."

"Whatever." She waved him off. "You're not helping. Sweet, but not helping. I was doing my job. That's all there is to it." She stood and walked into the back room to get away from all the activity. He followed her and slipped his arms around her waist.

"It's hard for any of us to shoot another person and not feel it deep in our gut, Jess. That's what this is all about, isn't it?" He held her tight against his side.

"Yes, I've shot a few people since working with

you. I don't know why this one is harder for me to take."

"Can I venture a guess?"

"Be my guest." She frowned. "I can use all the help I can get."

"You've never shot a woman before. You've fought for women for several years. But this time, you couldn't help that you had to shoot her. There was no time to think about it or talk to her—you made a split-second decision. If you hadn't reacted the way you did, I might be fighting for my life right now."

"You're right. I've been able to vilify a man, but never needed to do so to a woman before. This complicates things." She sighed.

"Not really. Sooner or later you needed to learn not all women are victims. Some women victimize other women. Not all men are bad. There are enough bad folks of both sexes to keep us busy for years to come."

"You always have a way of putting things in perspective." She leaned her head against his shoulder. "I was feeling bad that I shot her, and I know her injury was worse than merely shooting a gun out of her hand. It did damage. I will live with that image, but it would've been worse if it had been you." She shuddered at the mere thought of it.

"You saved me from a world of hurt. She'll recover, but I doubt the women she recruited will recover as quickly as she will. You need to keep that in mind. She's done a lot of damage to several women. She's not a nice person." He pulled her closer. "She's made a lot of money off other's misery."

"I know you're right. I probably would've had to shoot her, eventually. She was gunning for us."

"Was she acting alone, or is she even connected to the smugglers? It makes me wonder." Matt ran his fingers through her hair.

"I have no idea. Was she with the people who shot at us the night of Katie's party? If so, why did she come alone today? It doesn't make sense." Jessie pulled out of his arms and tilted her head to look at his face.

"I agree, we need to think this through. As soon as she's able, we'll have a chat with our suspect. Dylan is at the hospital now checking on her status." He reached for Jessie's hand. It trembled in his. "She'll be taken into custody as soon as she's released, which may or may not be today. Bartlett is coming to town to question her too. She's facing charges both here and in the Boston area." Lacing his fingers through hers, he pulled her toward the front of the store. He grinned. "You have to face your admiring public."

Her chin edged up, and a groan escaped her lips. "Yes, sir."

"Ready or not, here we go." He tugged gently on her arm again.

****

Matt sat back in the chair and watched her shine. She took every question thrown at her with grace and patience. If he hadn't seen her chin edge up or her clenched fist, he would have thought she was talking to one of her customers. He couldn't be any prouder of her than he was at this moment. All the strange things they'd been through since they'd met were the steppingstones to this point in time. She was the woman made for him. His equal. It was time to settle things between them and get on with life. As soon as this case gave them breathing room to celebrate, they would do

222

just that with their friends. For now, keeping them both alive to reach the day would be priority number one.

When things wrapped up, Matt took her by the hand and guided her out to Kip's waiting cruiser. "You managed to sail through that with flying colors," he said as he opened the car door.

"I'm grateful it's over."

"Not hardly. Every time an officer discharges their weapon in the line of duty there's an investigation into the shooting. There will be more questions to answer and reports to file. You'll have to talk to the police therapist." He saw her face pale and patted her hand. "You'll be okay because of all the eyewitness accounts. Still, it's a hurdle you have to get through."

"Why this time?" She turned her face to look out the window. "I don't remember going through that before."

"You didn't. It's all the new rules implemented by the state, and the fact that I'm involved makes it mandatory. Sorry."

"I get it. People can't go around shooting other folks anytime they want and say they're saving someone's life. I'll face it when I have to."

"Before I forget, Camilla will be fine and is on her way to lock-up. Dylan called when the police investigator was talking to you." He saw the question in her eyes. "Yes, he was on the scene. You'll still have a scheduled time with him." He placed her hand in his lap. "Don't fret. You did fine, and he was impressed with your quick response, just as I was."

Matt watched the struggle play on her face. She had a lot to digest for one day. There would be more. Sitting at the station for who knew how long during the interview was next. It was a good thing she was a trouper.

Chapter 30

Jessie listened in as Matt interviewed Browning, Crystal's "master". It sounded more like a one-sided conversation with Matt doing all the talking. Camilla refused to answer or even acknowledge him. Frustration rose with Browning's continued silence. Crystal and the others had told Jessie enough to make her want to see Camilla behind bars for a long time. As she paced, her fist clenched and relaxed at her side. The woman was unremorseful, arrogant, and being a total pain. Oh, for five minutes alone to talk to her. Jessie knew she could get her to talk. What kind of woman recruited women to become sex slaves for heaven sakes? Yep, given a chance, she would love to ask Camilla some questions.

"Jessie, the Chief wants you to come in the interview room with him." Kip startled her, bringing her movement to an abrupt stop.

"Tell him I'll be there in a minute. I need some water...and to calm down," she mumbled under her breath.

"Were you having a hard time watching him question her?" Kip asked after hearing her comment. "Matt thought maybe you'd like to get in on some of the action."

"I sure would, but first I need to get my anger under control. That woman is a piece of work."

"She is all that and a few more choice words.

Hurry. I think the Chief is getting exasperated." Kip turned to leave, and Jessie followed him.

After a quick drink of water, Jessie went into the interview room and sat in a chair near the door. Matt nodded at her and proceeded to ask a few more questions with the same results. "Hey, partner, what do you think of the suspect's answers so far?"

"I doubt she'd tell you the truth anyway. Jail is the best place for her. Remember I've heard the other side of the story from several eyewitnesses." Jessie's chin edged up as she folded her hands in front of her.

"I do remember hearing that." Matt glanced at her. "Would you like to refresh Ms. Browning's faulty memory?"

"I'd be happy to." She tightened her hold on her hands.

For the next ten minutes Jessie summarized the long list of complaints against Camilla, watching as several of the grievances she verbalized against the woman hit their mark. Browning's outward facade began to crack. Her arrogance crumbled, replaced by a knowledge she was caught and would be going to jail. Never mind the civil lawsuits that would be piling up from all the women she had sold out.

When Jessie walked out of the room a few moments after she had finished, she felt like a new woman. It was great to watch Camilla turn from a tough woman with no heart to a crying mess. She had ruined enough lives, and Jessie hoped she felt the remorse of her actions down to her toes. Closer to the truth, though, was that Camilla was only sorry she got caught and didn't think she had done anything wrong. Her repeated line was she was only trying to help Crystal and the other women become strong and successful like her. Jessie wasn't buying what she was selling with her big crocodile tears. With a little more work Jessie felt they might be able to get her to crack and turn on Corbett. Agent Bartlett might have a trick or two up his sleeve when he got to town. For her, it was simply satisfying to be able to say what was in her heart.

****

Matt had Camilla sent back to her cell and went in search of Jessie. She held it together well, but she was angry. He knew her well enough to know she would've loved to have said a whole lot more. She kept herself in check and had laid out her case against Browning like a pro. Jessie never ceased to amaze him. He had watched as Jessie confronted Camilla, and the perpetrator began to crumble. A few more interviews and he thought Browning would cave.

Matt understood Agent Bartlett wanted information on Corbett and how the operation worked. Who was supporting it? How many women were trapped in the bizarre cult? Matt had a few questions of his own. How did Corbett and Browning's group tie into what was going on in the tunnels at the Brass Lantern? For that matter, where did Kimberly and Hope's murders play into it, if at all.

Matt found Jessie in his office standing in front of the window. "A penny for your thought." A first, her silence puzzled him. He stood quietly beside her and waited.

She turned to look at him. "What makes a woman so desperate for money she would sell other women into slavery? What brings a person that low?"

"When you find the answer to that question, you

could solve half of the world's crimes. What drives a person to do what they do? I doubt they could tell you themselves." Matt put his arm around her waist.

"I'm sure no one says when they're young, 'When I grow up, I want to be a criminal.' What was her motivation—a bad day, a husband or father that abused her, or maybe she hates her mother? I want to understand." She turned to look out the window as darkness settled in.

"There could be any number of tipping points. Only time will tell if we'll learn hers."

"A criminal profiler must have an interesting job. They try to climb inside a suspect's head to figure out what's going on." Jessie turned away from the window and went to sit in a chair in front of Matt's desk. "I wonder if I could do the job."

"Of course you could. You deal with ghosts, and I never thought that was possible. You could probably do most anything you set your mind to."

"Thank you." She smiled at him.

"Only stating the facts. You're already good at knowing how people think when you study a case. Personally, I wouldn't want to crawl around in some of these dude's heads. Remember 'Silence of the Lambs?' " He pretended to shiver, a big grin on his face. "I'd rather analyze the case from the outside. I do admire those who do the job though. I've often called on them. The turnover in the position can be quite high, and I understand why." Matt leaned against the corner of his desk and folded his arms across his chest.

"Are we done here?" she asked.

"We're done. Kip told me they ordered pizza for the crew watching us tonight. They don't want us going out to dinner until the other suspects are in custody. Do you have enough clothes, or do we need to stop by your place?" He stood and extended his hand to her, pulling gently on her hand.

"I'm good for another few days. Tomorrow is Sunday, and the store is closed." She preceded him out of his office.

"That's good. We'll probably be here most of the day tomorrow. Bartlett will want me around when he questions Browning, and it's easier for our guys to keep an eye on us if we're together."

"Are you both ready to leave yet?" Kip asked as he met them in the hall.

"Yep. Let's go." Matt gave her a gentle tug to getting her moving.

"Dylan has the car at the back door. He doesn't want you walking out to the car in the parking lot. Too many places to hide in the dark for us to see." Kip handed them each a vest to put on. "We're all wearing them too. Today was a close call for you, boss, and we don't want to take any chances."

"Thanks, Kip." Jessie put the vest on.

"You'll get no argument from us." Matt slipped his arms into the vest.

"I hope you're hungry. We ordered pizza, and Kenny brought desserts and salads that Molly made. Kenny is one of the guys on duty tonight. I've already sampled the brownies, and the lemon bars look good too."

"You're reminding me I'm hungry. How about you, sweetheart?" She nodded.

Matt was happy when the car pulled into the garage at his house. He didn't like being a target for someone to practice on. Today was too close for his comfort. He wouldn't let his guard down again.

Chapter 31

Jessie had a fun evening despite the threats against them and the interviews on tap for tomorrow. Determined to enjoy this moment, she looked at each of their friends sitting in Matt's living room, a room that displayed Matt's great design sense. It was a masculine space with all its leather and chrome, making every man look at home in the surroundings. Yet the strong masculine edges were softened with candles, soft lighting, and the amazing floor-to-ceiling windows with great views to the lit gardens at night and the cove in the daylight. Their friends were giving up their own time to keep them safe. She loved this about Blue Cove—people cared about each other. Dylan had surprised her tonight by bringing Katie along for a visit.

Kip and Kenny were in rare form and had the group laughing through most of the evening with stories from their youth. Katie snorted at something Kip said, and Jessie laughed along with her. At one point, Jessie had laughed so hard she struggled to catch her breath. Kip paused, and with a roguish grin on his face, he told her to take a drink of tea. As soon as she did, he gave one of his punch lines, which meant everyone in a two-foot radius got sprayed. From that point on, she and Katie fell into a fit of the giggles. Maybe it was the stress of the case, or the fact laughter helped to relieve it, but Jessie felt better. Funny or not, everything made them laugh.

"Jessie, come and bring your computer. I have something I want to show you." Katie caught her breath and motioned to Jessie to follow her into Matt's kitchen.

"I'm coming." There was a knock on the door. Jessie grabbed her laptop and lingered in the doorway long enough to see who had arrived. Bartlett and another agent walk in. As she passed the switch, Jessie turned on the pendant lights hanging over the granite island in the kitchen. She sat next to Katie on one of the polished chrome stools with its comfy aqua cushions. With all the stainless steel and dark colors, the aqua was the surprise pop of color in the room.

Katie turned Jessie's laptop on. As soon as it whirred to life, Katie typed the name of the store into the search box. "This is a great room." Katie sounded surprised. "Most guys wouldn't know what colors to put together. Matt did a good job on the remodel. I could see myself cooking in here. I mean, get a load of that gas range. Trust me, this space is a cook's dream kitchen, and this color is perfect in here." Katie stood to point at the cushion she had been sitting on.

"Matt did an impressive job." Jessie rubbed her hand across the polished granite countertop. "What did you want to show me?"

"I almost forgot." Katie laughed.

"Please, no more laughing. My sides hurt," Jessie begged.

"I'll try not to laugh if you promise to try too." Katie glanced around the room. "Nothing excites me like a beautiful kitchen, unless of course it's wedding stuff. You will love this dress. I know you will," Katie squealed.

"I'm sure I will." Jessie glanced at the screen.

"With a garden wedding in the afternoon, I didn't want a long formal dress for the bridesmaids to wear. When I found this dress, it seemed perfect. Not long or short—" She pointed at the screen. "—see what I mean."

"Oh, Katie, I love it. It's perfect and wearable for another occasion. What color do you think?"

"With the gardens full of color that time of year I can see the coral, aqua, and yellow fitting in nicely. They seem right for the setting. I want the ceremony situated with the ocean as a backdrop."

"Perfect. We can arrange the chairs to face the cove, with the trellis at the front. It will be beautiful, and you will be too."

"I knew you'd see it. We think alike." Katie smiled and sighed. "I'm glad we can share this special time together."

"I am too." Jessie hugged her friend. "What color do you want me to wear?"

"Coral, definitely. Your looks and figure will pull it off perfectly. You're the only one I want in that color. The other girls will wear the aqua and yellow. I'm excited, but you'll understand when I say I'm also nervous. I can't imagine myself as a married woman. Only for Dylan would I even think about it." Katie glanced around the room, her voice soft. "Look at me sitting on a cushion the same color as I've chosen for my wedding."

"I get the nervous angle. As the years go by, I find myself wanting to cling to my youth. It's hard to see myself married, with kids—just the thought makes me feel like I'm morphing into my mom. On the other hand, that hunky cop of mine makes me believe there are happy endings in life." Jessie patted Katie's hand. "Our lives are changing. We're not teenagers anymore, and with it comes new things to experience in life."

"No more serious talk. I'm getting married, and we need to plan the centerpieces for the reception and floral arrangements for the ceremony." Katie opened a new site. "I love the look of this one." She pointed to a photo of centerpieces with her colors in the flowers. "What do you think?"

"You, my friend, have exquisite taste." Jessie spent the next hour poring over online bridal sites with Katie. Plans started to come together. She heard the guys talking in the other room, followed by a sudden burst of laughter.

"That's enough wedding for tonight. I want to find out why the guys are laughing." Katie shut off the computer. "Let's find out what's so funny. I hate being left out."

Jessie followed Katie into the living room. Talk about being a drag on a good time—the room got instantly quiet. "Katie, maybe we should try it again. Go out of the room and walk back in and see if we have the same effect." Jessie saw Matt squirm, and Dylan walked over to Katie, taking her by the hand.

"Did you get some of your plans done?" He put his arm around Katie's waist.

"Don't change the subject." She poked Dylan in the chest. "Something was funny until we walked in the room."

"It's probably better to leave it the way it is," he leaned close and told her.

"Be prepared to be annoyed all the way home until you tell me. I'm nothing if not persistent."

"How about you, Jess?" Matt asked her. "Is your interest piqued?"

"I think I'm safer not knowing."

"Jessie, you're such a wimp." Katie shook her head. "I want to know what was funny. I hate to be left out.

"If I'm reading the situation correctly, you'd have to be a guy to appreciate what they found funny. I'm willing to let them keep it to themselves. Don't you remember how it was with Liam and Connor?"

"Sure I do, but Dylan will tell me. Won't you, sweetheart?" Katie fluttered her lashes at him.

"We'll see." He smiled at her.

With Dylan's colossal fold, which is how Bartlett described it, Kip and Kenny were off to the races teasing Dylan, and the room erupted in laughter again.

****

Jessie crawled into the plush, comfy bed and shut off the lamp on the nightstand. It seemed lately that she spent more time in this guest room than in her own room at the cottage. Exaggerating, of course—it came naturally to her when she was feeling sorry for herself. She stacked her hands behind her head, and a frown settled on her face. She wasn't complaining exactly. The room was nice, like every other room in Matt's house. It was just the dumb, helpless feeling that came over her whenever her life was spinning out of control. She couldn't seem to do anything about the people who wanted to kill her. There were too many to count since moving to Blue Cove.

Her therapist would probably tell her she might be

235

conflicted. On the one hand, she wanted to make it on her own, and on the other, she loved the security that came with those watching over her each time. Yep, she couldn't decide what she wanted—independence or security. Either way, it was time to come up with a plan to solve Kimberly's murder. A plan made her think she was in control, and that's what she needed whether true or not. Reaching for the light, she found her pen and paper. It was time to take charge. Kimmie, Hope, Crystal, and the others were counting on her.

Chapter 32

A loud knock at the door roused her out of deep sleep. "Jess, are you awake?" Matt asked. "We need to get going soon. I need to meet Bartlett at the station in a while. Jess, can you hear me?"

"I'm awake, and the whole neighborhood heard you, believe me." She heard his annoying laughter. "How much time do I have?" She rolled to the edge of the bed and sat up.

"You still have time. Don't rush. I'll make the coffee."

"I'll be out as soon as I'm ready." She shuffled to the bathroom and began her morning routine. Forty minutes later she walked out of the room hoping she was presentable. She found Matt standing in the kitchen with Kip and Dylan, the steaming coffee cup halfway to his mouth when he caught sight of her. The look on his face made her wonder if everything was in place. "Good morning, sweetheart. Need I ask how you slept?" He smiled at her and poured her a cup of coffee.

"You mean besides the pounding on my door earlier? I slept fine." She noticed him watching her. "Is something wrong with me that has caught your attention, Parker?"

"No, but it beats me how you can look so good in the morning without any caffeine. You manage to all the time."

"You're too kind." She kissed his cheek. Pouring plenty of milk into her decaf, she took a sip. "Thank you. This is perfect."

"I aim to please. Weak decaf coffee with plenty of milk isn't for me, but I'm happy you are satisfied. I thought I heard you stirring late last night, or were my ears deceiving me?" He spread cream cheese on his bagel. "There's bread for toast or bagels if you want one."

"Thanks." She reached for the loaf of bread. "You heard right. I was going over the case. One thing led to another, and I had to work out a plan on paper that makes sense of the facts that we have right now." Jessie put a slice of bread in the toaster. She reached for the toast when it popped up.

"Don't keep us in suspense." He leaned against the counter, watching her butter the slice of toast.

"I'm not sure what I think. Last night I tried to figure out what ties all three of these crimes together. We have two murders, the strange cult-like group, and drug smugglers. Are they connected or three separate crimes? What are the odds of all three of these crimes taking place in the same location without any connection at all?" She took a bite of her toast followed by a sip of her coffee.

"I'd say at the very least, the drug smugglers and traffickers are connected. Kimberly's death was years ago. I have no idea how her murder can be connected to the other two. But stranger things have happened," Matt told her.

"The thing is, I believe all three are connected. There is an element I'm missing that connects them neatly together. Listening to Skylar that day at the commune and hearing Crystal talk about the teachings of Corbitt sounded uncannily similar to me. I admit it's a big leap to connect a mystery from decades ago to another event today, but I sense that they are. I'm still working on the how." She finished her slice of toast.

"Keep thinking about it. Write down every place you see as possible proofs of their connections. Maybe we can build a theory from it."

"Or I can hope for Kimberly's ghost to decide to visit our fair town and give me the answers I'm searching for." She poured her coffee into the travel mug he handed her.

"Yeah, and that too." The corner of his mouth turned up as he took her hand. "You arrange it, handle all the details, and fill me in if she responds. You're the expert in the ghost department." He reached for his coffee mug. "Okay, guys, we're ready."

****

Matt was exasperated with the tight-lipped woman staring blankly at him. She had clammed up again overnight. Nothing he said seemed to get through to Camilla about the trouble she was in. Her long red fingernails clicked repeatedly on the table. She frowned at him from time to time, acting as if the whole process was boring her to tears. He was getting ready to have her taken back to her cell. He was done messing with her attitude. They had her on attempted murder. She wasn't going anywhere.

Matt heard the door open. Bartlett came into the room waving a piece of paper. "I've got the arrest and search warrants." He handed Matt copies signed by the judge. "Agents are on the way now to pick Corbitt up and search his properties." He leaned over the table toward Camilla. "If I were you, sister, I'd start talking, or you'll be left holding the bag for this one." He sat across from her. "If you're willing to put your life in the hands of Corbitt and trust him not to rat on you, be my guest. He'll sell you out." He gestured with his hands. "Hell, you're going down for trying to kill a cop. What do you have to lose?"

"You may as well take your friend with you." Matt watched and knew the moment reality set in. She started talking and went on for a long time. He began to see the possibility of what Jessie had told him earlier. The connection between the three crimes seemed plausible. All they had to do was tie the evidence with what Browning told them. After Camilla was returned to her cell, Matt thanked Bartlett. "You came in at the right moment. She talked with Jessie a bit yesterday but wouldn't budge on anything today. Now I think she'll be singing for a while."

"You never know what the breaking point is for a person." The agent placed copies of the warrants in his folder. "Matt, you need to keep your guard up. Browning's arrest doesn't mean the threat against you is diminished. Camilla acted on her own or at Corbitt's command. We still aren't sure who the other shooters are, other than Doctor Gibbs and the suspect we've identified with the long rap sheet. It's possible the good doctor has ties to both sides of this crime." Bartlett followed Matt into his office. "I'll let you know as soon as we have Corbitt in custody. You might want to drive to Boston and sit in on the interview. It could be quite revealing."

"Sounds like a plan to me." Matt smiled when he said it. "I'm still trying to figure out how Corbitt pulled this scheme off. A lot of recruiting was done online. He was able to penetrate schools and social media accounts looking for the right women. Most of them were bullied and lonely—he did his research. Camilla's acting career made her seem innocuous, but she's a deadly combination of sugar and venom. Before they knew what hit them, the young women were trapped." Matt leaned against the corner of his desk.

"Believe me, we don't know half the story about the crimes being committed because of the internet. It takes a large team of agents working around the clock to track down hackers and to protect our computers. Cybercrimes are bigger than any of us can imagine. Our banking systems, our energy grid, voting machines, and most everything you can envision are now on computers and vulnerable." Bartlett stood in the open doorway. "Enemy states will and have tried to hack into our systems. This isn't a game—it's a war. There are people fighting twenty-four-seven to keep our country functioning without interruptions."

"It's even impacted us in our small town. I don't believe we can close our eyes to the threat. It's real." Matt agreed with Bartlett. Cybercrimes were like a plague exposing people's lives.

"You've got that right." Bartlett grabbed his jacket off the back of the chair, slipping his arms into the sleeves. "I need to get back to Boston, but I'll stay in touch and keep you up to date. We'll talk after we do the interview. You should keep your schedule open for the next several days." He shook Matt's hand. "Take good care of Jessie. She's good at her job. She understands people."

"I will. You should have seen her the other day.

Browning didn't know what hit her. When Jessie pulled out her gun, her move was damn sweet."

"You're not proud or anything." He clapped Matt on the back. "See you in Boston. Where's a good place to eat around here? You know the adage—ask the locals."

"You can't go wrong with Patterson's on Main Street." Matt walked with Bartlett to the door going out to the parking lot. "See you in a few days." Matt went in search of Jessie and found her in the lunchroom sitting at the table near the window. Her fingers flew over the keyboard as she concentrated on the screen and whatever she was typing. She didn't look up until he sat beside her. "Busy?"

"Not really. I'm trying to write my thoughts down before I forget them." She saved her work. "How did your interview with Camilla go?"

"It took a while, but she finally talked. Agents are on their way to arrest Corbitt and search his homes and office."

"That's good. Those two deserve whatever they get and more." Jessie turned the laptop off, slipping it into the carrying case. She collected her notes and other items, stuffing them in her purse. "I'm ready when you are."

"I'm past ready, but I still have a few things to do. I hope you don't mind waiting a little longer. We'll be out of here soon. I'm starving, and you must be too. Did anyone get you lunch?"

She shook her head. "I had a package of peanut butter crackers from the vending machine. Not a nutritious meal, I'm sure, but it took the edge off. This guy I know told me I had to stay inside and not leave, but then he left me for hours to fend for myself. He forgot me I think." She laughed.

"Some date. I don't know why you'd put up with a guy like that. There's plenty of other fish in the sea."

"True, but this fish is kind of cute and seems to suit me perfectly. I'm hooked." She reached out her hand and touched his cheek.

"This is one fish who is happy to be on the line." He smiled at her. "I'll be back soon. Sit tight. I promise you I'll get you dinner."

"I'll make sure you do." She waved at him and took her computer back out of the case to add more thoughts to them.

Chapter 33

Matt was true to his promise. He made sure she got dinner. Of course, half of the town's police force guarded them as they ate. Jessie enjoyed herself despite the police presence underfoot. The restaurant was packed tonight, and the billiards area in the back was filled too. Jessie loved watching the competitive nature come out in Matt as he played a game of darts with Dylan and then Kip. More than once during the evening Joe Patterson, the owner, had come over to their table to check on them.

"The mac and cheese are the best," she told him on one of his visits. "The cook always gets a nice, light, crispy, golden crust on it that makes it the best I've eaten anywhere." Her plate overflowed with her favorite comfort foods. A nice slice of meatloaf and green beans rounded out the food on her plate.

"I'll tell the kitchen staff what you said. I'm always pleased when my customers are satisfied, especially my sweet ones like you." Patterson squeezed her shoulder. He leaned closed to her. "Let's make that guy of your jealous," he whispered in her ear. A smile lit his face.

"Are you flirting with my girl?" Matt teased Joe.

"Who me? If I was younger, I might give you a run for your money. Of course, the missus might have something to say about that." He laughed and slapped Matt on the back. "Dessert is on me. I have a new pastry cook, and you can't leave here without trying one of his creations. Enjoy your evening, folks, and tell the waiter what you want for dessert."

After her high-calorie meal, Jessie wasn't shy she went with gusto for the chocolate cake, with a milk chocolate cream filling and a scoop of vanilla ice cream to top it off. Each bite was something to be savored. Matt chose a beautiful creation of chocolate cherry mousse encased in a white and dark chocolate cup. She had to admit it was yummy and amazing, but then so was hers.

She noticed the idling car across the street when they walked out of the restaurant. Something felt off about it. "Kip, look at that car over there." She noticed the driver roll down the window.

"Gun," Kip shouted before he slammed her to the ground. "Stay down."

Jessie watched as things played out like one of Matt's favorite TV shows. Matt dropped to the pavement and called for backup. Kip crawled along the ground, positioning himself at the front of a parked car. Matt inched toward the back of the same car. Dylan positioned himself out of the line of fire in front of the door into Patterson's to keep someone from coming out and being hit. The popping sound that followed she knew all too well.

Watching the action around her, she thought about the many times in the past few months she had been thrown to the ground. Twenty-some years she had made it through life without anyone pushing her down and out of the line of fire, but here she was down again. Jessie pulled her gun out of the holster hidden under her jacket and crawled over to the rear of the next parked car. Nobody could make her sit this one out. The gunfire exchange was heavy. Insurance companies would be paying to replace car windows in the next few days. Jessie waited, holding steady, her gun aimed and ready, waiting for the precise moment she saw the hand clearly enough. Then she took her shot. Hopefully, all her target practice paid off.

"Damn, Jess, you hit his hand or at least knocked the damn gun out it. You've perfected that shot," Kip exclaimed as the male voice screamed obscenities. The perpetrator dropped the gun to the street and started driving erratically down the road. A police car racing to the scene made a U-turn in pursuit of the suspects.

"How'd you manage it?" Matt reached his hand down and pulled her to her feet.

"You guys gave the cover. All I did was wait until I saw the hand holding the gun." She shrugged her shoulders. "It's no big deal. He practically posed for me, and I wasn't moving."

"I think she believes what she just said." Dylan motioned the people waiting to come out the door of the restaurant that it was safe for them to leave. People came out of several of the surrounding businesses. "It's a big deal, man. You stopped the gunfire with that shot at a busy time of night on Main Street. You probably saved a few lives with your quick thinking, and people's property as well. Damn good job, rookie."

Jessie smiled. No one had ever called her a rookie before. It meant the guys accepted her as one of their own. Matt always had, but now it seemed more official to her somehow. "Thanks, Dylan." Rookie. She liked the sound of that.

"Hey, Chief, it looks like you have a new officer.

When are you going to start paying her?" Kip patted her shoulder. "We're on your side, rookie."

"Sorry guys, we'll have to discuss this later. It's time to get to work. Kip, get the statements of anyone in Patterson's or surrounding businesses who witnessed the ambush. We need to find the owners of these cars. Names and addresses need to go in the report. They'll need copies of our finished reports for their insurance companies. Collect evidence in the area. Hopefully, we can pull some prints off the gun. Jess, I'll give you the honor of bagging the gun." He handed her a pair of gloves and a bag. "You did well." He leaned closer to her. "I'm proud of you."

She put on the gloves and opened the bag. Crossing the street, she bent down to pick up the gun splattered with blood. The suspect's blood. "Darn, that had to hurt." This was the one element of working with Matt that she didn't relish. She knew from their first case working together the force of being hit by a bullet. Even with a vest protecting her, it was bad enough She couldn't imagine a bullet ripping into her flesh or tearing up her insides. They might call her a rookie, but she was a long way from being there emotionally. Still, she had to admit she liked them praising her for a job well done. She picked up a cigarette dropped hastily to the ground. DNA maybe, along with the blood on the gun.

She marked the places where she saw bullet casings. How long had they been sitting in the car waiting for them to come out? Whoever they were, these thugs were serious about getting them even at the cost of being caught. They were either stupid, desperate, or both.

****

Matt watched her at work. She was good at making a suspect drop a weapon, but if he knew his girl, she wasn't happy about hurting the person with the gun. If she hadn't been protecting her friends, he wasn't sure what her reaction would have been. He would work on that with her. She was good, and he wanted her on his side.

"Matt, these guys are getting too close for comfort. Who are they? Have you heard if we got them?" Dylan asked.

"Not yet." Matt took the call from Kenny, who was working the desk. "Damn, how'd they get away." He listened to Kenny explain what the pursuing officer told him. Jessie watched him. "They lost them after they got on the highway," he told her. "Kenny put out an APB to notify agencies of the license plate number. With any luck, they'll be spotted."

Kenny's voice came through the phone. "It's taken care of, Chief. They sealed their fate when they started shooting at cops. It's only a matter of time. I'll notify you if I hear anything."

"Thanks, Kenny." He bent down to get a closer look at one of the bullets. He placed it in the bag Jessie was holding.

"A gun battle on Main Street is not a good thing. Innocent people could get killed. Who are these guys?" She glanced sideways at him.

"I have a theory on the who. It seems like we've faced the same kind of crime here. Someone in their town must know what's going on. These guys have operated too long in that area. It makes me wonder who has turned a blind eye to their operations. Are there cops or city leaders involved in some way? It isn't mine to solve except they keep coming to our town. Damn, they keep involving us whether we want it or not." Matt scowled, rolling an empty bullet casing between his gloved fingers.

"We should ask Bartlett to check for links. Your hunches are always correct when it comes to knowing something isn't right." Jessie handed him the bag with the gun as she stood.

****

He left Patterson's in stunned disbelief. Inept. They all were useless as far as he was concerned. They took an easy job and messed it up. Now what should he do? The damn woman created chaos wherever she went. From the first night he had laid eyes on her at the inn until she slipped through the portal, she had been a thorn in his side. All these years Kimberly and Hope were considered missing with no one the wiser. Damn woman. His easy life was vanishing before his eyes, and he couldn't trust anyone to take care of it. Hell, he was going to have to do it himself. He hid his face from view and shook his head when the cop asked if he had seen anything. "Not me. I was in the back room playing billiards." He scurried down the street before she noticed him.

Chapter 34

Thankfully, the next few days in Blue Cove were quiet. No gun battles on the streets. Of course, it helped that he and Jessie stayed away from public places except for their time at work. Matt had Bartlett working one of his theories of the case from his end. He promised to get back to Matt soon. He drummed his fingers on the desk. All the waiting bugged him. He wanted to get these guys before they killed someone.

Corbitt was in custody, along with Camilla Browning. Bartlett told him the FBI early morning raid had netted many boxes of evidence from each of Corbitt's properties. Orin Corbitt kept great records, which made their job a whole lot easier. There were names of thousands of women being held as slaves in his cult. The strange thing was that they found some of the records dated back over fifty years, which made no sense to the agents since Corbitt wasn't that old himself. Bartlett had also found some interesting facts about Orin that he would be sending in an email for them to examine. Any ideas to make sense of the information would be appreciated. Bartlett assured Matt that the FBI wanted their feedback. Matt smiled. If it was strange or unusual, it would be in Jessie's wheelhouse.

"Chief, you have a call on line one."

Matt picked up his phone. "Thanks, Collins." He

pushed line one. "This is Matt."

"I hear you're in the thick of it again." Chad's voice came over the line. "Do you have many gun battles on Main Street? If so, I might have to rethink moving here." Chad chuckled.

"Hey, Chad. I don't think you need to worry. It's rare." Matt turned his chair to look out at the park. "Are you in town?"

"I'm here to sign the papers on my new place. I'll be moving in first thing next week. As long as you think it's safe." Matt heard Chad clear his throat, not quite stifling the laugh that escaped.

"It'll be good to have you around," Matt told him.

"How's Jessie?"

"She's great. You'll have to ask her about her latest adventure the next time you see her. I can't even begin to explain it over the phone." Matt clicked the pen in his hand on and off.

"Sounds intriguing. Do you want to have coffee before I leave town?"

"Sure thing. What time?"

"I'll call you when I'm done and leaving here. The mayor told me you have escorts because of the attempts on your life. I figure you don't want to be waiting around for me to get there."

"It doesn't matter. I'm not about to put my life on hold to accommodate the suspects."

"It must be great fun having all these folks out to get you. You need to retire to a safer job."

"There are days lately when I wonder." Matt watched the young mother pushing her son on the swing. "It gets a bit old dodging bullets after a while."

"I'll take your word on the subject. As long as I

don't have to dodge them when I'm with you." Chad did laugh then. "See you soon."

"Okay." Matt smirked as he disconnected the call.

He turned his chair back around to study over the file on his desk. Damn, he wished they would have caught the suspects when they had the chance. He hated trying to second guess the next place or time an ambush would occur. It put too many innocent people's lives at risk.

Dylan knocked at his door. "Are you busy?"

"No. What do you need?" Matt asked. Dylan gave him a sheet of paper.

"Collins handed me this report to give to you. They pulled a print from the gun, and I thought you might want to see it right away. It doesn't mean anything to me, but I figured it might to you."

"I'll be damned."

****

Reba walked into Jessie's shop and paused at the front display to look at the books. "Hello, dear. I'm pleased to see you have the newest book in the series I've been reading."

"Yes, it came in my latest delivery of books. I've had quite a few calls asking if I had copies yet. People love to have their copy as soon as the books are out." Jessie walked to the front of the store where Reba stood. "It's tough to wait once you've read all the other books in the series."

"You're telling me. Waiting for the next book can seem interminable." Reba laughed. "If that's the worst we suffer in life I'd say we've had it good." She carried the book over to the table. "I'm going to look for a couple more titles."

"You're always free to browse. I love when you're here."

"How are you doing after your latest adventure?" Reba took her coat off and placed it on the table by the book. "Do you have time for a chat? I'll get us some tea and a treat."

"I always have time for a chat with you, especially when the store is quiet like it is today." Jessie went to answer her ringing phone. "Idle Time Books. May I help you."

"Hey, Jess, I wanted to make sure you're okay." Matt's voice brought a smile to her face.

"I'm good. The store is quiet today, although Reba went to get tea and will be back for a chat in a few minutes. How is the station?"

"Fine. I keep hoping the authorities in another jurisdiction spot our suspects, but we haven't had any calls. I guess they've eluded the roadblocks."

"We can hope they slip up soon." Jessie smiled at Reba and Molly coming through the open doors.

"Who's watching you, and where are they?"

"Kip is sitting in his car in front of the store, and the other guy is parked at the back door. Gary is in the coffee shop where he's keeping an eye on me. This is getting crazy having to use all this manpower to watch me work."

"I hope it doesn't last too much longer. Bartlett told me they confiscated a lot of evidence during their raid on Corbitt's properties."

"I'm glad. Did he say what they've discovered so far?" she asked.

"He said they found some strange stuff on his computer and sent it to me. Bartlett was right. It is hard to understand it, but I think you might be able to. I sent it to your email. When you get a chance, look it over and tell me what you think."

"I will."

"Enjoy your visit with Reba. I hope she is the bearer of good news. We could use some. I'm meeting Chad at Joe's later for coffee."

"He's in town?"

"Yep, signing the papers on his place. He'll be here to stay next week."

"Great. See you later." Jessie hung up the phone.

"Thank you for your help, Molly." Reba gave her money for the tip jar and Molly left to continue her work at the coffee shop. "Sit down, dear. The tea is hot, and these raspberry-white chocolate scones look scrumptious to me."

"They sure do." Jessie pinched off a corner, placing it in her mouth. "Oh my, these are delicious. I love her blueberry scones, but I think this raspberry might be my new favorite. Yum."

They talked about books they were reading and politics. Jessie enjoyed the conversation. "It's nice to hear your view on the state of the world. Anything is better than talking about how I saved Matt's life."

"It will wear off soon, and folks will move on to the next big story. You know, dear, something has been troubling me."

"What's that?"

"You were in two dimensions, and I keep thinking there may be others who have done it too. One of them feels compelled to kill you. I believe you met him when you were wandering in the sixties, and now he's here hovering around the edges. Waiting for his moment."

"I guess it's possible. If I went through the portal, someone else could."

"Can you remember meeting anyone that might be a threat to you?" Reba took a sip of her tea.

"There was Skylar, the cult leader at the commune. I knew my life depended on getting away from him. He could be a threat, I guess. How would it be possible, though? He'd have to be over seventy now. I met others too, but none of them age-wise seem right to me. I know you told me the past would meet the present, but I was thinking of one of their kids or grandkids maybe."

"Of course, it's hard to understand any of it unless you think of being in two time dimensions at the same time. You had real encounters, meeting living people in the time in which they lived, and yet your body was in a hospital bed in the here and now. It's possible one of the people you met was doing the same thing."

"Wow, when you put it that way, it sounds remarkable, and anything is possible. I'll have to think about it. I can't imagine going through the portal again. It left me feeling wiped out. It couldn't be good physically to do it often."

"Your entire experience was a mystery, and only time will tell you why. Still, you need to keep your eyes open. He's out there. I'm sure of it." She patted Jessie's hand. "Let's talk about something nice as we finish our tea. And then you can help me find a few more books."

"Sounds good to me. I could use a break." Jessie took another bite of the delicious raspberry scone.

Jessie helped Reba find her books, and Reba kept their conversation light and cheery for the rest of the time she stayed. Reba waved goodbye when the book club arrived. Jessie remained busy helping them pick their next book and ordering enough copies for the club. She waved at Matt and Chad when she saw them in the coffee shop.

"Hey cousin, what are you doing here? I thought I told you to stay away until it's safer." Jessie grabbed Peyton's hand as she came in the store.

"You did, but I promised Sadie I would stop by and see how you were, especially after the shootout the other day. She won't rest until I tell her that you look radiant as always." She followed Jessie over to the table of ladies.

"This is my cousin, Peyton." Jessie introduced her to the ladies in the book club. They made small talk back and forth for a few minutes. "I have someone else I want you to meet." Jessie grasped Peyton's hand and led the way into the coffee shop.

Matt stood. "Hi, sweetheart. Peyton, it's good to see you. This is my friend, Chad Bennett."

"It's nice to meet you, Chad." Peyton shook his extended hand.

"Likewise." Chad smiled at her.

"I have to get back. You boys enjoy your coffee," Jessie said as she heard the bell ring. She squeezed Matt's hand and walked back into her store while Peyton followed her.

"Is he married or single?" Peyton softened her voice and asked.

"He's single." Jessie's eyes twinkled with amusement.

"Are all the single guys around here so handsome?" Peyton sighed.

"There are quite a few. Such a nice dilemma for a single woman," Jessie said, her voice filled with laughter.

"Stop." Peyton put her finger to Jessie's mouth. "I was curious, that's all."

"Peyton, you're such a liar." They both laughed. "It's okay. I think Chad is handsome too, but then so are Matt, Evan, and Kip. Dylan is taken, but he's handsome too. Besides their great looks, they're all nice guys, and a girl couldn't go wrong with any of them. Although I don't know Chad and Evan as well as the others.

"I need to get back to Grams, and you have customers." Peyton walked to the door, and Jessie went with her.

"Tell Sadie I'm good, and she can call whenever she's worried."

"I will. Talk to you later." Peyton waved as she left.

Jessie straightened the display table. Who did she need to watch out for—Skylar, that strange little man, the man that Sue Ellen had described? Which one?

Jessie glanced at Matt and Chad talking. They seemed to be having a good time. Chad noticed Peyton all right. Jessie saw his eyes stray to her several times while she stood there. She hadn't thought of Chad when it came to Peyton. Or was her future in Arizona with her hot cowboy? Either way, Jessie was delighted by the possibilities for her cousin. She chuckled at the idea.

Jessie smiled at the lady who walked in the store. "Let me know if I can help you."

The woman nodded at her and went over to the display table.

Chapter 35

Matt stopped by to see her before he left to go back to the station. The book club was finished, and the ladies were gathering up their belongings. "Did you get a chance to look at the email I sent you?" He reached for her hand and missed. She bent down to get something under the counter.

"No, I'll look at it tonight. I've had a busy afternoon," she said as she stood back up with a stack of bookmarks. "Did you catch up on old times?" She straightened the basket and added new ones as she talked.

"Each time we talk it feels more like the relationship I remember. I'm sure you noticed Chad couldn't take his eyes off your cousin. I'd say he's interested."

"He's a man, she's pretty. Of course, he's interested, and Evan is too." Jessie smiled. "I told you if I remember correctly, and you were worried I'd be disappointed," she teased and patted his hand. A middle-aged woman with long auburn hair came to the counter with a stack of books to buy. "Did you find everything you were looking for?"

"More than I should have found. I'll be busy reading for a while." She handed Jessie her card to run.

"I'll see you later," Matt said as he leaned closer to whisper in her ear. "I owe you for bringing Chad back to town. It's good to have him as a friend again. Love you. I'll be back at five to get you." Matt followed Dylan out of the store.

Jessie smiled and waved as he left. She turned her attention to the woman at the counter. "A few of your books are on sale. You made some great choices." She placed the woman's books in a bag along with several bookmarks. "I know you'll have hours of enjoyment as you read these." Jessie handed the woman a pen.

"I had a friend suggest that I should come to your store. I've never been here before." She signed the receipt and handed it back to Jessie. "I admit I wanted to see the woman who shot the scum trying to shoot our police chief. That was him, wasn't it? He's as handsome as the pictures I've seen of him. He looks like a movie star, and those eyes of his are gorgeous."

"Yes, to both your question and statement. I think he's quite dreamy too." Jessie smiled at her. "Of course, I may be a wee bit prejudiced." She glanced at her empty ring finger. When would the jeweler finish with her ring? Matt said it had to be sent to the New York store to be sized.

The woman scrutinized Jessie, making her feel uncomfortable. "You're the one, aren't you?" the woman asked. "I would have been diving for cover."

"Yes, but it was out of character for me." Jessie put a copy of the receipt in the woman's bag.

"Only someone pretty like you could catch the eye of a hunk like him. I know you guys are an item. My friend tells me all the gossip and keeps me up to date. It was worth every penny I spent today to see you and him both right here together. Now I have something to tell my friend that she doesn't know. That man loves you. His eyes said it all. Better than any romance novel I could read." Her hand covered her heart dramatically. "I'll be back. My name is Theresa Goodman, and I'm not usually this nosey, but when I read your interview in the paper, I had to see you for myself." Theresa turned to leave. "You didn't disappoint. Sometimes real life is better than anything else. I can't believe he was here too. I swear he'd have kissed you if I hadn't been standing there." She sighed and murmured under her breath, "It was worth every dime."

"It was nice to meet you, Theresa. You're welcome anytime." Jessie hoped people's curiosity wore off soon. She'd be happy to be back to obscurity as soon as possible.

"I've had more people come in today to ask questions about the shooting, and you." Molly stood in the open doors. "It must be driving you nuts because it is me. They want to know where she was sitting, if I was scared, and how did you know when to shoot."

"I would rather not deal with it myself, but people are nice at least." Jessie walked over to where Molly leaned against the door frame. "Do you mind if I change the subject?"

"Not at all." Molly laughed. "I can only tell the story a hundred times a day. Still, I have to admit I love all those folks coming in to have a look and stop to buy."

"Same here. The last customer bought quite a bit." Jessie clasped her hands behind her back. "I should buy some of your brownies to take to the guys tonight, or do you have something else I should consider?"

"I'll make up a nice assortment of treats. Let me think about it, and I'll bring a box over later. I know

Matt likes the brownies, and I have some mini cream puffs and eclairs, along with the lemon bars. Oh, and the raspberry-vanilla chocolate scones are great too. I'll add a few surprises, and then you have to tell me what you liked best."

"I'd be happy to, but it might be a difficult choice. All your goodies are great." Jessie turned when she heard the bell above the door ring. "It's back to work for me." She made her way to the front of the store to see if she could assist the customer. She helped her find the author she was looking for and left her to shop on her own.

Once the woman had checked out, Jessie called Sadie to reassure her that all was well with her. She spent the rest of the afternoon waiting on customers who were more than a little curious about what happened after reading the paper. Whenever there was a lull in the action, she went over Reba's words in her mind. There was someone watching her who had followed her through the portal. She knew it was true, but she had no idea who he was. How would she know if he was nearby? She rubbed the sudden goosebumps she felt. He was either near, or her imagination had kicked into overdrive.

****

He could see into her store from where he sat. Feeling she was aware that he was near, he hid his face from view behind a newspaper. Hopping with activity, the coffee shop was a nice little hole in the wall. The locals liked the place anyway. The lady behind the counter talked up a storm with her customers. The coffee was hot, the food good, and to his way of thinking, not a bad place to hang out to keep an eye on her. Too bad he needed to deal with this damn problem, or he might like to stay in this town a bit longer. People were friendly, and given a few days he knew he could drum up business. From the buzz in the coffee shop, he learned about a shooting on the premises. Incompetence must be in the air. What did it take to eliminate one woman and a cop? How he hated to get involved. One slip-up and it could be lights out for him. He had a nice, tidy operation. He would walk out the door and not look back except his guide wouldn't let him. Damnation, what a mess to his quiet way of life. He'd hang out a bit longer. Maybe he could learn something more.

****

Jesse checked the clock. She didn't have long to wait for Matt. Molly opened the lid of one of the boxes to show her some of the luscious treats that were artfully displayed inside.

"Oh my gosh, these look wonderful. I can't wait to try this one right here." Jessie pointed to a small, creamy milk-chocolate mousse in a dark chocolate edible cup. A piece of art, almost too pretty to eat, but she'd be happy to try.

"Don't forget you have to tell me which one of the new desserts you and the guys like best. Keep track of their comments. It's important to me. That's how I determine what makes it to my menu."

"You simply must show Katie these delightful mousse cups. They'd be perfect for her reception. These petit fours too. You can put flowers in her wedding colors on top. I bet they're equally yummy." Jessie handed Molly the money.

"I will if you think they're good enough."

"I'll keep track of what they like best. I imagine it will be hard for me to choose only one. I'm partial to your scones and chocolate, of course. Still, they all look delish and gorgeous." Jessie told her to keep the change as her mind figured out which one she wanted to try first. She already knew the scone was good. Tonight, it had to be something new to satisfy her taste buds.

"Thank you."

Jessie waved it off. "You always go the extra mile to make everything perfect. I'm happy to pay and tip your staff well."

"I sure hope you get to go home soon," Molly said.

"I do too. I like my place, and I'm tired of living out of a suitcase. Don't get me wrong. I appreciate everything all the guys are doing to keep us safe. We have great friends."

"We sure do. Have a good night. It's time for you to close."

"You too." Jessie started her closing routine. She was happy to grab the box of treats from Molly and to finally lock the doors. As soon as she closed the doors, the strange feeling went too, leaving her wondering if someone in Molly's store could be watching her.

Chapter 36

Jessie opened the door and handed Matt the keys when he arrived. Dylan was driving, and Kip was in the car behind them. "Are you ready?" Matt locked the door behind her. "What's in the bag?" He opened the rear car door for her, quickly shutting it and getting into the front seat.

"Molly made some new desserts she wanted you all to sample. Don't worry, Matt. She made sure to put some of your favorite brownies in there too." Jessie latched her seat belt. "How did the rest of your day go?"

"Quiet, which suits me fine. I had time to go over the email that Bartlett sent me. I'm not sure what I'm looking for. I'll be glad for any help you can give me later."

"Sounds good." Jessie placed the bag on the seat beside her. "Reba stopped by to see me earlier with one of her warnings. She told me if I was able to go through the portal others probably have too. Someone followed me when I went through and is following me now. I did sense someone watching me all afternoon. The feeling went away when I closed the doors going into Joe's."

"Did you see anyone?" Matt turned in the seat to glance at her.

"Not really. But that doesn't mean anything. I don't know who I'm looking for. I'm trying to

264

remember some of the people I met, and that should help me if I see the same person again. I mean how many people would look the same today as they did in the sixties unless they went through the portal?"

"I can't believe we're talking about this casually, much less entertaining the possibility that it happened to someone else. I saw what it did to you, don't forget."

"I know. The memory is scary for both of us." Jessie paused, her face scrunched in thought. "It's possible the person has gone back and forth many times and that travel doesn't affect them the same way. I have no idea how it works, but it's something I have to consider."

Dylan interrupted their conversation. "This is the strangest conversation I've ever listened to. You both understand how strange this sounds. I'm your friend, and I know you're both sane, but I wouldn't talk like this in front of anyone else if I were you." He turned into Matt's driveway and pulled the car up to the garage.

"Are you saying we sound off the wall to you?" Matt enjoyed seeing Dylan's puzzled expression.

"You could say that. Let's get you both inside." Dylan opened the garage door so that they could walk in through the garage.

Jessie grabbed the bag off the seat and followed them in, with Kip and another officer standing behind them watching the street. "Are you worried there'll be more trouble?"

"Until we catch them, we aren't taking any chances. You've both had some close calls lately," Dylan said as he nodded.

"I guess that means yes." Jessie sighed. "People

used to like me before I moved here."

"We like you, Jessie, don't we, guys?" Dylan directed the question to Kip.

"Sure, we do. But you do have a way of bringing trouble down on our heads. We never had strange things happen like this until you came to town." Kip ruffled her hair.

"They're teasing you, sweetheart. Don't let them mess with you." Matt walked into the kitchen after Dylan checked the house to make sure it was safe for them.

"They haven't said anything that I haven't said to myself many times already." Jessie placed the bag on the counter, removed the boxes, and placed them in the refrigerator.

"While I fix dinner, I want you to sit at the counter and check your email. I want to know if you see anything in the information Bartlett sent," Matt said as he leaned close to her.

"I can help if you want." Jessie pulled her computer from the carrying case.

"No, I want you to plant yourself in the chair right there and start reading." Matt pointed to the place he wanted her. "Kip and Dylan will help me. Besides, Katie did most of the work. She brought by a pan of lasagna, salad, and garlic bread earlier. All I have to do is pop it in the oven."

"Katie makes the best lasagna. I'll leave you to your work." Jessie sat on the stool at the island and turned on her laptop. Reading the email, she scrutinized the information line by line, assessing what she read.

Matt put the lasagna in the oven. He sat on the stool beside hers. "What, if anything, can you make of it?"

"Before you get into the email, when do you want me to stick the bread in?" Dylan asked.

"When there are about ten minutes left on the timer. It shouldn't take more time than that."

"Okay, I'll take care of it. You two get to work." Dylan checked the clock and went into the living room to watch TV.

Jessie tried to make sense of what she saw. She couldn't believe what she read. Was it possible Corbitt and Skylar were related? The records dated to the beginning of the cult back in the 1960s. There were other comparisons. One of the teachings she read sounded similar to what she had heard Skylar say at the commune. Maybe they were related in some way. "Wow, I didn't expect this."

"What?" Matt asked.

"I'm still trying to figure out what I'm reading. I don't think Corbitt traveled through the portal, but he looks like Skylar. I wonder if he's one of his many sons or grandsons. Do you know how old he is?"

"No. I'll ask Bartlett." Matt moved closer to look at the screen with her.

"I pulled up one of Corbitt's teachings. Skylar said some of the same things to the girls sitting at his feet that day at the commune. It's uncanny how similar it sounds." Jessie opened the archive on Corbitt's site and began to read another teaching.

"Is it possible he's the one who went through the portal? Could it be Skylar?" Matt asked.

"I don't know. From the figures I'm reading, this group had its beginning in the 1960s. I can't imagine how many women have been trafficked during all these years. Held as slaves. I'm stunned, to say the least."

"How do we figure it out? There's nothing logical about what you're telling me." Matt shook his head.

"I need to know where he was born, who his parents were, and how he's related to Skylar." Jessie kept combing through the site. She called Jeremy, putting it on speaker so Matt could hear the conversation.

"Hi, sunshine. What's up?" Jeremy asked as he answered his phone.

"I'm about to send you some information." She explained to Jeremy what she knew and what she was looking for. "This is what I can see up front. I'm wondering if there's anything going on behind the scenes. See if you can find out who Orin Corbitt's parents are and where he was born. I want to know grandparents, where he went to school, and any general information you find on him." She glanced away from the computer screen when Dylan walked in the room to stick the bread into the oven.

"I'll check it out. What's your theory?" Jeremy asked.

"I'm not sure. Either he's related to Skylar, or he *is* Skylar, which would be mind-blowing in every sense of the word." Jessie tapped her fingers on the countertop.

"Trans-dimensional travel wasn't enough, eh, kiddo?" Jeremy sounded amused. "Now you're saying there may be others who are doing the same thing."

"That's exactly what I'm saying." Jessie continued to maneuver around the website while she spoke to Jeremy.

"Damn, I didn't expect that. Does Matt know?" Jeremy asked. "I got the information."

"He's listening along with me."

"What do you think, Matt?" Jeremy asked.

"Let's just say, it's a surprising twist to the case." Matt kept his eye on the computer screen as Jessie rolled from one area to another.

"I'll get back to you as soon as possible. We'll talk then," Jeremy told her.

"Sounds good." Jessie hung up the phone. "Now what?"

"Damned if I know. Man, you type fast." Matt leaned closer to glimpse what Jessie pointed at. "I'm not sure what I'm looking at, but I'm sure you'll explain it to me soon enough."

"It's time to take a break for dinner, you two. It'll still be here after dinner." Dylan tapped Matt on the shoulder.

"There's the answer to your question. For now, we eat, and after that, I have no idea. You're the one with the theory on this case. I'm along for the ride." Matt stood, pulling her up beside him.

Jessie leaned close to him and whispered, "When do I get my ring back?"

"Soon, sweetheart. Do you miss it?"

"I sure do."

"I'm happy to hear it. I miss seeing it on your finger. I want the world to know you're the love of my life."

"What are you two whispering about? Come on, we're hungry." Dylan took the bread and lasagna out of the oven. He set them on trivets on the counter as everyone gathered around.

Jessie placed a piece of garlic bread on her plate, with a slice of lasagna and some salad. "This smells good. I'll call Katie later to thank her." She walked into the dining room and placed her plate on the table. The chair across from Kip was open and she sat in it. Taking a bite, she remembered why lasagna was one of her favorite dishes.

"What is our next step, Chief? How are we going to get these guys off the street? I don't relish the idea of them coming to town every few days and shooting at you. Someone is liable to get caught in the crossfire." Kip took a bite of his garlic bread.

"We have to find them before we deal with them. Bartlett has identified one. He has an agent watching the house for the suspect to return. He hasn't shown up there in days. His wife hasn't heard from him and is getting worried. I have a theory or two about who else might be involved but have no proof yet." Matt drank a sip of water. "For now, we sit tight and keep following the evidence, which in this case might be the money."

"I enjoy hanging out here with you, but I wouldn't mind having a life again." Dylan laughed. "Damn, I'm marrying a great cook. I'll have to watch it, or I might lose my girlish figure." He stood. "I'm going back for more."

"Save room for dessert." Jessie called after him.

"I always have room for something sweet." Dylan brought his filled plated back in with him. "Does anyone want some coffee to go with their dessert? I looked in those boxes, and man they look good."

****

The longer Matt thought about the case, the more he wanted Jeremy to search for some info for him too. Somebody in the police department near the Brass Lantern was dirty. He was sure of it. "Follow the money" triggered another thought, and he wanted Jeremy to follow the trail. Opioids were in high demand. With a doctor who could write prescriptions, someone had a big cash operation going. Whoever turned a blind eye to their illegal venture had to be on their payroll.

He would let Jessie deal with the supernatural, illogical part, and he would handle the area he understood—the nature of a greedy human being.

Chapter 37

After they finished dinner, Kip and Dylan cleaned up. Jessie took her laptop into her room, and Matt opted to go to his room early. Once there, he called Jeremy. "Jeremy, this is Matt."

"What's up? I don't have much for you yet."

"I know what Jessie was asking you to do, but I want you to check out some things for me." Matt explained everything he knew about the case so far. "See if you find out anything about the police in that town. I believe someone may be involved, or at least turning their back on what's going on and getting paid to do it."

"Do you have some of the officers' names?" Jeremy asked.

"I do, and I'll send them to you when I hang up. I also would like as much information as you can find on a Dr. Ethan Gibbs. Is there any connection between him and any one of the officers or Carl Flynn, the owner of the Brass Lantern Inn? I think he's clean, but it never hurts to check it out."

"Sounds good. Do you think Jessie is in danger?"

"That's a loaded question. It seems to be the way of it, but she seems to be taking everything in stride. Right now, we both are. The possibility of a fellow time traveler poses another threat to her."

"I have found a few strange things about Corbitt.

I'm not done by any means." Jeremy explained the details he had.

"That's odd. It gives me something to think about." Matt put his pen down after taking notes. "Stay in touch. We're getting close, and our suspects are becoming bold."

"Only becoming? I say they're in-your-face bold." Jeremy paused. "Both of you be careful. Email me anything you get."

"Will do." Matt ended the call.

Matt leaned his head back against the headboard. As far as he could see, the case could be divided into three sections—the sisters' murders, the cult enslaving women, and the drugs. Added to that was Jessie's jaunt back in time, and someone who moved back and forth through some unknown portal. He had another damn mystery on his hands. Bizarre cases were their new normal.

He spent another thirty minutes on the phone with Bartlett, who confirmed what he was thinking. The main question he wanted answered was how all three segments were tied together. Flipping through the pages of his notebook, he started at the beginning. A clue that he was looking for existed somewhere in the notes.

****

Jessie closed her computer and stretched out on the bed. Corbitt's profile had several holes in it. She had exhausted every lead she could find. Maybe he was the dimensional traveler. The whole idea of being in two places at the same time confounded her. She doubted there was a person alive who could explain her experience. It was kind of cool though to get a first-hand look at the time she had only heard or read about.

Adjusting the pillows behind her head, she closed her eyes. Kimberly knew her killer. Now, if only her ghost could talk. Maybe she needed to spend another night in the Brass Lantern to see if Kimberly was still around. With her body found, it was possible she was resting peacefully. Although, her murderer was still walking free. If this worked anything like their other cases, Jessie doubted Kimmie had found peace yet.

A sudden chill caused Jessie to reach for her blanket, and that's when she saw Kimmie's reflection in the mirror. She shot up to a sitting position and wrapped the blanket around her. "What is it with you and mirrors?" she mumbled under her breath. "At least your presence answers one of my questions. You're a long way from home, but I guess there are no rules in your world."

Jessie closed her eyes for a moment. She opened them slowly, thinking Kimberly would be gone, but she was still watching her. Their eyes locked. A vivid scene flashed through her mind. Kimmie was afraid of someone Jessie couldn't see. Who was it? When the second set of hands pushed her into the large shipping trunk in the attic and locked it, the fear Kimmie felt pulsated through Jessie. It was dark, stifling, and getting harder to breathe as time ticked by. Surely someone would come back and let her out. Hard to breathe. She needed fresh air. It was too hot, and she was entombed. Unseen, she slowly began to suffocate, listening for the steps that never came. Each time the scene unfolded in Jessie's mind, she saw a little more detail and felt more deeply what Kimberly went through.

Jessie wiped away the tears running down her

cheeks. Kimberly knew her murderer. Jessie was sure of it. Her suffocation may have been an accident, but her broken heart was real. That's when Jessie saw a shadow hit Kimmie's lifeless body—an attempt to make it look like a crime of anger. The person hadn't meant for her to die. Another mystery to solve. Maybe Patrick's feeling that there was somebody else might have been true. Reflections of Kimmie's broken life and heart were scattered among the shards of glass in every mirror she broke.

"I will not forget your story. You were too beautiful for your own good." As Kimberly watched her, Jessie pulled out her computer and began to write. Several pages later she laid her head back. Max and Neil would print this one. They had to. Everything was different when you could see murder through the victim's eyes. "Kimmie, I can feel your pain. Please help me see. I know why Hope was murdered too," Jessie whispered. She shut off the light and went to sleep.

****

"Are you awake in there?" Matt knocked on her door as he walked down the hall.

She cracked the door open. "I'll be out in a minute," she called out to him.

He followed the smell of brewing coffee into the kitchen. "You're up early."

Dylan handed him a plate filled with pancakes. "I was awake most of the night. I thought I might as well get breakfast going. The coffee is hot, the bacon is ready, and my pancakes are light as a feather. Katie taught me her secret, and I swear it works every time."

Matt grabbed a fork and the syrup on his way to the

table, sat, and began to eat. "Who knew you could cook like this." Matt took another bite of the pancake. "These are great. I might need to get her secret too."

"I thought I heard Jessie talking to someone last night. Her light was on quite late too. I think she was having a hard time sleeping." Dylan put another stack of pancakes on Matt's plate.

"I heard her crying. I'll see if she tells me what was going on or if I have to pull it out of her." Matt placed some butter on the top of the hotcakes. "Did you brew a pot of decaf for Jessie?"

"I sure did. I would never forget Jessie's preference. I can't see why she bothers to drink it, but if it works for her, it's okay by me."

"Works for who, Dylan?" Jessie walked into the kitchen. "Something smells yummy."

"Grab a plate. You're about to have a real taste treat this morning." Dylan placed a few hotcakes and a strip of bacon on her plate. "Do you want more?"

"No, this is more than enough." She put her plate on the table.

"There's a fresh pot of decaf. Do you me to bring you a cup?"

"Thanks, Dylan, but I can get it." Jessie went to the counter and poured a cup of the steaming hot brew. She added the right amount of cream to make it perfect.

"Are you sure you have enough cream?" Kip walked into the kitchen and ruffled her hair when he passed by her. "Good morning."

She slapped at his hand. "No one messes with my hair." Jessie took a sip and laughed over her cup. "It's spot-on." She smiled at him. "Dylan, these pancakes taste like Katie's. Did she share her famous secret to getting hotcakes light and fluffy with you?"

"She sure did. We have to keep it in the family."
He grinned as he sat with his full plate. "Kip, you had
better fill your plate. The hotcakes are going fast."
Dylan slathered his with butter and syrup. "You were
up late last night, Jessie. I thought I heard you talking to
someone."

"I had a visitor last night. Let's leave it at that."
Jessie sipped her coffee.

"Would you care to elaborate?" Matt studied her as
he took a bite of his bacon.

"I'll talk to you later. Right now, I want to eat my
breakfast while it's still hot." Jessie placed her napkin
on her lap and began to eat.

"Sounds reasonable to me." Matt finished off his
second stack of hotcakes.

"I know who'll be cooking breakfast at the inn
when Katie doesn't want to." Jessie smiled at Dylan.

"Who, me? Say it isn't so." Dylan laughed.
"Honestly, I never saw myself cooking anything until
Katie worked her magic on me. I swear that woman can
talk me into doing anything."

"I know, my friend. You'd better learn to say no to
her, or you won't have a free moment to yourself."
Jessie laughed.

"Too late. I'm a goner." Dylan took a sip of his
coffee to wash down the hotcakes.

"Jess, I want to spend some time at your store this
morning. I'll bring my computer. We have work to do,"
Matt told her between bites of his breakfast.

"It will make our job easier," Kip added. He gave
Dylan a thumbs up after he tasted the pancakes. "Does
getting engaged turn every guy into a regular Suzie

homemaker?"

"I wouldn't know," Dylan said. "I'm a macho cop who can make pancakes as light as a feather. It doesn't make me no Suzie."

"We'll be ready to leave in about twenty minutes." Matt said as he stood. "Does that work for you, Jess?" He put his plate in the dishwasher.

"That gives me plenty of time to get the store ready to open." She finished eating her breakfast.

Matt walked down the hall to his room. He gathered his notes and laptop. His gut told him it was all about to come down. His conversations with Jeremy and Bartlett confirmed it. This case shouldn't be theirs to solve anymore, but it would be. He knew it. Jessie was at the heart of this one too. He couldn't wait to hear what had taken place in Jessie's room last night. It would add another piece to the puzzle.

Chapter 38

Jessie began her morning routine at the bookstore while Matt walked over to one of the leather chairs, got comfortable, and started working. Joseph Collins was helping Jessie, and another officer sat in his cruiser at the back door.

"Is it okay, Chief, if I go to the coffee shop before the store opens?" Collins asked.

"Works for me."

Jessie unlocked the doors going into Joe's. She waved at Molly before closing them again.

"Did you survey what they liked best?" Molly popped in and closed the doors.

"We didn't taste everything last night, but I did hear several comments. You already know I love the raspberry-white chocolate scone and that your lemon bars are a huge success along with the brownies. But the chocolate mousse cups were a big hit, and the banana cake squares with banana icing were awesome. I made sure we would have the chocolate peanut butter bars, along with the cream-filled chocolate cakes and eclairs, to try tonight. Honestly, Molly, everything was delish."

"Thank you. Wait until you try that cream-filled chocolate cake. It tastes similar to the cupcakes I ate growing up. I think it's my all-time favorite."

"Take it from me, Molly, I would have a hard time

picking my favorite out of the box you sent. They were all good." Matt added his two cents.

"Thanks, you guys. I'd better get back to work." Molly beamed when she left Jessie's store.

Jessie went to sit by Matt. She still had twenty minutes before she needed to open. "That was nice of you to tell Molly. She had the biggest smile when she left."

"It's all true—every word of it." Matt smiled at her. "Are you ready to tell me what happened last night? Even though you were trying hard to be quiet, I could hear you crying."

"Kimberly showed up last night. I saw her in the mirror." Jessie covered her face with her hands. "At one point our eyes met, and I saw what happened to her through her eyes." She took the tissue Matt handed her. "I didn't see who murdered her. I wish I would've. When whoever it was shoved her in the trunk, she was still alive. She slowly suffocated, and her heart was broken waiting for the steps bringing the person back to her. At least two people were involved. There had to be."

"She was hit after she was dead. Is that what you're saying?" He saw her nod.

"Yes," she replied. "But Kimberly knew who it was, and it broke her heart, which might have hastened her death. The killer was angry, but I don't think they meant to kill her." Jessie shook her head. "That's why I could see her in the pieces of the broken mirror. Maybe Patrick was right. There was someone else who loved her. He was always jealous of her. Perhaps he had a reason to be."

"It's possible." He handed her the box of tissues.

"You constantly surprise me."

"If you're surprised, you ought to hang out in my shoes for a few days."

He shook his head. "No way. Besides, your shoes would never fit. You did give me something to think about and a possible motive for the crime. I'm wondering how the three of the segments to this case fit together, if they do at all."

"I almost forgot to tell you. There were a lot of information gaps in Corbitt's profile. I have no idea where to look next. I hope Jeremy can dig up some more information."

"Let me tell you my theory." Matt explained to her what he was thinking. "Bartlett's investigation is following the same path. Jeremy is digging into it, and hopefully he'll have something for us soon."

"I wonder if Radar could track the suspects we're looking for. We have one of the perp's blood on the gun, and anything is possible."

"I'll ask Frank." Matt pulled his glasses out of his pocket and slipped them on.

"I have to open. I'll let you get to work. I feel better about having you near. I know the guy Reba told me about is close and watching me. I don't know what he has in mind for me, and I'd rather not find out."

"Believe me, sweetheart, I would rather you not find out too." Matt opened his computer and read over the emails he had from Bartlett and Jeremy.

Once the store opened, Jessie kept busy. Someone from the bus tour that came in must have read the interview in the paper because several people gathered around her asking questions.

She finally told them to ask the chief of police

himself and pointed to where he sat.

****

Matt impressed himself with how calm he was. Jessie had done that on purpose. He didn't blame her—all the questions could drive a person to distraction. She needed a break. He'd be happy to take over for a few minutes. Matt chuckled to himself. She had got him good. He'd have to be creative with his payback.

Matt answered all their questions to their satisfaction, making Jessie seem like the heroine he thought she was. He smiled as several people bought more books, all to be able to talk to her. He was already coming up with ways she could thank him later. His story was good for her bottom line. Sales would be great in her store today.

That's when he noticed the strange man scrutinizing Jessie from the coffee shop. The man must think he was inconspicuous, peering out from behind his paper, but Matt saw past the man's pretense. He continued to monitor him for the next several minutes, and Matt's gut told him to keep his eye on this one.

Maybe he should have a little talk with him. Matt stood. "I'm hungry. Can I get you something, sweetheart?" He walked past where Jessie was talking to a customer. "Think about it and let me know. I see someone I want to talk to first." As soon as Matt started through the doors into the coffee shop, the man folded his paper and stood to leave.

"Excuse me, can I ask you something?" Matt approached him, giving him no room to make his exit.

"Who me?" The man nodded. "Ask away."

"I noticed you watching the bookstore most of the morning, and I couldn't help wondering what you're up to. Do you know the owner?"

"No, can't say that I do. I'm a people watcher is all. I enjoy observing how people go about their day. I find folks interesting, that's all." The man fidgeted with the paper in his hand.

"I can't say that I believe you. You might want to move along." Matt motioned and made room for him to walk by.

"Are you telling me I can't sit in a coffee shop as a paying customer and watch the people who come and go? I didn't know I was breaking any law." The man sneered at him.

"Nope, no law, unless of course you're plotting something against the owner of the bookstore, which I happen to believe that you are. I stopped you from committing the crime, and I think it's better if you move along." Matt moved aside as the man swept past him and toward the door.

Damn, it was too bad he couldn't arrest him on a hunch.

Matt went to the counter and ordered two sandwiches, iced teas, and a couple of chocolate chip cookies. He was buying her lunch whether she wanted it or not. Still troubled, Matt was sure he was the man that Jessie felt watching her the past several days. How did he fit into this case?

****

The man scurried out of Joe's and down the street. Too damn close for comfort, and his cover was blown. Now, what should he do? This moved up his timeline considerably. He couldn't afford to sit back and be Mr. Nice Guy waiting for the perfect opportunity. The cop saw through him and suspected something. Damn, he hated when things went wrong. He'd have to pull out the big gun and get his guide involved. He didn't want to—things could escalate out of his control fast, but with his cover busted he needed to handle this fast. Blue Cove, no longer a haven, needed to be behind him as soon as possible.

Chapter 39

Matt had bought her lunch, which was nice of him considering what she had done to him. Frankly, she was ready to eat and wanted to sit for a minute. Her feet were aching. The morning flew by, and sales had been brisk. She sat across from Matt at the table.

"Thank you. I appreciate this." She pointed to the sandwich. "It's nice considering I sent all those folks over to talk to you. I have no excuse except that I didn't want to answer any more questions." She took a bite of her sandwich. "I was done, and you looked nice and too comfortable, if you get my drift."

"I get it. I knew what you were up to, and I'll pay you back some time." He smiled at her. "First I want to make you squirm for a while wondering what it will be and when." He chuckled. "A little something I learned from my brothers. Paybacks must be original, creative, and well-planned. I'm going to put a lot of thought into this one." He leaned forward and kissed her cheek. "You need to see my resourceful side."

"There's not a doubt in my mind that you are quite capable, but so am I. Let's see who can win at this game."

"Oh, sweetheart, I hate to tell you there's no competition. You're stubborn but sweet. I'm tenacious and resolute with a determination to win. It comes from never wanting to be bested by one of my bros. It's a guy thing."

"Another character trait about guys that makes no sense at all." Sipping her iced tea, she shook her head at him.

"There's nothing to get—you either got it, or you don't, and sweetheart, I've got it." He grinned his lopsided grin. "I'll win hands down."

"Okay, I believe you, Mr. Braggart. Not to change the subject, could we please. Who were you talking to in the coffee shop earlier?"

"I wondered when you'd get around to asking me that question." He took a swig of tea. "I noticed this man in the coffee shop watching you all morning and decided to have a talk with him."

"What about?"

"First of all, I wanted him to know I saw him. He was trying hard not to be noticed, which made him more visible. I also wanted to know why he was scrutinizing you."

"Did he tell you?"

"No. If I remember correctly, I told him."

"What exactly did you tell him? I can't believe you're so cavalier about this." She pinched his hand playfully.

"I had a serious discussion with him. I accused him of plotting against you and requested that he move along, which he promptly did."

"Do you think he's the man who has been watching me?"

"My gut told me he is, and I'm going by what it tells me." Matt devoured his sandwich in a few bites. "I don't hear from ghosts." He flashed her another smile.

"Well, here's to him leaving and staying away."

She lifted her cup and tapped the cup he held in his hand. "He may be the one Reba warned me about. She said he was like Irwin, the professor in the Palm Spring case, who had dabbled in the dark arts too. All that means is, he'll be back to war with me sooner rather than later. I do appreciate you challenging him and sending him on the way. I don't want to deal with him today."

"I doubt that he'll be back today." Matt finished his cookie.

"Where was Dylan while you had this chat with the said suspect?" Jessie pushed her cookie toward him. "I'm full. You can have it."

"He, my dear, was taking a picture of the man. Now, all we need to do is find out if he's in the system." Matt bit into the second cookie and polished it off.

"You're brilliant." Jessie jumped up. She leaned across the table and gave him a kiss on the forehead. "Let's check it out. I want to see if we can get on ID on this guy."

"Brilliant might be carrying it a bit too far, but I thought it was rather clever of the two of us." He gave Dylan a thumbs up.

"She liked our idea I take it." Dylan smiled as he walked up to them.

"Yes, she did," Jessie answered him.

"I'm glad I could help you out, Chief. From where I'm sitting you need all the help you can get with your girl. You're much too slow."

Jessie looked at the photo on the phone. She recognized him as the man outside the café when she was in the sixties. Her excitement built. "I've met him.

He obviously has gone through the portal."

"I've sent the photo to Tom, Gary, and Jeremy. Now, all we need is a name to go with the face."

"I wonder how many times he's been through the portal. He threatened me outside the café. Did I tell you that?"

"You didn't mention it. I'm sure I would remember being told you were threatened in a different decade."

"I was sitting outside the café feeling sorry for myself. That's the place where I had the best chocolate malt ever."

"Focus, sweetheart. Although, that was a happy moment for me." Matt reached for her hand.

"He told me maybe my friend didn't want to be found and to let it go. He also twisted my wrist." Jessie pulled the event from her memory. "I remember the day clearly. Nervous and sweating profusely, he seemed out of place in the moment and yet it was as if he had been waiting for me."

"He probably followed you in and was searching for you. I can't believe I spoke that aloud as if it were a hypothesis of the case." Matt looked at an incoming text.

"Have I told you that you're brilliant? You're right, of course. Now what Reba said makes sense. I'm a threat to him and his lucrative operation. It's time to put a stop to his enterprises."

"We have a name to go with the face. Garrett Massey." He tugged her with him to the counter and the laptop.

Jessie typed his name in the search box. "He lives in the right town." She began to search through his records and suddenly stopped. "Wow, I was expecting to read this." She pointed at a paragraph on the page.

"What?" Matt asked.

Dylan whistled when he read what she pointed at. "Damn."

"How the hell is it possible?" Matt looked at the photo of the two men standing side by side smiling.

"Would you look at those two as cozy as can be. This paragraph says Garrett died a few years ago. A lie, since we saw the living breathing version only an hour ago. The proof is on my phone." Dylan brought up the photo again. "Yep, that's the same guy.''

"Where's he living now is the question." Matt shook his head. "How could he be dead? I just talked to him. He was breathing all right."

Jessie continued to read and follow the threads where they took her. Slowly she was getting a picture of something completely out of her league. She had no idea how any of it was even possible. There had to be a simple answer. Garrett was alive and not dead. Yet this said he had died. According to this article, he was nearly eighty years old, but obviously, he was closer to his fifties. She couldn't believe what she read. It wasn't true. It all had to have been made up. How did she find the real story of Massey?

"What are you thinking?" Matt rubbed her shoulders.

"I find this to be window dressing, covering the truth. Presented in such a way to lead people off track. Remember in our last case Trevor Valentine's site had all the protections that kept you from getting to his real operations? A false narrative is what we have here. Jeremy can break through this if anyone can."

"I'll call him and get him on it." Matt picked up his

phone. Jeremy was on his favorites list—he called him often.

"Hey, Jeremy, I'm here with Jessie."

"Hi, Jeremy," Jessie called. "I'll let Matt tell you what we need." She listened to Matt tell him to add a few words here and there.

As she concentrated on what she was reading, she felt there had to be a key to Kimberly's story and the crimes they were investigating connected to this man. He had been through the portal more than once—the whole story revolved somehow around him. Garrett Massey was the one link that tied it all together. Maybe she would need to go back through the portal and have him follow her again. Not a discussion she relished having with Matt. One way or another Massey and she were destined to meet again. It had to happen. Matt would figure it out eventually, but he wouldn't like it. That's when the grumbles would begin. It might be best if she met Garrett on her home turf. Massey's cover was blown when Matt talked to him. In her heart, she knew it was all about to come down.

Chapter 40

"I can see your mind at work." Matt's voice startled her when he walked up beside her. "Jeremy is going to do research. Don't even think about going through the portal again. I want no replay of the past few weeks. Once was enough for me." He pulled her to his side. "You were thinking it, weren't you?"

"I may have thought about it for a moment. But even I know it would be better for the confrontation to take place here where you can all help me." She smiled sweetly at him.

Matt shook his head. "We aren't going to talk about a confrontation."

"You may not want to talk about the subject, but the fight is coming whether you want it or not. His cover was blown by you, and he's feeling desperate with nothing to lose. I'm a danger to his operation because of the portal."

"Okay, let's talk about it."

"Massey is coming for me, and I need to be ready. I need a plan. He is as skilled in mind-games as Irwin, and he isn't alone in his strength. Don't ask me to explain—you're better off not knowing."

Matt scowled. "We'll plan," he grumbled. "There's no way I'll let you face him alone." He squeezed her tighter. "I'm going to do my best not to let you out of my sight.'

A subject change was needed, and she took it. "There are too many holes in Massey's profile to get enough information from these pages. I'm confident that Jeremy will work his magic and I'll soon know enough to understand how Garrett came to have his ability and what I'm up against."

"Why is it important to deal with him at all?" Matt's frown intensified.

"I won't go looking for him, but he will come after me, and that's all there is to it." She turned when the bell of the door rang. "It's time for me to get to work."

****

Matt went over several reports as he watched her at work. Damn, as much as he hated to admit it, she was right. Massey's beef was with her. They were linked by their travels through the portal. She had proven herself strong enough, and it was time to let her do it. Garrett was the only one with possible connections to all the cases. Matt understood he held the key to answers that they were in search of. His abilities, Matt had never had to deal with, but Jessie had experience. She had faced and stopped Irwin when several men couldn't.

He'd support her because he had no clue about this side of the case. If he was going to survive being with her, then he had to get over this crazy idea that he was the one who needed to keep her safe. She did a damn fine job on her own. She had faced circumstances that would make grown men tremble.

He needed to listen to her. Decision made. He would ask her again about what she saw on the other side of the portal. Together maybe they could figure out the steps she needed to take to be one step ahead of Massey. He wanted her opinion. Matt had a working theory of the case, and so far it seemed to be panning out. If his gut was right, this one would soon be solved. He returned all the calls and emails that Kenny had handed him earlier. Taking the case notes out of his briefcase, he searched for the links between Massey, Corbitt, and Kimmie's murder.

When the last customer left, Matt watched Jessie lock the front door. He glanced at the clock—it was after five.

"I'll be ready after I finish my closing routine." She sat on the arm of his chair.

"I'd be happy to help you." Matt put his arm around her waist. "I've been sitting too long."

"Give me something to do." Dylan stood. "I need to move. You can only read and drink so much coffee."

Jessie placed the feather duster on the counter and Dylan went to work with it. Matt cleaned the tables and threw away the trash. Jessie closed the doors into Joe's and put the money in the safe. In a matter of minutes, they had made short work of closing the store for the night.

"I'll take you two home," Dylan said. "Kip and Collins are on their way there now." He pulled his car keys from his pocket. "What do we need for tomorrow?"

"I have to go to the station. How about you, Jess?"

"Audrey isn't feeling well. She sent me an email, so I will need to be here. I know it makes more work for your officers." She shut down her computer.

"It can't be helped. I'll make the arrangements." Dylan opened the back door. "Jessie, would you like a visit from Katie tonight? She has more plans for the wedding she wants to show you, and she made me promise to ask you."

"I'd love to see Katie. I've missed her. We're used to popping in to see each other for a few minutes whenever we can." She shut the door behind her and followed them to the car.

"I'll bring her by."

"Great, and thanks, Dylan." Jessie pulled the seat belt across her when he closed the door.

He tipped his head. "You betcha."

"Jess, we need to talk. Don't worry. I'm not going to lecture you," Matt said when he saw the look on her face. "I did some thinking about what you told me earlier, and I know you're right. I trust your abilities. They've never led us wrong in any of our cases. I'm ready to hear your reasoning and any ideas you might have. I also want you to go over what you can remember from your time following Kimberly's trail. We need to put our heads together and get this right."

Jessie pulled out her notebook and told him what she could remember and had written down. "Massey was the man I saw outside of the café, and Sue Ellen had described another man that she saw with Kimmie. I don't think Garrett is the man she described, but I don't know that for sure. Skylar also knew Kimmie and wanted her to be one of his wives. One of these men might have killed her." Jessie flipped through her notebook.

"Who knew that Kimberly had a twin sister?" Matt turned to look at her.

"Their father and mother, the stepfather and his brother and wife. Obviously, any grandparents, but I'm not sure if anyone else knew. My theory is the person who killed Kimberly didn't know about Hope."

"Why do you think that?" Dylan asked.

"The dream I had of Kimmie's murder gave me the feeling the person didn't mean to kill her, and there may be more than one person. The killer was mad at her and was stunned when they came back to find her dead, then in a panic hit her after she was dead to make it look like she had been brutally murdered. My theory is when the murderer saw Hope, they thought they saw Kimberly's ghost and struck her the same way." Jessie sniffed, and Matt handed her a tissue.

"Damn, that sounds awful and yet feasible." Dylan shook his head. "What I want to know is why would the girls' parents tell them they were cousins? They were identical, weren't they? People make no sense to me sometimes."

"Yes, they were twins. The girls knew they had a strong attachment, and I believe they realized they were sisters and not cousins."

"I suppose that's why the parents raised them in different towns and kept them apart most of the time." Matt frowned with his comment.

"Still the girls managed to have a bond the way twins do. Hope went looking for her sister, and that's when she was killed. She was aware something was wrong."

"Jess, who do you think is the killer?" Dylan asked.

"I'm not ready to say yet. I need to see if Jeremy finds more information on Skylar or Corbitt. I'm still looking for a link."

"I have no idea yet. We'll figure it out." Matt glanced at her.

She smiled at Matt. "We usually come to a meeting of the minds. You get there thinking logically, and I get there riding on my emotions and feelings. We're perfect together."

"Absolutely." He reached for her hand.

"Okay, you two. I'm in the car too. Let's just figure out how to keep you both alive until we catch our suspects. The whole town wants to celebrate your wedding someday. We already know you're perfect together." Dylan pulled the car into the garage. "I'll go get Katie and be back in a little while."

Matt and Jessie walked hand-in-hand into the house. He wanted to hear more. As soon as he was inside, he made her go over the whole story again. If necessary, he would do it again until she remembered something that could change the nature of the case. He wrote several pages of notes as she told the story again, remembering new details as she did.

Chapter 41

Kip and another officer assigned to watch Jessie went about checking her store as she got to work the next day. She took the cash from the safe and placed it in the register. On her wish list for today was Corrine Clark's new book. She crossed her fingers that it would be found in one of the boxes being delivered later. It was a tradition for her and Katie to read the book and discuss it late into the night until they were finished. She hoped their custom would continue after Katie was married and would someday be passed on to their daughters—if they had them, of course.

Katie's wedding plans were coming together. Last night they laughed their way through wedding details. Oh, Katie was serious about what she wanted all right, but she was no bridezilla. She could make a joke about anything with her witty, carefree personality. Katie didn't seem to have a nervous bone in her body. Dylan kept checking on them to make sure they were okay, which made them laugh more. In the light of day, she had no idea what they had found funny. They could create their own reasons anytime they were together.

Jessie waved at Molly when she opened the doors between the businesses. Molly was busy with the morning crowd but waved back. "I've got great coffee and fresh scones hot out of the oven," she called to Jessie.

"Sounds good. I'll be over in a minute." Jessie went to grab her purse under the counter.

"I'll take care of it. You stay here, and don't unlock the front door until I get back." Kip slipped through the open door. "Promise me."

"I promise." Her chin lifted. *What's up with these guys always telling me what to do?* She knew Kip meant well, but still, it was rather annoying. She heard him the first time and would have waited. Now she wanted to go unlock the door simply because he said not to. She walked to the front of the store and did just that, although she locked it again immediately. When provoked, she could get stubborn.

Kip carried in two cups of hot coffee. Placing them on the table, he went back to get the bag with the scones in it. "I hope you like a raspberry-white chocolate scone. Molly said you do."

"I do. It's one of my favorites." She reached her hand into the bag. "Is the coffee decaf?"

He nodded. "We all know you drink decaf coffee in your milk," he said with a grin. "What's on your agenda for the day? I don't want to worry about everyone coming into the store."

"There's new-book club meeting here today. They're not as rowdy as the mystery book club. The Blue Cove Literary Club reads literature and classics, and they're a bit more dignified, if you know what I mean."

"Stuffy is what I'm hearing." Kip sat back in the chair sipping his coffee.

"I didn't say that." Jessie sounded like she was scolding a child.

"Nope, but you meant it." Kip chuckled. "I only

put the words to the vibe I was getting from your description."

"You're incorrigible." Her laugh came close on the heels of her words. "I need to unlock the door. It's time to open."

"Go ahead."

Jessie smiled all the way to the door, her secret still intact. Let Kip think he was in control. She knew better as she unlocked the door for the second time and turned the sign around to "Open."

****

Matt had several calls waiting for his attention when he arrived at the station with Dylan. First on his agenda was Bartlett.

"Hey, Matt, the print you pulled from the gun was who you suspected. You won't see him around anytime soon, though. He's underground—his injury would give him away. I've been checking every day to see if he's back on the job. The secretary tells me he's recovering from emergency surgery."

"I bet he his." Matt turned his chair to look at the window.

Dr. Gibbs hasn't shown up either. I have agents staking out his house twenty-four-seven." Bartlett cleared his throat. "Are you sure you don't want to come back to work for the agency? Your gut instinct can't be trained. You've got the goods, man."

"I'm sure. I may have some more information later about Corbitt. I have someone doing research. He's trying to track down the holes in his profile. Jessie has a theory on him, but she'd have to explain it to you. It makes no sense to me logically, but it's a damn good theory nonetheless."

"I'll wait to hear from you," Bartlett told him.

"Sounds good. I'll call you as soon as I have the info for you." Matt hung up the phone and dialed Jeremy's number.

"Matt, I was about to call you. I sent the info to Jessie in an email. Corbitt has some interesting secrets he's been hiding." Jeremy spent the next thirty minutes telling Matt what he had found.

By the time he got off the phone, Matt's head was spinning. How could any of this be real? It was right up there with Jessie being in two time periods or in the past. It wasn't the way he knew how to solve crimes. Jessie would get it, but he didn't.

Dylan knocked on his door. "Do want to go to lunch? You've been on the phone all morning. It's risky to get out, I know."

"Yeah, so is driving. I'm sick of hiding. If they're coming, at least we're aware of it. I have a few ideas we can try." Matt talked to all his officers on duty before he went to lunch. Together they developed a plan that could be implemented in case the suspects were sighted in town again. They were to pass it on until everyone in the department was up to speed on the idea.

"A great meeting of the minds. I think it'll work," Dylan said as they walked out of the station and entered the car.

"I agree. No more surprises." Matt fastened his seatbelt.

"That's for damn sure." Dylan pulled out of the station's parking lot. "What sounds good to you?"

"How about Joe's? I can get Jessie's thoughts on the info Jeremy sent to her." Matt glanced in the side mirror. "I don't think we have long to wait."

"You're usually spot on with this stuff. The next few days should be interesting." Dylan pulled in the spot in front of the bookstore. They walked in the door. Jessie was with a customer. Matt waved at her and walked into the coffee shop, followed by Dylan. After ordering lunch, they sat at a table where they could watch the store.

"Her store is busy today. It's become a gathering place for book clubs. She loves it and is in her element." Matt watched her scurry from one person to the next.

"Others gather besides the living too." Dylan chuckled. "I swear she should write a book. I'd buy and read it. Her real life is better than most novels I've read."

"I doubt she'll write it. She doesn't like attracting attention." Matt smiled when she smiled at him.

"You can't look like her and not attract it." Dylan took a bite of his sandwich.

"Don't I know." Matt stood when she walked into Joe's. "Hi." He gave her a quick kiss.

"What are you two up to? I was surprised to see you." Jessie stood beside him. "Please, sit and finish your lunch."

"I wanted to get out. Our suspects are coming back whether I'm inside or not. We might as well have a plan when they do. It seems a beautiful lady I know spoke those very same words a few days ago. I happen to believe she's right."

"I know she is." She grinned at him. "I have to get back to work."

"I'll be in before I leave." Matt realized he hadn't asked her if she had looked at Jeremy's email. Damn, all she had to do was walk in the room, and he couldn't hold a thought long enough to find an answer.

"Come on, lover boy. You'll have to say goodbye and ask her later. She's too busy to take the time now." Dylan walked toward the door. "Catch you later, Jessie," he called.

"Sorry I didn't get a chance to talk with you. It's been like this all day. Not that I'm complaining. Busy days in retail are good days." She walked over and went with Matt to the door.

"We'll talk later." He followed Dylan to the car.

Dylan made a U-turn and headed toward the station down Main Street. He checked the mirror a couple of times. "We have a tail. I'm calling for backup," Dylan told him and called it in. "We have officers in their own cars, and they're following behind the suspects. It's working so far. This could be our lucky day."

"Let's hope our plan works the way we designed it." Once the call came over the radio, everyone was in place. Matt gave the order. "Let's take these guys out while we have the chance."

Dylan turned onto Blue Cove Drive and drove a few blocks. He made a sudden right turn into the seaside village, causing the guy on his tail to make the turn and to quickly slam on his brakes. Before the driver could back up, the car was pinned in by several of Matt's officers' cars. The officers took cover behind their cars, guns drawn, as they kept the suspect's car in their sights. After a short standoff, the driver stepped out of the car, threw down his gun, and raised his hands above his head in surrender. He was followed by two other men. Matt cuffed the first man, giving the Miranda rights as he placed him in one of the patrol cars. The three suspects were in custody with little resistance.

"Damn, that went well. My next question is why? It was too easy." Matt had a sinking feeling in the pit of his stomach.

"I for one am grateful." Dylan glanced at him. "Don't go looking for trouble."

"I'm not looking, but I'm not sure it hasn't found us." Matt got in the car and shut the door.

"Why?" Dylan asked.

"Call it instinct. Something was off, but I don't know what." They drove back and pulled into the station. The suspects were booked. Kip brought Jessie to the station. Matt would be there for a while, and now she would be too.

Chapter 42

The longer Matt interviewed the suspects, the more he knew they were dealing with something unusual. The three they had arrested earlier were all involved in the sale and trafficking of opioids. There were more people involved. One of the men confirmed what Matt already knew.

"Who is the leader of your group?" Dylan asked Dr. Ethan Gibbs, one of the men arrested.

"I can't answer you." He put his head down.

"Are you saying you don't know who it is?"

"I'm telling you I won't. You have no idea what this guy can do. I've always been a law-abiding citizen and a family man, with no record. I lived and worked in my community with no problems until the day he walked into my doctor's office. I fear him more than anything you can do to me."

"I don't understand." Matt wrote notes on the pad in front of him.

"You couldn't possibly. All I know is that my wife must be devastated by what I have done. I am. I came to your town to kill you because I was told I had to. I've tried fighting the impulse, but this man controls my actions, and I have no idea how. I won't tell you who he is because I hope you never meet him. You seem like a decent enough fella." Gibbs covered his face with his hands.

"Gibbs, be upfront with me. What are we dealing with?" Matt frowned as a memory rushed into his mind.

"I wish I knew. Although I wrote the prescriptions, I wasn't privy to inside information about where the drugs came from. Believe me, the people operating this scheme are making a boatload of money. They pay us on a regular basis." He paused to wipe the tears forming in his eyes. "I haven't spent one cent of what they gave me. I can tell you where at my house you can find it. I want every penny to go the rehab groups that help people addicted to these awful drugs."

"Why should we believe you?" Dylan's hand slammed down on the table.

"There's no reason for you to. I wouldn't. Hell, nothing I'm saying or have experienced the last several months seems real. I'm living in a nightmare. But if you ever meet the man, you'll understand. If I talked, my family would be dead, or before the words left my mouth I would be. He doesn't even need to be in the same room."

"Take him back to his cell," Matt told the officer standing by the door. It sounded similar to the case in Palm Springs. Irwin did it through voodoo. How did this man operate? There was mind control happening. The fear on the doctor's face was real.

"I don't believe a thing Gibbs said." Dylan, who had been silently watching, paced around the room.

"I do. I've seen something like this before during the case in Palm Springs. We need to talk to Jessie. This is beyond how you and I think." Matt went in search of Jessie and found her in his office reading the email from Jeremy.

"Jess, we may need your help with this." Matt

explained what Gibbs had told him.

"I'll see what I can do." Jessie followed Matt to the interview room, going over in her mind what she knew she had to do.

One of the officers escorted Gibbs in and motioned for him to be seated. Jessie listened to Matt question him.

"I already told you I can't answer you, and you know why." He laid his head on his folded arms and shut down.

Jessie reached across, touched his hand, and quietly spoke to him. "Massey has no hold over you or your family. His power is temporary. Listen, can you hear him in your thoughts? You can't because he's not there." Jessie repeated the question to him several times as she spoke to him.

Matt knew the moment something in him changed. Ethan's head snapped up, and he glanced at her. "What did you do to me?"

"Why?" Jessie asked.

"My mind is quiet for the first time in several years." The doctor sobbed. "You can't imagine how great it feels. Can I talk to my wife?

"As soon as we are finished here." Matt turned on his recorder. "You can start at the beginning. How did you meet Massey?"

"It all started when Mr. Massey came to my office as a patient." Free, Gibbs sat up straight, looked Matt in the eyes, spoke directly to him, and spilled his guts.

"Did you ever meet Corbitt, his partner?" Jessie asked. "Were women often left in the tunnels?"

"Yes, to both of your questions. Corbitt was Massey's protégée. He was more ruthless than Garrett."

Gibbs cited details and examples.

Matt found it hard to believe what Gibbs said. If he hadn't seen Irwin in action in the Palm Springs interview, he wouldn't have. Jessie's quick thinking saved the interview. When Gibbs finished, Matt allowed him to make his phone call. Mostly Matt heard him cry. Gibbs was a broken man.

Matt told the clerk to transcribe what was on the tape into a confession. "Listen, it might not make sense to you, but those of us in the room know what he was telling us was true." Gibbs made it clear where he had hidden the money. The fact that he refused to use the money would make it better for him with the judge. Still, he was facing plenty of time. Matt had seen the mind-control actions first-hand, and even still he struggled to believe Gibbs's story. How would any jury buy it?

After the officer took Gibbs back to his cell, Matt sat by Jessie. "What did you do to him to make him talk?"

"You know—a little of this and that." She smiled sweetly at him.

"Exactly what this and that are you talking about?" Matt touched her arm. "When you touched him and talked quietly to him, something changed. It was visible on his face and in his body language."

"I simply reminded the entity around him that he wasn't in control until I felt it lift. I don't know how to explain it to you in logical terms. Remember when Reba told me about being the gatekeeper and not letting Irwin into my thoughts? I did something similar for Gibbs. This case is unique but has a few similarities to the Palm Springs one. The doctor's description of being afraid for his life reminded me of the same mind games Irwin played. He held people and controlled them through fear. Call me naïve, but I still believe love trumps hate. We've seen the truth of it play out somewhere in each of our cases. I tried and beat Massey in this round."

"Do you still believe he's coming for you?" Matt stood and pulled Jessie close.

"It's not a matter of if, but when. We'll meet."

"Let's get out of here. Tomorrow will be another long day. Bartlett is coming."

"Can I go home tonight?" Jessie asked.

"Not until we're sure we have all of the suspects in custody. For you that includes Massey." He reached for her hand. "We're going to Sally's for burgers and a shake. Ever since you told me about the café, I've wanted to have a chocolate malt."

"You'll get no argument from me."

Dylan pulled the car up to the back door and Jessie and Matt got in. "Where to?"

"Sally's Place." Matt secured his seatbelt.

"I'm down with it. Junk food sounds like the way to end the day." Dylan glanced at Matt. "You have to admit it went better than you expected it would."

"Definitely. No complaints from me."

"I haven't heard the story about how you managed to take the suspects into custody yet. Would you care to enlighten me?" Jessie asked as she reached in her purse for her lip gloss. She glided the wand across her lips.

"You never know. The evening is young, and this was one time when everything worked like a charm." Matt proceeded to explain how smoothly it went.

Chapter 43

After Sally's, Jessie talked Matt and Dylan into stopping at Liam's and Connor's bar. They were in the area, and the sign said they had live music tonight. Katie met them there, and anytime she showed there was bound to be a party. The day ended perfectly to Jessie's way of thinking. The band sang a lot of folk ballads which brought back memories from her time traveling through the sixties. Everyone in the bar joined in on the Beatles tune "All You Need is Love." She had needed to unwind—the music was good, and besides, the Donovans knew how to push all her funny buttons.

"I'm happy you came tonight. This was fun." Jessie said as she stood and hugged Katie, who was getting ready to leave. "Whenever you show up it's always a good time."

"I enjoyed myself, even though my goofy brother was a pest." Katie reached for her purse. "I have to get back to the inn and make sure my guests are taken care of for the night."

Dylan held Katie's coat while she slipped her arms into the sleeves. "I'll talk to you later."

"You'd better." She kissed him goodbye and they walked hand-in-hand out the door. Katie stopped and turned around. "You too, Jessie. Call me later. I'm in the mood to talk girl talk." She waved as she left.

"We'd better get going." Matt stood beside her.

"Tomorrow is liable to be a long day."

"I'm ready." She reached for her jacket. "Thank you for a pleasant evening. I relaxed and forgot for a while that we are in the middle of a case."

"Did you like the music? I saw you singing." Liam reached for her coat and held it for her.

"I thought the music was terrific. We had a fun evening. What's better than hanging with friends and listening to great music?" She smiled at him.

"Which is the reason that Donovan's and Murphy's, is the perfect enterprise for us. Having a good time is the name of the game." He kissed her on the cheek. "And you know me. I'm always down on having a good time."

"True, there's not a serious bone in your body. I've often wondered how you made it through law school. It's hard to joke about the law."

"Jessie, I can be dignified when I need to be. The problem is that being serious-minded gets boring after a while. You know how us Donovans are."

"Yes, I do, and I always loved hanging out at your house when I was young." Jessie reached for her purse.

"You were always a somber little thing." He tapped her chin. "Who knew you'd grow up to be you?" He paused. The smile on his face was replaced by a more serious expression. "I always felt like I disappointed you. I had the feeling you could see my deepest thoughts, which at the time weren't extremely profound. I had a one-track mind. All those teen hormones raging in me. I knew you liked me, kid, and believe me, I saw you were a beauty then too. I never wanted to let you down, but somehow I knew I would. I took the honorable way out for me and left you alone.

And now look at you. You're everything I thought you were—sweet and kind. I'm happy to have you as a friend."

She smiled at him. "Thank you. I often wondered why I couldn't get your attention."

"You had my attention, but I didn't want to corrupt you, lovely lady." He gave her a hug.

"Okay, Liam. I draw the line at hugs longer than a few seconds with other men." Matt walked up and grabbed her hand.

"I don't blame you, man. But she's safe with me. I know she's given her heart to you." He stepped back from her. "Thanks for coming in tonight. Come again on a Friday night when you can stay." He leaned in and whispered in her ear. "You've grown into a terrific woman. Don't let anyone tell you differently."

"What was that all about?" Matt asked when they were in the car riding back to his house.

"Liam was getting something off his chest. In the long run, he answered a question I've had for a long time." She leaned forward and touched his shoulder. "Do you have more interviews tomorrow?" She changed the subject. She wanted to savor the words Liam said to her. It didn't change anything now but made her memories of years ago somewhat sweeter.

"With Bartlett coming to town it'll be a long day." Matt turned to look at her. "We may have to go back for a few days to the Brass Lantern and the Boston area. I hope not, but we'd better be prepared."

"Okay, I'll arrange for people to be available at the store if I need them," Jessie told him.

A while later, as she snuggled beneath the blankets, she realized it felt great to relax. Matt hadn't questioned her any further about what Liam had said to her. How could she explain what it meant to her without Matt feeling threatened? Liam would always be only a friend and a happy part of her memories growing up. Knowing he had found her attractive as a teen gave her a warm feeling in her heart. Smiling into the dark room, she closed her eyes and went to sleep.

****

"Gary and Kip are here to help you if you need them. I'll call you as soon as my day permits it." Matt reached for the keys she held and unlocked the door to her bookstore. "Don't go looking for trouble."

"Now Matt, have I ever gone in search of trouble? It's always been the other way around." She touched his cheek as she passed by him through the door he was holding open. "I'm sure I'll be fine. Don't worry. I have a busy day ahead of me."

"Kip will bring you by the station after work if I'm tied up." He gave her a quick kiss and walked to the front of the store. He paused before he went out. "Be careful, sweetheart. You saw the fear that Gibbs had. Garrett isn't a pushover."

"I will. Go, you'll be late." She motioned him on his way.

Matt got in the car, and Dylan pulled away from the curb. He was bothered by the possibility of Massey being in the area and Jessie having to deal with him. No one else would know how to handle him, though. Until Irwin, he never believed any of the stuff he had heard about voodoo and the dark arts.

"You're quiet, Matt." Dylan put on his signal and moved into the turn lane. "What's on your mind?"

"Massey and the fear that I saw on the doctor's

face until Jessie talked to him. Garrett had control over him. He made Gibbs do things contrary to who he was as a man. I'm wondering how something like that is even possible."

"You're asking the wrong person. I know nothing about the weird and the unusual. Other than what we've had to deal with since Jessie came to town." Dylan chuckled.

"I've never thought about this stuff before, but I'm intrigued by it. Gibbs couldn't speak, and when Jessie touched him and talked to him, it was like the floodgates opened. He couldn't turn it off. I hope he's still talking today for Bartlett and the others."

"Speaking of the agent, are you ready for today?" Dylan pulled into a parking space at the station.

"I'm ready. I want this case solved, and we're almost there." Matt closed the car door. "I like to see how the pieces fall together and how close my theory was to being right."

"I admit I can't wait to see what strange new thing unfolds that I had no idea even existed. Your girl has taken our cases to a whole new level of strange." Dylan said as he followed Matt into the station. "First stop for me is coffee. Do you want a cup?"

"I'll be in to get a cup in a few." Matt went to the front desk. "Hey, Joe, has Bartlett or any of the agents arrived yet?"

"Not yet, Chief."

"I'll be in my office. You can send them back when they show up."

"Will do."

Matt filled his coffee cup and made his way to his office. Sitting at his desk, he opened the file and added

313

the newly signed confession that had been placed on his desk. Matt read through the document line by line. One statement led to several thoughts and questions. His mind was off and running, building the case against Garrett, Corbitt, and the person who might have killed the twins. The knock on his door interrupted his thoughts.

"Hey, Matt, are you ready?" Bartlett walked into Matt's office and sat in the chair in front of his desk.

"Let's get started. You'll find Gibbs an interesting suspect. We didn't get much from the other two. Your agents might do better." Matt stood and handed him a copy of the signed confession. "I have a few ideas rolling around in my brain. I'll tell you as we walk." The two men walked out of the office to the interview room. On the way, Matt discussed with the agent where the evidence was taking him.

Chapter 44

Jessie's store had only been open ten minutes when a woman in her early forties—she was guessing on the age—walked in from the coffee shop. Her chestnut brown hair lay in waves over her shoulders. Jessie noticed she was tall, maybe an inch or two shorter than herself. The woman's eyes were pretty and yet sad.

"May I help you?" Jessie asked her, wanting to throw her arms around the woman and to hug the sadness out of her.

"I talked to my husband for the first time in weeks, and he told me about you. I had to come and meet you. Do you have time to talk?"

"Yes, please have a seat." Jessie walked with her to the chairs. "I'm not sure I understand. Who is your husband?"

"I'm sorry, I've never done anything like this before. My name is Amanda Gibbs. You met my husband yesterday at the police station." Tears filled her eyes. "I've been worried for several years that the man I married was lost to me forever. I have no idea what he was involved in, but he changed dramatically over the last few years. I hired a lawyer a few months ago to start divorce proceedings. I didn't want our children anywhere near him. He's been so erratic. When he called me last night, he sounded like the man I once knew. He said it was because of you." Amanda covered her mouth with her hand, but the sob escaped anyway.

Jessie tried to explain how she helped and what had happened to her husband. "When I took hold of his arm and began to talk to him, the control that Massey had over him was broken." She wasn't sure the woman understood what she told her. "I know none of this must make sense to you, but there are things in life for which we have no answers, and this may be one of them." Jessie handed her the box of tissues. "Your husband was controlled by two men. He feared them and what they might do to you and the kids. He couldn't tell you because he didn't know how to."

"I don't understand any of this." Amanda sniffed, swiping at the tears on her cheeks.

"Of course, you don't. I have no idea how to explain it to you either. I can only share with you what has happened to me." Jessie explained some of what happened to her in Palm Springs where Irwin had practiced his dark arts. "What I'm trying to tell you is that there are some bad people out there who control people through fear. Your husband was a victim of one. Massey met your husband when he came into his office as a patient. He controlled him with mind games and threats."

"What will happen to Ethan?" she asked.

"A judge and possibly a jury will decide. He'll need a good criminal attorney. His confession and testimony against Massey and Corbitt will be taken into consideration. But a lot of people were hurt by the opioids they moved and that he wrote prescriptions for."

"I'm happy you helped him. He sounded like my

old Ethan again. I'm not sure I can ever trust him again, but hopefully he can pick up the pieces of his life."

"Maybe you will be able to as well. I believe you should talk to the Chief of Police, Matt Parker. He could tell you more about the charges against your husband, and perhaps he'll let you see your husband." Jessie texted Matt. She read the message he sent back. "He said to have you go to the station. I know he'll be able to answer more of your questions."

Amanda stood. "Thank you. Do you mind if I hug you?"

"Please do." Jessie wrapped her arms around the woman and hugged her tight. "I'm sorry for what your family has gone through."

"I still love my husband, but I hate what he's become. I would rather have him in prison and be at peace than driven the way he's been the past several years. I hope that doesn't make me sound awful." Amanda placed her purse over her shoulder.

"Not at all. I think Ethan is lucky to have you." Jessie walked with her to the door and gave Amanda directions to the police station. "Feel free to call me anytime you need to talk." Jessie handed a business card to her.

She watched Amanda drive away. That's when she noticed Kimberly and Hope in front of the church. Separated in life but united after death, came to her mind. *What are you two doing in town? I hope you're here to help me. I have a feeling I'm going to need it.*

"Hey, rookie, can I buy you some lunch?" Kip asked as he stood from his seat in the store.

"That would be nice."

"What sounds good to you?"

"I'll take a chicken salad sandwich. Molly makes the best." Jessie turned to help a customer who came in the front door. She felt the sisters come in the store. The chill in the room was palpable. Pulling her sweater tight around her, she rubbed her arms. Something was up, and more than likely she would soon find out.

Jessie ate her lunch while looking over her shoulder. She jumped every time the bell rang above the door. A confrontation was coming, and she didn't want to be taken by surprise.

"Are you okay, Jessie?" Kip asked her. His forehead wrinkled into a worried expression.

"Sure, why?"

"Let's see—Gary asked you a question three times, and you never answered. There's also the fact that every time the bell rings you jump. It might make a casual observer wonder what's going on. I, on the other hand, know something isn't right. What gives?"

"I sense something is about to happen, and I don't want to be taken by surprise."

"You should have told us the moment you started feeling this way. We don't want to be caught off guard either." Kip gathered his trash and reached for hers. "We are here to help you. Tell us what we need to do and what you think might happen."

Kip was right, of course. She explained about the ghosts in her store and her concern about the impending confrontation with Massey. "You may see me do something that seems strange to you, but I know what I'm doing." She smiled at him and then said under breath, "At least, I hope I do."

"Did you hear what she said, Gary?"

"I heard. We'll keep our eyes open and be here to

back you up."

"The thing is, Massey isn't normal, and I'm not sure this will be like any situation any of us has seen before. I'm giving you a fair warning." Conversation stopped when two customers came into the store.

As the clock ticked closer to closing time, Jessie began to think she had dodged a bullet. She was straightening the counter when the atmosphere in the store changed. The sisters were worked into a frenzy.

Suddenly the loud crash propelled Gary and Kip to their feet. Massey kicked the front door hard enough for it to bounce against the wall. He rushed in and made a beeline toward Jessie, picking up speed as he came. Jessie began to sing in her mind as Massey grabbed for her arm.

"What in the hell?" Gary yelled out. "I can't move. My feet feel like they are weighted in cement."

"Mine too." Kip was stuck in place.

Obscenities flew out of Massey's mouth as he strained to grab her arm, but she resisted him. "You know I'll win," he said. His hand fisted to hit her, but his arm turned awkwardly, and his clenched fist hit his own face. "How in the hell did you do that?"

"I didn't." Jessie continued to sing the words in her mind. She reached for his hand and knew when his power began to weaken. "Why?"

"You came through the portal, and my guide told me to follow you. You were trouble. How did you find the portal?"

"Kimberly led me through." Jessie stood her ground, her hands on her hip.

"You're lying. She's dead." His hand raised with his anger.

"Dead to you means gone. To her, it means seeking justice for her and her twin sister, Hope." She stayed his hand with her thoughts. "The girls are here, you know."

"You're lying."

"You know I'm not. The cold you feel swirling around you is the sisters. It's their way of telling you they know the truth."

"I didn't kill them."

"You played a role in it."

"You can't possibly know," Massey screamed at her.

"That's where you're wrong. I do," Jessie said. Massey writhed in agony. His hands clutched for something to grab onto.

"What the hell? Now I can move," Kip said. Gary and Kip rushed to subdue and put the cuffs on Massey.

As Kip latched the cuff, he was left holding an empty cuff. "Where did he go?"

"Jessie, what just happened? I can't write this in a report. No one would believe me. Damn, I don't believe it."

She plopped down in the chair, trying to wrap her head around what had taken place. She knew Matt would want her take on the events. There was no way even a smidge of logic could be found in the explanation she gave him.

****

Matt arrived as soon as he could get there. He found Jessie sitting dazed in the chair. She wasn't answering any of the questions Kip and Gary threw at her.

"What's going on, guys? Take it easy on her." He smiled at them to take the sting out of his words. "She's not ready to talk yet. You guys will have to tell me what went down."

"I'd be happy to if I knew how," Gary told him.

"You can say that again." Kip leaned his elbow on the counter. "I've never seen anything like it. The guy is gone. All I know is when I went to cuff the guy after I could finally move, he disappeared."

"What do you mean? He left the store or what?" Matt frowned.

"No, I mean he vanished. Gone, no trace, melted into thin air." Kip shook his head.

"If I hadn't seen it with my own eyes, I would've never believed any account of this." Gary stood next to Kip, thumping him on the back. "It was crazy, man."

"Back up a minute. What did you mean once you could move?"

"It was the damnedest thing. My feet felt like they were encased in cement. Massey came crashing through the door headed for Jessie. I jumped up but couldn't move, and neither could Gary. I couldn't reach for my gun or anything."

Gary nodded. "Jessie warned us earlier that she might do something strange and that we wouldn't understand. We were helpless to stop the guy from hitting her. Hell, we were worthless. She took care of the guy herself. Whatever you do, don't ask me how."

"Why not?" Matt asked, clenching his lips

"I couldn't tell you and don't want to venture a guess." Gary pulled out a chair and sat.

Matt would get to the bottom of it somehow. He sat on the arm of Jessie's chair. He rubbed her shoulder. "It looks like you had a time of it. Can you explain?"

"No, but I promise I will soon. I'm still trying to

process it and can't believe it myself yet."

"Okay, I know you'll tell me when you're ready." He reached for her hand. "Was it Massey?"

"Yes, but there's more to it than that. I'll tell you when I've figured it all out in my head and I have proof."

"That's fair enough." He smiled at her. "Thanks for sending Amanda to the station. She helped us understand the changes he underwent. She also brought all the money Gibbs said he had in his safe. It was all accounted for, which should help him with the judge a bit." Matt rubbed his thumb across hers. "Everything about this case is strange. I have no idea how we bring some of the evidence into a trial."

"If you think what you have will be hard, wait until I eventually tell you what I have. There's no way anyone will believe what I've found out." Jessie shook her head, frowning as she did.

Chapter 45

They did end up going back to the inn. Jessie waited in the lobby of the inn while Matt was closeted with Carl and Bartlett in a meeting. The Brass Lantern felt like a whole new place—no more crashing mirrors or strange sounds, according to Evelyn, which made Carl happy.

They had a few loose ends to tie up. Most of the case was solved, and they were setting a trap for the next few arrests that would be made. Matt told her she would be the one making the summation this time. Lots of research and writing were a part of her evenings since the incident in the store, and she was almost ready to lay it all out the way she saw it. If Matt knew who killed the twins, he wasn't saying anything, but she knew. At least she thought she did.

This was the time she loved in a case—all the pieces falling together until a clear picture emerged. It felt like magic to her. She saw what the guys loved about their jobs. If her instinct was right, this case still had a few surprises left for them.

"Jess, are you ready?" Matt walked out of the room. "Bartlett will wait for our call."

"Let's finish this." Jessie stood and followed him out to the car.

"I'm still waiting for the whole story," he told her as he closed the door.

"You won't have to wait much longer." She turned in her seat to so she could see his face. "I think you'll find it was worth the wait and probably the strangest case we've worked to date. Kimberly was the catalyst into a mystery that I won't soon forget, if ever." She paused. "Aren't we leaving?"

"I'm waiting for Bartlett and the others. We're headed to the police station first."

"Sounds good. If you arrest our suspect, he won't be able to warn anyone." She smiled and touched his arm. "Smart plan of action."

He grinned. "You've got that right, rookie, I'm glad you approve."

"What's not to like about your insight?" She fluttered her lashes at him and squeezed his biceps playfully.

They followed the agents to the station and waited in the car. They watched until the agents walked the suspect out in handcuffs and they got the okay from Bartlett. Then it was their time to move. Matt drove first to Patrick's house. They questioned Kimberly's old boyfriend for a while. He held firm to his story, not wavering at all.

"What do you think?" Matt held the car door open for her.

"I have a theory if you'll trust me."

"Okay, where do we go next?" He turned the key in the ignition. She leaned toward him and whispered the answer in his ear.

"Are you sure?" he asked.

"I'm positive. I have an idea." She glanced at him. "Whether it works or not remains to be seen." She fiddled with the purse in her lap. "If it goes the way I think it will, we'll know who Kimberly's murderer is before the day is over."

"I'll let you have the lead." Matt parked in front of the inviting house. The garden was awash in color with all the pretty flowers in bloom. Linda answered the door when he knocked.

"Come in, both of you. It's so good to see you again, Mr. Parker, and you too." She glanced at Jessie. "I figured you'd be around soon."

"Why is that?" Matt sat in one of the chairs and Jessie in another.

"I read the newspaper. I couldn't believe you found the tunnels were open at the inn again and being used in a crime. Poor Mr. Flynn must have been mortified when the dog found the bodies. I figured you'd be back to see me. I watch enough police shows to know how you guys work a case. I assumed you'd want to check with me to see if I remembered any new detail. Am I right?"

"Yes." Jessie looked around the orderly tiny house. "Something like that."

"I'm sure I've seen you somewhere before. I know it isn't possible, but still, you seem familiar to me. I told you the last time you were here, didn't I?" She sat on the couch. "Can I get either of you something to drink?"

"We're fine, Linda. My partner and I would like to ask you a couple of questions, and then we'll be on our way." Matt sat back in the chair

"Okay." Linda smiled at Matt. "Fire away."

"Where was Patrick the day Kimberly went missing?" Matt asked her. "The three of you were so close I figure you must know where he was and why he was late." He took out his small notebook and jotted something on the page.

"I don't know. I wish I could tell you." Linda crossed her legs. She fidgeted with the tassels on the throw over the arm of the chair. "He was late that day, but he wouldn't have called to tell me. I wasn't his girlfriend."

"No, he wouldn't have called, but you did call him." Jessie studied her reaction closely.

"Now, why would I do that? He was Kimmie's guy, not mine."

"Because you needed to tell him that Kimberly wouldn't be ready until five-thirty. Why did you do that, Linda?" Jessie looked directly at her.

"I did no such thing." She pressed her hand to her chest. "Why would I do that? Kimmie was waiting for him to come."

"That's where you're wrong. Your friend had already been locked in the trunk in the attic for several hours in the heat of the day. You called Patrick but never got him. Skylar was there, though, because you promised to give him Kimmie. He wanted her, and you promised to help. You told me once you were Kimberly's best friend, and you told me you suspected her stepfather. What you didn't tell me was how jealous you were of Kimberly."

"I never told you anything." Linda stared at Jessie. She frowned in concentration.

"I'm afraid you did. But you didn't tell me you were in love with Patrick. Was he worth killing her for? You planned to make him angry by having him catch her with Skylar. That's why you locked in her in the trunk. You never thought she'd die. Your plan failed,

Kimmie died, and Patrick still didn't love you."

"Why are you saying these awful things to me? Patrick did love me, and Kimberly didn't deserve him," Linda sobbed. "She didn't care about him."

"We've met before, Linda, as hard as that might be for you to believe. You not only murdered Kimberly by locking her in the trunk, you and Skylar killed Hope when you thought she was Kimberly's ghost haunting you." Jessie frowned at Linda. "The only thing I can't figure out is why you bashed her head in after she was dead."

"I hated her. We'll leave it at that." She didn't leave it at that. She spilled her guts.

Matt watched the volley between the two women like a tennis match. "I'll be damned. It was her." He spoke the words aloud. "How did you know?" he mouthed at Jessie.

"I'll tell you later." She smiled at him. "Thanks for trusting me."

"Anytime, Jess."

****

Matt read Linda her Miranda rights as he cuffed her. He walked her out to the car. He called the police to tell them he was bringing in a suspect who had confessed to the murders of Kimberly and Hope Ryan.

When he was finished at the station, he grabbed Jessie's hand on the way out of the building. "The locals will take over the case now. This is their jurisdiction. We are free to go home. We'll have to testify when the time comes, but we're done for now." He opened the car door for her.

"I can't say I'll miss this place," Jessie told him when he got in the car.

"Too bad, because I promised Carl that we'd back to stay for a weekend soon. I mean, there are no ghosts so we should be able to have a nice stay."

She laughed. "I wouldn't count on it. If I'm near one, they seem to latch themselves to me."

"I'm not turning this car on until you tell me how you knew it was Linda." Matt turned in his seat to look at her.

"I had my doubts about her when I talked to her back in the sixties. The fact that she kept telling me I looked familiar made me wonder. She also talked about Kimmie in the past tense. But the main reason was the look on Kimberly's face when she was locked in the truck. She felt betrayed and completely wilted. Seeing someone die through their own eyes changes everything. I knew it had to be Patrick or Linda. Patrick's love seemed to be real. He was jealous of other guys, but I couldn't see him hurting her."

"What made you suspect Linda? How did you know about the call?" Matt fired off the questions as they came into his head.

"There's nothing meaner than a jealous girlfriend. Girls can be so catty with each other. I've seen it up close and personal. Skylar dealt the fatal blow to Hope when she came to the attic looking for her sister. High on acid, he was sure she was a ghost." Jessie paused. "The call was a lucky guess."

"It was pure genius." He leaned across the seat and gave her a kiss. "I'm patient to hear the story about Massey, but I won't wait forever. I need to know how to add him into the case." He started the car. "We'll have dinner and celebrate the job you did first."

"Sounds good to me. I say since we're in the

Boston area, we should eat here before we leave for the cove."

"I know the perfect place." He drove to a little bistro that Matt knew had great food. He would let her have a quiet dinner. They had a long drive ahead of them and plenty of time for him to ask questions.

Chapter 46

"Thank you." Jessie said as she reached for Matt's hand as they walked out the door of the bistro. "How did you know about this place?"

"One of the nurses at the hospital told me that it was a great small place. She was right on." He closed the car door once she was in and got in the driver's side "We have a drive ahead of us, and this would be a good time for you to start talking."

"You don't mince words." She glanced at him and smiled.

"I'm direct. I've waited long enough to hear what happened to Massey."

"I know how one of your suspects must feel." She fiddled with her purse strap. "One question. Why do we have to do this tonight? We have time."

"That's easy for me to answer, sweetheart. I want to know. I'm tired of waiting. Besides, when we get back, I'll be tied up for the next few days."

"What about Friday night? You could come for dinner." She turned to look at him, and he shook his head.

"Not Friday. You and I have plans."

"Are you asking me or telling me? I don't remember you mentioning that we had plans." She leaned toward him when he mumbled something. "Did you say something?"

"I said, I made plans, and they're a surprise." He started the car and pulled out of the parking space.

"I do like your surprises—they've been great every time. I can trust your instincts on this one too. Could you at least give me a hint on what to wear? A girl likes to be dressed right for the occasion." She patted his arm.

"You always look nice, but this calls for something snazzy."

"I don't do flashy." She laughed. "You do have a way with words, Mr. Parker—a real silver tongue."

"You're stalling." He squeezed her hand on his arm.

"I like to see you sweat."

"Not me. I'm cool. I want answers, and you have them. For some reason, you don't want to tell me, and I want to know why."

"Because you'll never believe what I'm going to tell you. Before we start, I have a question for you." She pulled her hand from his arm and moved closer to the door.

"How did you know Sam Macintyre was dirty? I wouldn't have suspected him." She pulled her notebook out of her purse.

"He left me on my own to investigate. No police chief lets another cop come into his territory and doesn't look over his shoulder. He had too many excuses for his department and didn't seem to know what was going on. Sam had no initiative when it came to the case."

"Is that all?" she asked.

"No, I asked around town. He was spending plenty of money and drove a high price car. He told people he had come into money, but his bank accounts told a different story of consistent payments every month. He also had been away from the job for a couple of weeks recovering from emergency hand surgery." Matt paused and looked quickly at her. "Due to a gunshot wound to his hand, if I'm not mistaken."

"Are you kidding me?"

Matt shook his head. "Not hardly. It turns out Sam was double dipping. Massey and Corbitt both paid him. He had an arrangement with Camilla to use the tunnels whenever she needed to, and she paid him plenty to keep his mouth shut. Here's one for you. How did you know it was Cranston that murdered the twins?"

"I talked to Linda on my travels. Something about her bothered me. It wasn't what she said, but how she said it."

"What do you mean?" Matt signaled his turn, winding his way through the Boston area.

"Girls can be spiteful with each other. Linda told me she got Kimmie's leftovers or what she thought of as the throwaway guys. She said she wanted them, but she didn't. Her face lit up when she talked about Patrick. He was the only one she wanted."

"Did you figure it out right away?"

"No. I would have told you if I had. I thought it was a possibility for the past few weeks but didn't figure out how she did the deed until we were sitting in her house."

"I knew you wouldn't hold out on me. Do you know how proud of you I am?"

She smiled. "I do, but only because you've told me at least a hundred times at dinner."

"Be prepared to hear it a few times more." He

flashed her a smile.

"I can live with the compliments coming from you." Jessie took a deep breath and exhaled. "Did you know Sam Macintyre is Linda's nephew?"

"I had no clue." Matt stopped at the red light.

"He's her sister's son." She flipped through the notes she had written.

"Do you think he covered up the case for her?" Matt turned onto the freeway back to the cove.

"He's a few years younger than she is, but not by much. Linda was six when he was born. Her sister was much older than her. Sam is scheduled to retire in a couple of years. I'm sure it didn't hurt having him in charge, although Linda was never a suspect." Jessie took out her notes.

"She'll be going away for her crime, and she'll die in prison. Skylar helped her kill and bury Hope's body in the rose garden. He'll go to jail if he's still alive. I doubt that he is, but there's no statute of limitations for murder. Corbitt, Browning, and the others will be right there with Linda. We have enough evidence to put them away for a long time. Bartlett is following the trails to all Corbitt's groups operating in our country. Gibbs is working with the prosecutor, and Massey will serve time if we ever find him." Matt glanced at her. "Which brings me back to you. It's your turn. No more hedging."

"You'll have a hard time believing what I'm about to tell you. When all is said, I have as much proof as I could find, but this will remain between us. I'd like to think others could accept this as fact, but there is no way. I'm still struggling with what I've found. You'll understand soon enough why I delayed before telling you." She looked out the window. The sun was setting.

"What's this? The girl who's seen dragons and angels fighting in the night sky doesn't know how to tell me about a missing suspect? Another strange phenomenon for the record books, is that what you're asking me to believe?" Matt patted her arm.

"I'll start with the easy part first. Corbitt and Browning were trained in mind games by Massey. They were his protégés you could say. They had mastered his skills by any means." She reached for the bottle of water she had in her purse. "With Jeremy's help, we were able to trace Orin Corbitt's lineage back to Skylar. He is Skylar's grandson. I'll let that sink in for a minute."

"Damn, there really is a connection." Matt shook his head.

"Skylar brought him through the portal when he was old enough to live on his own, and he was training him to take his place. I'm not sure how, but Skylar mastered moving through time. I have some ideas which I'm considering. Orin Corbitt and Camilla Browning used mind control to convince the women to follow them."

"This isn't too bad, yet. Still, I'm not sure the idea of time travel would be permissible in court." He grinned.

"Duh. Wait until you hear what's next." She took another deep breath and blew it out forcefully. "Here's where it gets tricky. As I researched Garrett Massey, I found out he died several years ago, like we read that day. The same man that we saw and that you spoke to died but suddenly was resuscitated after they had given up working on him after a lengthy time. His brain had been deprived of oxygen for too long. In the same hospital, and several minutes after the head doctor called the time of death for Garrett, Skylar died."

"We're talking coincidence. Right?"

"I wish. Skylar jumped into Massey's body. Skylar continued living in Massey's body until the other day in my store. How I know that is that everything about Garrett changed after the incident. The doctor who worked on Massey said there was no way his body could continue to live. His heart was beyond repair. He was dead.

"The orderlies who were sent to move the body to the morgue went nuts when the monitor suddenly began to beep again and Massey started breathing. His breathing commenced at the precise moment that Skylar died. Garrett managed to beat all the odds and walked out of the hospital in a few days. Every test the medical team did on him convinced them that Massey wasn't the same man, but they couldn't explain it medically."

"Are you kidding me?"

She shook her head. "Do I sound like I am? That's why Massey disappeared when they cuffed him. Skylar jumped. Skylar had only used Garrett's form and went in search of another temporary house. Massey's empty body will never be found; it was only an illusion, a mirage. Skylar needed to escape. His gig was up here."

"Where did you find out the information on Massey?" Matt asked.

"After researching his life, Jeremy read about his case in a journal of unexplainable medical events. Massey's was a must read. They wanted to test him further, but they couldn't find him. He simply disappeared."

"How convenient for him. There's no damn way this can be used in a court of law."

"No, this part of the story will never be told. Who'd believe it? Skylar died. He did too many drugs—his body was shot. He needed another image because he couldn't walk around as himself. He had learned in his study of mysticism and white and black magic how to transport himself. He found a way through a portal in time and into Massey with the help of someone he called an attendant. Not an angel, I can tell you that much."

"Damn, Jess, it's a bit hard to swallow this."

"I know, believe me." She frowned. "Let me give you an example. I had a chance to view life on the other side through the mirror. I saw you in the room and felt your emotions. I could hear you, but you couldn't see me. I can't explain how it happened any more than I can explain this."

"How does Kimberly fit into this story?"

"Skylar was obsessed with Kimmie. He hung around her constantly, and it made Patrick angry. Patrick thought about breaking up with Kimberly Ryan. Linda saw it as the perfect opportunity to make Kimberly disappear and tell Patrick she ran off with Skylar. She didn't believe Kimmie would die. When Linda found Kimberly dead, Skylar went nuts and used a clawfoot metal post from a dressmaker's frame in the attic to hit her and make it look like a brutal murder."

"A strange twist to the story. It's hard to believe Linda capable of killing anyone." Matt glanced at her.

"I agree. Linda may have been a jealous friend, but she didn't mean for Kimberly to die. It was an accident.

She became an accessory when Skylar killed Hope and they buried her. I find it ironic in the end—the only peace Linda Cranston had was working in her garden. After burying Hope in the rose garden at the inn, you'd think she'd hate gardening. All along, when I thought of her as a possible suspect, I kept wondering if someone helped her, and now I know it was Skylar."

"Makes perfect sense." Matt turned on his signal. "I'm only kidding. I don't get how any of it is possible."

"Neither will anyone else." She reached for her water bottle and took a sip. "All three of these cases were connected to the sixties, and I guess that's why I had to go there."

"I don't know what I expected, but it wasn't what you just told me." Matt turned off the highway toward Blue Cove. "How does this end? Any idea?"

"Skylar traveled through the portal many times over the years. He trained his grandson to be what he was in the sixties to keep his legacy going. Massey was only a temporary house for him."

"What about Massey?" Matt asked. "Where is he?"

"Garrett won't be back. He was only an image Skylar used. The real Massey died that night in the hospital. As to whether it was Skylar's or Massey's body that went to the morgue on the gurney we may never know for sure. All I know is Skylar walked out of the hospital several days later looking like Massey, and I have no idea how he managed it." She paused, folding her hands on her lap. "As for Skylar, he may show up somewhere, someday, as someone else."

"I don't know what to say." Matt frowned.

Jessie glanced at him. "Strange huh? Some of it I'll

never understand. Like when I saw Garrett and Skylar together in my travels. How could that happen? Of course, they really were together in every sense of the word, but not in the past, only in the present. The man that the waitress, Sue Ellen, saw with Kimberly is still a mystery to me, a part of the details I may never know." She forcefully blew out her breath. "Unless, of course, Corbitt could also travel through the portal. I never thought of that possibility."

****

Matt stretched out in bed after dropping Jessie off at her cottage. All that she had told him rolled around in his brain. She was right—it was a story that would stay between them. Unless he could talk to the doctors who had worked on Massey. He wondered if any of them were still alive.

Life certainly was more complicated since Jess had come into it. He wouldn't trade one minute of it with her for anything. Still, he had to admit this was the strangest summation of a case that he had ever heard. He grinned into the dark room. Those words had been spoken or thought about in every case since her arrival. His girl made his life a whole lot more interesting. He had it bad—he was in love.

Chapter 47

Friday had been beautiful, and the sunset promised to be spectacular. Jessie stood at the window looking out. Matt would be on time. He always was. They had talked every night since getting back to town. Somehow, he had managed to convince her that he wasn't going anywhere after her crazy summation. Even to her ears the whole premise sounded bizarre. How could she prove it unless, of course, Skylar showed up again as someone else? Corbitt had already confirmed Skylar was his grandfather, and he believed Garrett to be his grandfather too. Agent Bartlett didn't agree, but Jessie knew from what she had read in the file Garrett Massey was Skylar, and it was her and Matt's secret for now.

Why did she have butterflies in her stomach? No accounting for them. Matt was shaken by what she told him, but he wasn't running. Jessie went into her bedroom and glanced at the mirror one more time. She had opted for the red dress that Katie made her buy in New York. It was a tad shorter than she was used to wearing, but as Katie told her, she looked killer in it. The ruby necklace Matt gave her for her birthday was perfect with the dress and complemented the earrings from her dad. Her hair was down, the way Matt liked it. Funny how she was taking his likes into consideration now. Something she told herself that she would never do for a man.

Matt's knock at the door brought her to her feet. He was breathtakingly handsome, and all coherent thought flew out of her mind when he walked in. She searched for the right words. They stood staring at each other. "Wow, you're a feast for my eyes." The words popped out of her mouth, and her cheeks flushed.

"You stole my line. You've left me speechless. Damn, Jess, I remember the night you wore that dress." He smiled. "It was the longest night of my life, sitting near you and unable to touch you." He opened the door. "Shall we go, beautiful?"

"Nice recovery." She slipped into her light coat that he held. "Hmm, you smell nice."

"Another one of my lines stolen. I'm slow on the draw tonight." He gazed into her eyes and held her hand as they walked to the car. "I want to tell you something about the case and then the subject will be off limits for the rest of the evening." He shut the car door after he slid into the driver's seat.

"I'm all ears." She turned to look at him.

"Besides being proud of you, I'm impressed with the way you handled yourself all through this case. I read Skylar's grandson, Corbitt's file. He repeated some of the same things you said to me verbatim. I believe your theory. I have no idea how it's possible. Some things simply don't have pat answers." He shook his head. "Honestly, I have no idea how you were in two dimensions, but I know that you were." Matt reached for her hand.

"I really was, as hard as it is to believe." She squeezed his hand.

"One last thing." He took a deep breath. "I talked

to the hospital team who worked on Massey that night. They remembered every detail, and all of them from the head doctor on reported there was no way that Garrett Massey could have lived. They didn't believe he was the same man they had worked on. Massey may have looked the same, but according to every test the medical team ran on him, he wasn't the same man. Skylar may have had Massey's body, but he had his own essence. I'll leave it at that."

"Thank you." She unlatched her seatbelt and leaned close to him. Holding his face between her hands, she kissed him. "The fact that you went to the trouble to confirm what I said makes me love you more."

He kissed her back. "No more shop talk. Let's celebrate. I can't drive until your seat belt is buckled." He grinned. "Although…" He stopped. "We have reservations."

"What were you going to say?" Jessie reached for his hand.

"I'll tell you later." Matt started the car.

****

"Did you enjoy dinner, sweetheart? It appeared to me that you did." He reached for her hand when they walked out the door. "I love watching your facial expressions. Seeing them on your face at the hospital gave me hope. I knew I'd see you again."

"I did. I've always liked the Chowder House, since the first time we went there. Tonight seemed to be extra special." She stopped and kissed Matt before they reached the car.

"This was the place you first wore that dress. It still gets the same reaction too. Every man in the place was staring at you."

"You're sweet, but you need to wear your glasses."

"I don't need glasses to see other men noticing you. It makes me damn proud that you're with me."

Jessie felt the familiar heat on her face and smiled. "Look." She pointed toward the heavens. "The sky is clear enough to see thousands of stars. A perfect night, a great meal, and you. A girl couldn't ask for more. Except maybe for this night to never end."

"I'm one lucky guy. It doesn't take much to please you. Still, I have a few more surprises before we call it a night." He opened the car door for her.

"Where are we going?" she asked, slipping into the front seat.

"Another mystery, one I think you'll approve of." Matt turned onto Main Street. A few minutes later he pulled into the driveway on his property. "Let's go in the front. I like the gardens in the moonlight."

"They're beautiful." She stopped beside him. "Listen, you can hear the water singing. I never tire of the sound of the ocean. It sounds like music to me—at times soothing and calming, and sometimes wild and free."

"Dance with me." He took her in his arms and began to sway. Alive, is how he'd describe it. With her gazing up at him and love shining in her eyes, this was life. "I love how the moon lights your hair and how you're looking at me right now. It's a heady feeling." He could've remained with her there and honestly wanted to… When Matt finally opened the front door, she saw the champagne chilling in an ice bucket on the coffee table.

"If this is your surprise you've read my mind." She

slipped out of her coat. She moved to the couch and sat.

****

He seemed nervous to her, and she couldn't imagine why. She patted the couch beside her.

He shoved his hand into his pocket as he walked toward her. Leaning down close to her ear he whispered, "Remember I told you when I took your ring to be sized that the next time I slipped it on your finger it would be there for all our friends to see and celebrate with us?"

She nodded. "I do."

"That's the answer I'm looking for." He knelt before her. "Jess, you know I love you, and I want the world to know it. I love the faces you make, the way you twist your hair when you're nervous, and how fearless you are at facing your new normal. Ours will be a unique marriage, I'm convinced, with never a dull moment. I only know I want to live life with you by my side. You're my equal in every way. Will you do me the honor of wearing this ring and marrying me—" He paused and finished so only she could hear. "—in front of our friends?"

Before she could answer, the lights flew on, and people came from several directions yelling their responses. Sadie's voice was the loudest. "Say yes, girl. Don't let him get away. He's a keeper, just like my Max was."

Jessie looked around the room at all the beaming faces anticipating her answer. "You know, I wouldn't want to disappoint our friends." She gazed at his handsome face.

"Naturally, you wouldn't. You have a kind heart." Matt reached for her hand.

"Grams thinks you're a keeper, and she's usually right." She squeezed his hand, drawing out the drama a little longer.

"That's important." Matt grinned.

"And you did promise me that I could work with you and you'd try not to lecture me."

"Yes, I did." He chuckled, pulling the ring out of his pocket.

"Besides being handsome, I kind of like hanging out with you."

"I feel the same way about you. Life is more exciting with you around."

"In that case, of course, I'll wear this beautiful ring and marry you." She smiled at Matt as he slipped the ring on her finger for the second time. She held her hand to the light and sighed at its beauty.

"It's our secret that this is time number two," he said softly. "Did I surprise you?"

"You know you did." She pulled his head down and kissed him right there in front of everyone. She blushed as the cheers were a reminder they weren't alone.

"I do believe my charm campaign did its job and I won the challenge outright." He grinned and kissed her back. "Yep, it's a sealed deal with a ring and a kiss right here in front of all our friends as witnesses. I won."

"True, but only because I let you." She chuckled, taking a sip of the champagne Dylan handed her.

"My little feminist to the end."

"Not the end. This is only the beginning." She patted his cheek. "I do believe your proposals get better with practice. You wouldn't want to try for three," she added for his ears alone before she went to talk with friends.

He had managed to overwhelm her again with his thoughtfulness. How had he planned all this with everything else going on? She showed off her ring while all the ladies swooned about how romantic it all was. Peyton had her laughing as she told her she was heading for Arizona to find her a cowboy, and Sadie had her crying when she told her she could die happy once Jessie was married. Between all the well wishes and her emotions, Jessie needed a moment alone and some fresh air. She stepped outside knowing he would look for her, and she wanted him to find her. Her breath caught when she heard the door close, and his steps brought him closer.

"Here you are." He pulled her into his side. "Are you happy, sweetheart?"

"You know I am." She leaned her head against his shoulder. "For the record, I will always love the first time you proposed best. I can still see the panic in your eyes when I almost beat you to it. Tonight was a close second and perfect in every way. I mean, what could be sweeter than celebrating with all our family and friends in Blue Cove?"

"Not much except dancing alone with you in the moonlight?" He held her tight against him. "Winning the challenge is right up there too." He grinned.

The music coming from the house filled the night air with the sounds of "Crazy Love."

She snuggled closer. "I may have let you win the challenge, but I only did it because I knew from the beginning you were the prize. That makes me the ultimate winner."

Jessie felt the tremor in his chest, heard his chuckle, and sighed with contentment.

A word from the author...

I am a multi-published Amazon best-selling author who writes romantic suspense with a touch of the paranormal. I enjoy writing fiction. The character development, their stories, and the twists and turns in the plot intrigue me. Once I let the characters loose I can't wait to see where they take me. I'm hooked from the first words on the paper, and I have to keep writing to see how the story ends. Layer by layer I build it until I come to the happy conclusion.

I live in Colorado with my husband and family. I am a member of the RMFWPAL (Rocky Mountain Fiction Writers Published Authors League) and have enjoyed becoming involved in my community as one of the many authors living in Colorado. I invite you to read one of my Blue Cove Mysteries and see for yourself why Blue Cove is a special and unusual place.

http://www.ionamorrison.com

Thank you for purchasing
this publication of The Wild Rose Press, Inc.

For questions or more information
contact us at
info@thewildrosepress.com.

The Wild Rose Press, Inc.
www.thewildrosepress.com

To visit with authors of
The Wild Rose Press, Inc.
join our yahoo loop at
http://groups.yahoo.com/group/thewildrosepress/